S0-BEQ-660

Captive Heart

*Also by Linda Chaikin
in Large Print:*

Behind the Veil
Endangered
Golden Palaces
Swords and Scimitars

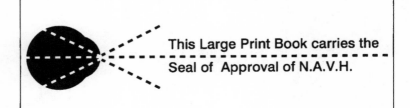

Captive Heart

Linda Chaikin

Thorndike Press • Thorndike, Maine

Published in 2000 by arrangement with Harvest House
Publishers.

Thorndike Press Large Print Christian Romance Series.

The tree indicium is a trademark of Thorndike Press.

The text of this Large Print edition is unabridged.
Other aspects of the book may vary from the original edition.

Printed in the United States on permanent paper.

Library of Congress Cataloging-in-Publication Data

Chaikin, L. L., 1943–
    Captive heart / Linda Chaikin.
        p.   cm.
    ISBN 0-7862-2719-2 (lg. print : hc : alk. paper)
    1. Barbados — Fiction.   2. Pirates — Fiction.   3. Large
type books.   I. Title.
PS3553.H2427 C3 2000
813′.54—dc21   00-032601

Captive Heart

1

"Even There Thy Hand Shall Lead Me"

Ashby Hall, Bridgetown, British Barbados
Eventide, September 12, 1661

The trade wind embracing Devora Ashby blew warm and lush, wooing her forward with the anticipation of something unexpected awaiting her. The promise shimmered from the low yellow moon, sighed in the brisk rustle of the palm fronds, gently swayed in the waltz of the giant blooms of the crimson hibiscus.

She paused, her satin slippers going dead on the walkway. Footsteps! But not the ones she anticipated. The sharp click of slippered heels beat upon the mellow pink-brick walkway that meandered from the opposite side of the Great House. Devora grasped the yards of cool parrot-green muslin and darted, as swiftly as the cumbersome crinolines would allow, behind a leafy banana tree. Her heartbeat slowed painfully, then took off racing as though the king's hounds were after her as she listened to the voice of her mother, Countess Catherina Radburn.

"Really, Barnabas, you're behaving the offended Puritan!"

It was followed by the assertive voice of her mother's cousin Barnabas.

" 'Tis not I who am offended by these selfish plans, Catherina, but heaven."

But her sharp rebuttal parried as a dueling sword.

"You've ruined my daughter with your religious soul-lashing. We'll have no more of it. We've come for Devora. You might as well accept it. With Cromwell dead and a Stuart on the throne again, Robert is going to become the new ambassador to the court of Castile."

"Spanish devils. Inquisitors, all!"

"You're hysterical. I must say, I was treated splendidly in Madrid these five years, despite your warnings of religious terror. It was Cromwell who instigated a reign of terror in England!"

"She'll not agree to this, Catherina. She has better sense than to seek a husband from Spain!"

"My dear Barnabas," came the wearied voice, "Devora will have very little say in the matter — no more than I had in mine."

For a startled moment, Devora held her breath. She gripped the folds of her skirts. *Spain?*

"Robert has decided," said the countess.

"Robert! The man cares for nothing except his plans. He blends well with the dark intrigues of popish Spain!"

"Dribble. You dare dispute our parental right to arrange her future?"

"In Spain? Yes! Yes! Exactly so."

"One would think she was your child. Or do you intend to argue for that as well?"

"Of course not. It's Robert's insensitivity, his willingness to barter her away that grieves me. You may look the other way, but you know why he wishes it so, don't you? His plans —"

"I'll not discuss *that* with you," came the tense voice, the pitch growing higher.

"Will you discuss it with Devora?"

"I'll do no such thing. It isn't true. I know what you're going to say. It's just religious hysteria, Barnabas. In your old age you grow worse than a prattling Quaker."

"Hysteria, indeed, that he uses the family fortune on ruthless expeditions to cheat and destroy!"

"It is not her father or the conquistadors who will frighten her, but you and your lurid tales."

"Tales, is it? Bah! Is it a tale that Robert has sponsored Favian Valentin to trick the Inca Indians into leading Spanish adventurers to their mountains of silver?"

"I know nothing of that!"

"And whose are those new ships that bring slaves and prisoners to work the silver mines? They belong to the Valentin family — and Robert. The Valentins! And you will allow Robert to give Devora in marriage to their son!"

"Barnabas, you're laughable. It's typical of Puritans to paint every Spaniard as a diabolical inquisitor. Devora will learn differently, even as I did. And it is not Favian she will marry, but Nicklas. I want to see Devora tonight. Where is she? Or do you intend to try to deny us the right to take her?"

"I would if I could," came the suddenly weary voice. "I'm an old man, Catherina. I've no strength to fight you both. But I will fight in my prayers for her. She's only 17!"

Catherina's voice also fell, as though her energy had sunk with her cousin's. "Seventeen," she said wistfully, as though remembering. "She's far older than I was when brought to the London court."

"A pity Warren didn't live. . . ."

"Let's not talk of the past, Barnabas. At least we had Devora. As they say, life must go on, and Robert and I are successful."

"That depends on your definition of success, my dear Catherina."

"I've no intention of abandoning his plans now. As for Devora being too young for marriage, she's two years past the proper age. It's our duty to arrange a suitable partner for her, worthy of the Radburn and Ashby names. The son of the Spanish viceroy is becoming a respected military and political figure in Madrid, despite your disdain of him. Anyway, his mother, I hear, may have been English . . . and the Valentins are a strong ruling family on the Spanish Main. They have a great hacienda in Lima, with the most beautiful horses in the world!"

"Spain's right to rule the Caribbean," came his scoffing voice, "is highly debatable, as King Philip must surely know by now, with the buccaneers scorching his beard."

"Despicable behavior, which is why Madrid will use Nicklas Valentin to see the rogues all hanging. And Nicklas is a very proper caballero. With the uncivilized manners she's cultivated in this wretched environment while under your guardianship, I can see to my regret I've already waited too long. I cannot see to her marriage too soon."

Devora's soul shriveled. In the letter that Catherina had sent the year before, telling of plans to visit Barbados, there had been no hint of plans to arrange a marriage for her. Now that Charles Stuart was back on the throne, she was coming (so Mother had written with brief hand) to claim Devora again into her rightful position as the daughter of the Earl and Countess of Radburn. Until now, Devora had believed she would be returning to England.

Even the thought of returning home to a life at the court of King Charles had not thrilled her as it might have the heart of other young women her age. Devora was at peace with Barbados, Uncle Barnabas, and his work as a physician. For the last three years she had been in training at his side and had helped deliver the baby of Emily, the wife of an indentured servant. She had even anticipated marriage to Edward and taking over raising sugar at Ashby Hall. Life was pleasant and spiritually meaningful. How could it all come crashing down in an emotional upheaval. Marriage to the viceroy's son! Barnabas was right. It appeared as though the countess cared little for her good. Leaving with her mother for the Spanish Main would be like leaving with a stranger. And her Shepherd and Father — how would He care for her with all these dark and foreboding plans threatening her? The plans of the earl and countess came sweeping in on her like a hurricane: unexpected, destroying everything. Had her heart been far from Him, she could better understand why this was happening. But it was not so! Her best dreams had been wrapped up in wishing to serve Him. And now the Lord seemed to be allowing darkness to close in about her, bringing her to certain ruin!

She closed her eyes, holding back tears. This couldn't be happening to her. Her mother's return was a nightmare. Her mother. *Mother?* Devora bit hard to keep back the resentment that wanted to bubble up from a heart that Uncle Barnabas said she must keep with all diligence.

Her first recollection of her mother was of an indifferent woman who came to visit her now and then when Devora was a young child at her grandmother's country estate outside London where she had spent the first 12 years of her life. When her parents did come for a few days' visit, Lord Robert was preoccupied with the king's business. Her mother would ask for her daughter to be brought to her, but only long enough to see if Devora was growing into an "attractive and educated girl, fit for an advantageous marriage."

"Be sure she speaks French fluently, Mother, and Castilian. Madrid cannot be worse than Paris. Now, Devora, give me a kiss on the cheek. That's it, Sweet, don't muss my hair. Gretchen — here, take the child," she would tell the governess. "I will see her again before I leave for London."

Barnabas had stopped on the walkway near the banana tree where Devora hid.

"You'll destroy her if you marry her into the Valentin family."

"You don't know what you're talking about, Barnabas. There is English blood in Nicklas. Have you forgotten who his mother was?"

"No, but from what I hear of —"

"And it is well that he has," she insisted. "He makes a grand name for himself with King Philip."

"But she's not like any of the other children of the nobility. She reads a book of sermons before she goes to bed at night. She never fails in her prayers. And she wants a simple life here in Barbados, married to Sir

William's son. Edward is a good boy. He aims to be a physician like me. So does Devora."

"William Townsend's son? Edward, that backward farming boy! I've seen him. He has the breeding of an ox. I shall not shame the family."

Devora winced, as though slapped across the face.

"Catherina —"

"Did you think I could approve of this? Do you think I've given her up to you for nothing for all these years when the war kept me in Madrid? Be reasonable, Barnabas. A match with a West Indies planter is totally unsuitable." Devora felt as though the final nail had been hammered into a box that confined her.

"One thing you and Robert have forgotten," came his hopeful voice. "Her religion is anathema to King Philip."

"Do not think to use piety against our wishes. As my daughter, she will remain loyal to the Church she was brought up in. I do not care what you may have taught her. Anything less will not be tolerated. Robert insists there will be no discussion of religion. It only causes division."

"We have much in common. However, truth and error cannot be mingled. And truth, my dear Catherina, must prevail. It is wiser to not offend God than to pamper the sensitivities of those in error."

"How inflexible you sound, so unsympathetic!"

"I love Devora. I do not want her destroyed by your selfishness — or Robert's."

"Don't be absurd. She may pray as she wishes in private, but she will be required to behave herself in public."

"I've dreaded this hour. Yet I see my hands are tied and I can do nothing to alter your plans."

"No, Barnabas, nothing. We will join Robert for a brief visit with Governor Toledo at the Isle of Pearls. The viceroy comes to interrogate a dreadful pirate imprisoned there. It will also present an agreeable time to introduce Devora to the man we hope will become her father-in-law. Then we will sail for Madrid. It is said that Nicklas will soon appear before King Philip. If Robert can arrange an introduction at that time, he will do so."

Barnabas sighed. "You will have to tell all this to Devora."

"I will speak with her tonight."

Devora's hands went to her mouth. She blinked hard to keep the tears from running down her face.

Their footsteps faded as they walked on toward the Great House.

Devora bit her lip in apprehension as she stood concealed behind the banana tree. The voice of one of the house slaves brought her back to the moment.

"Miss Devora! Is you out here? Miss Devora? De countess is callin' for you!"

Devora held her skirts against her to silence the crinolines and backed cautiously away, her heart thudding so hard that she felt breathless.

She knew that change drifted in with the trade winds that would forever alter her future.

The Isle of Pearls, and then Madrid! I'll never see Ashby Hall and Barbados again. Soon I will be Señora Devora Ashby Valentin. The thought that she must endure the social gathering tonight seemed impossible. The countess may guess that somehow she had overheard the conversation with Barnabas, or even that Barnabas had warned her, making matters more unhappy between them.

I must see Edward, she thought. Yet, what could he do? What could anyone do? She might flatly refuse to go with her mother, but life did not afford her such an independent spirit. To disobey the earl and countess was unheard of and deemed rebellious. She knew her parents well enough to realize they would not understand her wish to not go with them to Madrid. They would arrange the marriage regardless, for it was entirely in keeping with the custom that also ruled in England, Spain, and France.

The Lord — yes, He was her confidence. And had not Barnabas said he would seek to defend her in prayer? Yet despite this hope, how swiftly life's plans came tumbling down in ruin.

She walked briskly toward the shelter of the clump of palm trees. The trade wind began to shake the crisp leaves overhead, and some parrots screeched noisily. If she didn't seek out Edward tonight, by tomorrow it may be forever too late.

"Miss Devora?"

She was torn with the desire to see Edward as they had planned when last they saw each other on Sunday at Christ's Church in Bridgetown. She must make an opportunity to speak with him, for she may never see him again.

With tears in her eyes and the desire to pour out her torturous news, she ran through the garden. She went past the hibiscus bushes, where the crimson blooms no longer appeared as inviting as they had earlier, before her mother arrived. Devora ran past the palm trees whose tall, weaving fronds might as well have been waving good-bye as she saw herself boarding a ship for the Isle of Pearls.

The tall cane rippled in the wind, the sound rushing in the evening twilight like a large flock of doves in flight. The stalks concealed the road from the house, and it would be easy to run to the stables and have Percy saddle a horse. She would ride to see Emily at the overseer's bungalow and wait for Edward to arrive from the Townsend plantation as originally planned.

Suddenly the notion of sitting in Emily's little cookroom sipping tea and eating gingerbread, while the overseer's wife talked to her of how well the new baby John was getting along in the month since Devora had delivered the infant, drew her as a bee to the garden of honeysuckle that rambled beside its porch.

Devora hurried ahead, her skirts billowing behind her like a white sail on Carlisle Bay. She ran down the dusty road with a darkening sky stretching across the horizon.

She would need to do some explaining when she returned home, since the countess would demand to know where she had disappeared to, but Devora could endure no more. Even without overhearing the argument between her mother and Barnabas, she had planned to see Edward and discuss the illness of the slaves on his father's plantation. Was the outbreak local to the Townsend workers alone, or was the sickness ready to spread to Ashby Hall and the other planters' estates? Now her own tragedy weighed as heavily.

She had been up early, seeing several sick children belonging to the new indentured servants arriving from Ireland. The dirt road cast up golden-brown dust beneath her shoes and soiled the hem of her pale, cream-colored crinolines in her haste to escape.

The wind blew against her face, loosening her honey-colored hair from its pins, warming her cheeks, and bringing a touch of color to her fair skin. She slowed to a brisk walk. Nearing the stables, she saw the groom, Percy. He was leading the golden-brown mare toward its pen for the night.

"Wait, Percy!"

The brawny, silver-haired stable master in an oil-stained jerkin apron looked up.

Devora rushed up, breathless. "Never mind, Percy, I've decided to ride Honey. She's been in the stables for a week."

He glanced toward the Great House as if

expecting to see someone coming to thwart her. Did he know the countess had returned? He looked toward the road leading to the fields and the overseer's bungalow.

"Ye be sure, miss? 'Tis gettin' late, and they say a buccaneer's ship arrived this afternoon."

She hardly heard, thinking of her dilemma.

"They say it were the pirate hisself, miss! T'wouldn't mind seein' the rogue, though. All them Spanish galleons he done sent to the bottom of the Caribbean." He laughed merrily.

She came awake. "Pirates? Well, they're not likely to come here, Percy. They'll be hanging about the bawdy houses and throwing away their pieces of eight on the dice tables. A pity," she said in a wry moment. "I could use some of it to buy new medical supplies from the Boston ship. It arrived yesterday."

She wondered who the pirate was that the countess had mentioned being held on the Isle of Pearls. Whoever he was, the Spanish viceroy Maximus Valentin must think him dangerous to Spanish rule in the Caribbean, since he was coming all the way from Madrid to interrogate him.

He rubbed his chin. " 'Tis none of my

business, but does the countess know ye be leavin' now? Look to me like they just be gettin' ready to receive the guests for the dinner."

She took the leather reins from his gnarled hand. "I've a reason to call on Emily. It's been four weeks since she's had the baby. If anyone asks for me, tell them I'll return later tonight. I won't be up to the social gathering."

"If'n ye say it so, but —"

"Tsk now, Percy — no squabbling. I've had enough chatter for one day!"

The grizzled old man smiled and touched his cap respectfully, his eyes twinkling.

"Yes, Miss Devora, I be sympathizin'. No need tellin' ye how to be careful with Honey. Ye be one of the best horsewomen about."

"Coming from you, I'm flattered. Is she ready?"

"Aye, miss, she is."

Devora swung herself into the saddle as Percy adjusted the stirrups. She touched Honey's flank with a bone-handled whip and sent her trotting swiftly toward the bungalow. Moments later they vanished down the road between the palm trees and left the Great House behind.

Farther down the dirt road, the cane swayed and tossed as if trying to reach out green hands to grab her from the saddle. The trade wind blew sweet and warm, bringing the humid fragrance of sea, moist earth, and flowers. The palm trees lifted their fingers toward the sky. . . . "Even there thy hand shall lead me."

The overseer's bungalow loomed ahead. Devora rode up, dismounted, and after hitching Honey to a tree, ran toward the lantern light to take temporary refuge from the gathering dark clouds that threatened to break over her future.

2

My King, My Enemy

Madrid, 1661
Court of King Philip

"You know what your fate will be if the truth is discovered," continued Tobias in a low voice, glancing toward the ornate door leading into the corridor of the palace of King Philip. "Do not appear before His Majesty. It is surely a trap."

Bruce Anthony Valentin — called Nicklas by his father — made as though he did not take seriously the warning of his uncle, a friar of the Franciscan order; instead, he continued the elaborate preparation required in his dress to make an appearance before one of the most powerful monarchs in the Western world: His Most Catholic Majesty King Philip of Spain.

Bruce, six feet of muscle, slipped into the black-velvet jacket with silver embroidery and pearls at cuff and collar. His hair, the color of ebony, was worn in cavalier length, and his eyes, a gray-green, flickered with a touch of ironic humor beneath lashes as dark as his hair. Now his gaze turned granite as it fell upon the Spanish scabbard that Tobias had brought from Viceroy Don Maximus Valentin with the message that Bruce was to use it in the knighting ceremony. He would not use it; he would use the scabbard from the English house of his mother, with a sword he had used many times to frustrate the Spanish cause.

"Take it away," he said, gesturing with a strong, tanned hand flashing with gems.

"Do not behave the reckless, audacious pirate you are!"

Bruce couldn't help but laugh as his uncle's face flushed with exasperation. He threw an arm around his broad shoulder. "You worry too much, my uncle. His Majesty is so preoccupied with the building of his new palace that he could not tell a Spanish blade from the scepter of King Charles! There is no way he could know Don Nicklas Valentin is the English pirate Captain Bruce Hawkins!"

"Hah, you jest; a dangerous and clever fox is he. You tempt all the angels of heaven to protect your head by refusing this scabbard. Even if His Majesty did not notice, do you think Maximus will not? This is the hour of your father's pride."

Bruce's handsome face remained unyielding. "Which is why I would not use his scabbard, though it would keep me from the inquisitors."

"Stubborn," growled Tobias.

Bruce looked at him. The Franciscan friar was a husky man, as round in the middle as he was across the chest. He pulled back his brown faded cowl from his wide forehead, showing his thatch of silver hair. His cocoa-brown eyes glinted, as did the silver cross hanging about his thick, muscled neck. Bruce had found his friar uncle both a father, a confidant, and a friendly spiritual antagonist, and so he smiled at him reluctantly.

"All right, Tobias. For you I wear it because you, too, are a Valentin, and you do the name honor. But the sword I place inside this scabbard will be my own — one with which I will eventually destroy Maximus."

Tobias relaxed somewhat, but his tired face retained a look of concern. "You have come far in your ambitions since those childhood days in the adobe hut."

Bruce thought of the West Indies and the Valentin hacienda in Lima, where the silver

26

mines once belonging to the Inca Indians were now controlled by the conquistadors and, ultimately, King Philip.

"If your hatred toward Maximus does not burn itself out into ashes soon, I fear the road that has brought you to success at last will break beneath your feet, taking you down with it. I understand your anger, for I have known its sting through the years, but he is your father."

"He is not my father," said Bruce carelessly. "He sired me is all." And he added sharply, "Should he be commended for forcing my mother and siring me? Even a bull sires his offspring more honorably than he."

Tobias appeared to be accustomed to Bruce's anger and did not rebuke him. He lifted the Spanish scabbard with the insignia of the House of Valentin off the excessively carved table and handed it silently to Bruce.

Bruce hesitated, then forced himself to belt it on. He withdrew the English blade from his own scabbard — a sword given to him by a relative on the Caribbean island of Barbados, Lord Arlen Anthony — and sheathed it firmly.

"What if Philip notices the sword?" hissed Tobias. "Instead of knighting you, he may thrust it through your heart."

"He will not notice," said Bruce with affected calm. *But what if he does?* Bruce thought to himself. *Would he actually draw sword against the Spanish king?* Despite his malice toward the worldwide kingdom, he could not bring himself to assassinate its head.

"You forget I've been summoned," stated Bruce. "Would you have me insult our illustrious king?"

"It is the protection of our merciful God that has saved us both from the dungeons of Cadiz thus far. Do you think you can perpetually deceive the court with your 'victories' against the enemies of Spain? Pay heed, my son Bruce: The truth will be known. One day a Spaniard will escape to bring the shocking tale home to Madrid. They will learn that, like David, you secretly raid the Philistine camps."

The illustration did not go unheeded by Bruce, who knew the Old Testament. David, in fleeing from King Saul, had taken refuge in the land of Israel's enemies where he was befriended by the Philistine king. David, living at Ziklag with his 600 mighty men and their families, would come and go making raids. The raids were not against Israel as reported to the Philistine king, but against the outlying Philistine villages.

Bruce was returning to Madrid after two years of serving the king of Spain in Florida and the West Indies. Secretly, he had done much harm to the Spanish cause. But it was not this alone that had Tobias so concerned. While at Saint Augustine, Bruce had been returning from a secret raid against a Spanish ship when the general he served was waiting for him on the beach. The general had discovered the truth. A duel between them had cost the great general his life. Tobias had watched from the white beach near the palm trees and later reported that the general's captain had slipped away before he could stop him.

"And do you think he will not report this to His Majesty?" said Tobias as he paced the gilded room in the palace.

"No one has heard from him. His ship sank in the storm."

"My bones tell me it is not so." And Tobias mused to himself as he rubbed his elbow and looked from the curved balcony onto the magnificent plaza below where Bruce knew black-and-white royal horses were gathered for the parade. Spanish soldiers and horsemen were everywhere, for after the knighting, there would be a fiesta to honor Spain's present victory in Europe. New troops were being sent to Holland to bring the heretical kingdom back into the Spanish fold.

Bruce cast his uncle a smile. "Careful — reading your bones will see you answering to the Dominicans for heresy. Then I will need to raid Cadiz to save you. Not even the English buccaneer Bruce Hawkins could be successful."

Tobias cast him a look, his mouth twitching at one corner. "Do not mention that name here, lest you breathe it for the last time."

Bruce offered him a bow. "Anything to waylay your fears, Tobias. I am, as you wish, the loyal Don Nicklas Valentin!"

Tobias watched him with an even stare. The friar looked more a soldier than a man given to religious ritual. He frowned, his hands stuffed inside his loose-fitting brown habit, but Bruce knew he carried a dagger there — a dark secret from King Philip and his fellow friars.

Tobias had befriended Bruce when the boy was all but abandoned by his father, Don Maximus, outside Lima near the silver mines. Maximus was now the new viceroy of the Spanish Main and would soon leave for Cartagena, as would Bruce's half brother Favian and his second cousin Doña Sybella Valentin Ferdinand — a recent widow with a month-old child. Sybella did not grieve; Bruce knew she had always wanted him rather than her deceased husband, Marcos. And Bruce had wanted Sybella . . . but so did his brother Favian — a temperamental and spoiled but very proper caballero. His courtly airs, his horsemanship, and his expertise with the sword were much talked about among the other caballeros — all young men that Bruce secretly disdained with a contempt he could conceal with as arrogant an indifference as their own.

But it had not always been so.

Bruce gazed at the Spanish scabbard with its Valentin insignia. His grip tightened about it as he thought of the man who had sired him, Don Maximus Valentin. The cool, dark eyes that stared back emotionless from his childhood memory would be deeply injured if Maximus knew that the man called the English Devil Hawkins among the Spanish nobility in Cartagena and in Madrid was his son Nicklas Valentin — the buccaneer Hawkins among the Brethren of the Coast on the Caribbean island of Tortuga.

He walked to where Tobias stood on the balcony. Bruce's fingers closed about the black wrought-iron railing as he stood looking every inch a gallant Spanish soldier

31

of the king. He wore an exquisite uniform of black, the jacket opulent with silver, and beneath he wore fine chain mesh. His woolen hose were also black, worn over muscled legs with calf-length Cordovan boots. He appeared oblivious to prancing horses below preparing to parade before the Spanish king and his court. Bruce stood with his gaze fixed upon the coach that arrived, for the viceroy had stepped out.

Bruce's green eyes smoldered as he saw his father, who had come to share in the glory to be bestowed upon the illegitimate son whom he had once abandoned. As he looked down at him from the balcony, he saw his father not as he was now, but as he remembered him when a child hiding in the adobe house in Lima. . . .

Maximus — tall, darkly handsome, and ruthless — was raging at Bruce's English grandmother, Lady Lillian Bruce, and Bruce was a small child in the corner near her rocking chair, still trying to gather the piece of linen cloth and embroidery thread that Maximus had snatched from her hands and in a moment of unbridled temper had tossed angrily aside.

Maximus, wearing the leather of a cowboy with silver-butted pistols in his bandolier, for he had come in from training a new group of horses he had brought from inland, demanded, "I will not have him molded and shaped by your heretical views. For speaking of the Lutherans I could have you arrested to stand trial. It is my mercy that holds me back."

"Mercy, Don Maximus? What mercy did you show my daughter!"

Bruce saw a flash of gold and emeralds in the rings on the strong hand connect with the side of his grandmother's face. In a flash, Bruce lunged at his father like a ferocious cub, trying to beat against the strong chest. Maximus flung him across the room. Bruce's head struck the adobe wall, and he lay there barely conscious, hearing his grandmother's weeping and Maximus shouting for Tobias in a voice that was both frightened and angry. His uncle came running in from the field, and Bruce found himself gathered into the friar's strong arms. He could smell the fragrance of the field, of horses, feel the rough friar cloth against his cheek, the hand on his head in prayer.

He awoke. He was on the floor on a llama rug, and Tobias and Maximus were arguing again.

"He is your son as much as Favian!"

"He will never be my son. He is a coward. It is the English blood in him."

"There is not a speck of cowardice in the boy. It is your treatment, your neglect, the way you speak of him in front of others that makes him fear you. Look at this hut! Why do you not bring him home to the hacienda and dress him as a Valentin! Put leather on him, give him a horse —"

"So he will fall off again? He will soon break his neck!"

"You nearly killed him now, Maximus! Touch him again, and I vow before God that I'll take him and raise him!"

"Will you take him and make him your sniveling brat? Then take him, Tobias! And neither of you show your traitorous faces to me again!"

"I will," breathed Tobias, standing, his broad chest behind the friar's tunic heaving with emotion. "You are a fool, Maximus," he said, walking to the bed and looking down. Bruce looked up, his green eyes burning, his face wet with sweat and secret tears. Tobias's eyes also filled with tears. "He cannot be moved yet, Maximus. Señora will need to care for him. His head is hurt."

"I did not hurt him," said Maximus, his breath coming as though he had been running. He paced, his boots sounding on the adobe floor. "I would not hurt him —"

Soft weeping sounded from his grandmother as she sat in the chair, bent over, face in her hands. She could not rise, for her ankle had been injured in the shipwreck years before when the ship from England had blown off course and landed on a stretch of Spanish beach. Maximus and his soldiers from the guarda costa had found her and her daughter, 15-year-old Lady Marian Bruce, his mother —

Tobias turned to look at his brother Maximus. "You treat him like King David treated Absalom, and like Absalom, Bruce will one day turn to overthrow you."

"Overthrow me? He has neither the will nor the courage! He hangs to his grandmother's skirts like a whipped mongrel puppy, preferring foolish wives' tales of the suffering of his mother, or of my supposed cruelties. Of 'black deeds' of Spain in Europe and here on the Main. He is a poet, a boy who prefers the bull to live and the matador to die! He is a sissy. Favian my son will excel. Ah, if any of the two will prove himself a man, it will be Favian!"

"Your pride blinds you, because you will not confess the evil done to his mother."

"I will not hear of it! I treated her as well as a man treats a woman! She was like the son she gave me: weak, frail, weeping. Was it my fault she could not bear a son without dying?"

"What did she have to live for as your slave? You would not even marry her, but shamed her! Your sin —"

"Shut up, Tobias! She had the baby to live for!"

"Did she? Had she lived, you would have taken Bruce away from her!"

"You don't know what you're talking about. I loved her."

"Did you?"

Maximus whirled as if to strike Tobias. Their gaze held. "In the end, Maximus, you will make Bruce your greatest enemy. But turn to him now, throw aside your pride, confess your guilt, tell him you love him. I know this boy! He will make you prouder than Favian ever will. He will yet outdo Favian. Then what?"

"Then I shall make him my firstborn."

"And Favian will despise you for it. And Bruce will not be won. It will be too late."

"It will not happen. The child is sullen and dim-witted. He runs from me like a mouse. He can hardly hold a sword!"

"Then leave us," gritted Tobias. "Return to the city and come no more. I will see to both the child and the Señora!"

Maximus stared at him, his handsome face grave and angry. The silence grew, and Bruce had been compelled to try to sit up from the llama rug to look at Maximus, but he could not move, for his head ached and his eyes were blurry. What if he could never move again? What if he became like Grandmother Lillian, unable to walk? In a moment of childish terror, he imagined himself forever doomed to the cramped darkness of the small adobe hut, unable to run among the grasses, to see the llamas again, to meet his Inca Indian friend, Tupac — last of the Inca princes from the royal house. Tupac, older than he, was teaching him to ride wild horses, to use the bow, the sword. He could not bear it if he could not see him again — "Oh God of my mother and grandmother! Help me! Help me now. I will serve You if You will but help me —"

A cry of anguish escaped his childish lips, but it came out as a sob. The sound broke the tense silence between Tobias and Maximus and must have angered his father, for he hissed something.

"You see? He is a girl! Take him then! I will see his English face no more!" And he strode from the adobe hut.

Bruce had heard him shouting for his servants, mount a stallion, and ride away back to Lima. The sounds of the horses thundered across his emotions. His heart tore in two, hating him yet loving him in some way he could not understand. The sound of the horse hooves trampled his self-esteem into the dirt outside the hut.

Hearing other horse hooves prancing below in the courtyard of King Philip, Bruce stirred from his reverie. He looked at Tobias. It was his Uncle Tobias and the Inca Tupac and Lady Lillian who had raised and trained him for the first 15 years in Lima and Cuzco in the mountainous regions of Peru. For the most part, he had been ignored by Maximus. Except for once a year at Favian's birthday. Everyone in Lima was invited to the fiesta and games on the grandee's plantation. Each year from his twelfth birthday on, Tobias had brought Bruce on a mule to the Valentin home. The first time Bruce had gone there he had been astounded. The house was large and pink and black, with rooms and patios and gardens and stables and horses — great and magnificent horses that were bred and trained and sent to Spain, the best of which would be chosen by the king himself.

"Castile has always had a history of horses and horsemen," Tobias had told him as they journeyed along by mule, coming ever nearer to the large iron gate of the Casa Valentin.

Bruce already knew how to ride.

"I also want to compete," he told Tobias.

Tobias had chuckled. "You cannot enter the contest. You are too young."

"What of Favian?"

"Neither will he ride. He is there to watch. Next year he will ride."

"You can arrange for me also, Uncle."

Tobias's eyes twinkled. "Maybe."

The following year, Tobias had somehow accomplished it. They had arrived early, Bruce on the back of the golden-brown stallion that he and Tupac had tamed and trained. He was astride the horse in front of the house when Maximus appeared on the railed porch, not waiting for Tobias to come up the steps. Maximus would not look at Bruce, nor would Bruce look at his father except out of the corner of his eye as he leaned over to stroke the sweating horse they had named Aztec.

Maximus said shortly, "You insist on going through with this, Tobias?"

"He has trained long and hard — two years."

"If you wish to make him look a fool before all, it is your decision," and he turned and strode away toward the fiesta plaza.

Bruce had looked after him, gritting his teeth. He had competed that day not only in riding, but in all the games, even wrestling in the fashion Tupac had taught him. And Bruce had tasted the cup of glory for the first time. The screams and shouts of the audience, the clapping hands, the squeals of the lovely Señoritas had fired him to behave his best. He had won. But it wasn't that which satisfied him; he had proven Maximus wrong. He had proven Tobias right. And he had honored the memory of his English mother and would bring joy to his grandmother. He wished she could have been there to see him defeat Favian!

He had ridden home wildly on Aztec to tell her, bursting through the front door and going down before her on one booted leg while he snatched up her frail, wrinkled hand and kissed it. Her eyes, a lighter green than his own, had rimmed with tears.

"You won," she stated. "You need not tell me. It is written in your eyes, my son."

"You should have seen Favian," he said, out of breath and sweating from running. "I knocked him from his gilded saddle into the dust of the field. He lay there stunned in his fancy black suit. He wept, Grandmother. And everyone heard and saw. But I didn't laugh. I — I even felt a little sorry for him.

Don Maximus was silent. He said not a word. He walked past him toward me, and when Favian reached for his hand, expecting him to lift him from the dirt, Don Maximus ignored him. I thought he would come to me on the horse and strike me with his whip, but he would not even look at me. He walked over to Tobias and spoke to him. I don't know what happened. I galloped away to come and tell you I honored you today. And my English mother."

She reached out her hand and laid it gently on the side of his face, smiling. "You did well, Bruce. And now that you have proven you are a young man, you need not be unhappy and angry anymore. You must go with Tobias away from here, away to —"

The door had been flung open with a thrust that sent it slamming against the adobe wall. Lillian looked up, her face tense, and Bruce arose and turned to face Don Maximus. His father stood there, his hands in fists at his side — stood there without moving, looking at him.

Bruce expected to feel those great fists come slamming into him, and he was wondering if he could restrain his seething inside long enough to endure it without fighting back.

41

"You made me proud today," Maximus said.

Bruce, stunned, stared at him. The words brought no joy, nor did they bring sadness. He felt nothing.

"Come. I am bringing you to the house."

Bruce had heard his own voice coming calmly, surprising even him. "No. I will stay here with Tobias and my grandmother."

Maximus looked at him sharply, equally stunned.

Tobias came hurrying across the dusty yard, out of breath. He seemed to know what had happened, for he saved the moment from a great battle of wills.

"Be not foolish, Maximus! The boy is worn out. Look at him. He is dusty and sweaty. He needs rest, food, water! You overwhelm him with your sudden embrace. Give him time to understand what just happened. You ask too much."

Maximus said nothing, his dark eyes holding Bruce's. After a moment he nodded, then turning away started out the door. "Have him packed and ready to sail on Saturday. He is going with Favian to the academy in Madrid."

"Yes, Maximus."

Maximus turned and looked at Bruce. "From this day onward your new name is

Nicklas. Don Nicklas Valentin, my son."

Bruce had stood there in a daze listening to his father's horse's hooves gallop away from the adobe hut. Twice he had heard them in his memory: when his Father had walked out on him, and when he had come to claim him.

He heard horse hooves again — and came alert. He lifted his eyes, still burning from the memory, and saw a hundred soldiers with the name of Nicklas Valentin echoing on their lips in the hot Madrid sunshine. He saw the coach of the now Viceroy Maximus Valentin arriving in the courtyard for the ceremony, saw his half brother Favian also alight from the coach, and Doña Sybella in her black mourning clothes with a long mantilla. . . .

He looked at Tobias and, as their gazes met, Bruce could see that the friar had guessed what he was thinking. Bruce turned and left the balcony, going into the chamber. It would soon be time to meet with King Philip.

Tobias followed, frowning. "Are you certain you wish to go through with this meeting?"

"As certain as a man could be about anything. Have we not planned and worked for this hour?"

"We have, and none know better than I, but things have gone wrong. Things that worry me. Favian for one. His envy of you has grown far stronger than even I had suspected. What if he reports the truth to your father about what happened in Florida?"

Mention of his half brother brought concern, but not enough to convince Bruce to abandon his plans in the Caribbean.

"Favian knows very little."

"He is clever. More a conniver than a soldier. He has wit."

He had come to care about Favian and did not wish to think disparagingly about their relationship. "You imagine the worst. Our childish competition has long been put aside."

"Already jealousy burns like the flames in Hades in his soul. He will destroy you if he can, Bruce. Do not ignore my words. It is no simple matter. You should know what it can do to a man."

Bruce knew Favian envied him. He knew well the story of how envy among brothers could destroy and ruin a family. He had read about Jacob and Esau, about Cain and Abel. But it was not his half brother who concerned him now, nor even his father, Don Maximus, but his audience with the king.

"Favian has never felt the rejection I have.

He never will. He is back in Maximus's good favor."

"One does not get over bitterness and envy. One deals with it, as one would deal with a boil on a hand; you must cut it open. And Favian has not forgiven you, any more than you have forgiven Maximus. Only God can work so great a grace in either of your hearts."

Bruce knew all this. Both Lady Lillian and Tobias had taught him the Scriptures while he was growing up. And while on his own away from Spain, where heretical books were banned on pain of death, he had read the works of Calvin, Luther, and the Puritans. He knew about grace, forgiveness, atonement, justification by faith alone. As Martin Luther had so profoundly put it, *sola fide* — justification by faith alone, and *sola scriptura* — the Scriptures are the authority.

"Have you forgotten Favian was there that night in Florida? The captain who saw the duel and escaped must have gone to see him in the camp," continued Tobias. "Favian may know you killed Don Demetrio. And he would presume to guess why, because Demetrio discovered you sank that galleon off the coast of Saint Augustine."

Bruce set his wide-brimmed hat upon his

head. "Favian is easily deceived, even as Maximus now is — and our illustrious king will be also."

"You jest, but I tell you Favian is your enemy. That you refuse to take him as a threat will be your final undoing."

Bruce turned to him impatiently. "Was I not always the outsider, little better than the offspring of a slave? That he resents me now changes nothing, nor surprises me. Yet he believes as does the general of the guarda costa that I captured the French settlers in Florida and sold them into slavery on the Main. For now, that is sufficient. When and if they learn that I permitted them to sail home to France, I shall have a ready answer. There is nothing Favian can tell Maximus."

"In ignoring Favian, you make the same error as Maximus did when I warned him about ignoring you as a son."

"It matters not what Favian may think. I do not seek to replace him as the choice of Maximus to head the family at Lima. I no longer want that position. I have other plans," he said vaguely.

The hard lines on Tobias's face deepened. "You walk among lions. If the truth of your allegiance is ever suspected, Maximus will not hesitate to send you to Cadiz."

That his father was now viceroy of the

Spanish Main brought Bruce a moment of cool reflection. "You are wrong. If Maximus learns, he will not send me to Cadiz. He will seek to put a sword through my heart himself. And then," he stated softly but with indifference, "I will need to stop him."

Tobias shook his strong head tinged with iron-gray. "Let us leave here, my son. We will slip away now, before the ceremony. We will leave Madrid. We will go to Paris, a neutral city — neither English nor Spanish. You've jewels enough to live well, and you have the finest of educations. And your grandmother is well taken care of now."

She was, thought Bruce, satisfied. While she lived apart from the family by choice, she had fine and comfortable chambers in the Casa Valentin, and serving women to attend to her needs. She lived in peace with her memories. Having her provided for was one of the high pinnacles of his life. But it was not the only matter on Bruce's mind that drew him back to Lima. He would turn against the man who had destroyed his mother. The plans were yet in the making, but with each victory he forged to please Philip, the closer he came to the final realization. For years he had planned it — since the time he had been sent with Favian to the famous academy here in Madrid to train as a soldier. He had done well there — better than Favian. When he realized his military capabilities, Bruce had planned to rise in the ranks of Philip's soldiers. It had taken years, but he had succeeded. In the last five years since his graduation, he had won the acclaim of the military, and at last, the king, and all for one purpose: He would use it as a weapon to destroy the house of Valentin.

Lady Marian Bruce had been a young girl of 15 of the family of Lord Anthony in England when she had landed on the beaches near Cartagena with her widowed mother, Lady Lillian. His mother had become an unwilling victim of Maximus's lust. She had died a year after her captivity, giving birth to Bruce. Even now there were times when he felt as divided as a man without a country, for his heart was bound to his mother, but much of his courage and ambition had been inherited from Maximus. Little did his father know that the ruthless courage from his own blood would be turned against him and Madrid in the end.

Bruce was secretly Captain Hawkins — a name he had adopted from a buccaneering friend from Bristol who had gone to the gallows at Santa Domingo. Bruce was able to behave as English as the rest of the Brotherhood, thanks to his grandmother Lady Lillian Bruce, who had remained captive in Cartagena even after his mother died in her arms.

"Then you will go through with this? You will risk getting caught?"

Bruce lifted a black brow, and his green eyes turned thoughtful. "It is not often the son of an English slave wins knighthood from King Philip. I will take the position to serve in Cartagena."

Tobias sighed. "Then I will go with you, even as I have been with you all these years. But I will not enter the throne room of the king. I go back to our rooms and will wait for you there."

Bruce looked at him, refusing to show his disappointment. If there was one man he wanted to witness his knighting, it was Tobias, not Don Maximus. Bruce made light of the moment, not wishing to force the friar.

"I never thought I would see the day you walked away from a banquet."

"This is not the hour to celebrate your honor," said Tobias gravely. "Not when I know you intend to use it to try to destroy Maximus."

"And I never thought I would live to see the hour you would defend his evil ways!"

49

"It is not Maximus I worry about, but you. In destroying him, you destroy yourself." And Tobias snatched his cowl over his head and strode from the gilded room.

Grave and thoughtful, Bruce looked after him, then with determination he also left the castle chamber to be called before King Philip.

3

Don Nicklas Valentin

Bruce paced in a palatial pavilion of marble and crimson brocade, his boots silenced on thick Turkish carpets. He walked to one of the great walls and gazed up at hangings he recognized to be woven of famous Flanders tapestry. The gruesome scenes were all depicting various Roman saints undergoing martyrdom. He thought this somewhat ironic since Rome was the persecutor, not the victim. The atrocities now going on in Holland and in Protestant France were overlooked. Religious Rome used the secular sword of Spain in "the act of purging the church of devilish heretics." He turned away, only to see more statues of more saints standing on either side of a large stairway. The king's guards stood like statues themselves beside a strong door inlaid with silver.

The ascetic hush of the pavilion settled upon his senses as oppressively as too-sweet incense. He longed to be through with the business at hand that he might voyage to the West Indies.

Religious officials from Rome came and went with somber faces. He should not have been surprised that there were so many. The pope had found an obedient monarch in the kings and queens of Spain from the time of Ferdinand and Isabella, and the king and his armies carried out religious policy with un-flinching and — in Bruce's viewpoint — mindless fanaticism. Church and state were so mingled under the banner of the Vatican that it had become a double-headed mon-ster. The struggles in France, Holland, and England were also of peoples and monarchs striving to free themselves from the mastery of religious Rome. Bruce had plans to aid Holland financially by diverting the great wealth of the Spanish treasure fleet so as to feed, clothe, and supply weapons to the Protestant soldiers. Could it be done?

He turned, hearing quiet steps. A somber-faced secretary in purple-and-black silk ad-vanced toward him with a bow of his head.

"My orders, Señor Valentin, are to bring you to His Excellency. This way, if you please."

He followed the man down a maze of cor-ridors until they came to a doorway draped with purple and gold cord. Bruce went through into a darkly furnished chamber. He glanced about, expecting to see the king, but was greeted by even more tapestries of martyred saints, more silver — probably stolen from the Inca Indians in Peru — and more marble.

The secretary returned. "His Majesty will see you, Captain," and he stepped back with a bow to let him pass.

Bruce walked toward large double doors of carved wood. These swept open wide, and he looked into a great purple-and-gold chamber smelling of incense. Robed men sat writing on parchment at a long, dark table, their candles burning with a cool, steady flame. Guards stood beside more austere doors. A guard drew back a velvet drape, and Bruce wondered wryly whether a dungeon might await him instead of the king.

The secretary was speaking to someone behind the drape. "Captain Don Nicklas Valentin, sire," and bowing very low, he then drew back to allow Bruce to pass through.

Bruce entered the royal chamber with a faint clink of metal, and the drape slipped back into place behind him. A bishop stood near a window. As Bruce glanced toward the king's throne, he almost expected to see the pope himself, but alas, it was King Philip.

The monarch sat behind a long, glossy table on a high-backed chair that was all black except for the arms covered with red velvet.

Bruce had seen the king at other functions where he had walked about greeting officials, so he knew him to be a rather tall man. He was also slim, with thinning dark hair and a sallow complexion, and with eyes that appeared hooded because of sagging eyelids. His short, pointed beard was trimmed, and there was white lace around the cuffs of his dark clothing. His feet were on a red stool with a gold fringe.

Bruce found himself the object of the king's scrutiny. Was it his imagination, or were those eyes unfriendly? Or did they merely lack emotion? Perhaps his impression of the king of Spain was affected by his prejudice toward the man.

Bruce swept off his hat and sank gracefully to one booted knee, despairing of the moment, but affecting sobriety. He bowed low, his handsome, dark head nearly touching the marble floor as custom demanded, but neither the danger nor the irony of the tense moment was lost on him. He smiled briefly to himself. *The king of Spain and I in the same room, and he doesn't know I'm the English dog pirate he searches for in order to hang!*

"Captain Nicklas Valentin," came Philip's low, harsh Castilian. "I bid you rise and welcome, my son."

Your son? No. Your enemy, sir! thought Bruce as he rose on his polished boots, hand resting officially on the hilt of his sword. "Your Excellency, I am humbly honored!"

Philip studied him for a long, tense moment, and Bruce began to wonder if there hadn't been something of truth to Tobias's warning about Favian. Had he reported anything about the fighting at Florida? Could he know about the duel between himself and Don Demetrio?

Bruce, whilst under cool scrutiny, remained expressionless, but his fingers tightened on the handle of his English sword. Their eyes locked; the moment eased past as though he had only imagined its tension.

"Your success against the enemies of Spain has come to my ears with excellent report, Captain Valentin."

Bruce bowed his head.

"However, it is unfortunate you did not take a few prisoners from Florida that we may interrogate them of future plans to unlawfully colonize Spanish territory. Next time see you leave a handful alive, Don Valentin."

"At your wish, sire."

Philip watched him, seemingly in no hurry. "At least the flag of Spain waves without further disdain to her sovereign rule. Then the colony was altogether destroyed?"

"It is destroyed. The colonists were removed."

"And sold as slaves then, or dead?"

He dare not hesitate. "It was the wish and command of General Don Demetrio, sire."

"And General Don Demetrio, your commander — I have a report that he was killed in the resistance?"

"He resisted to the bitter end, sire," he said truthfully. "I can attend to the fact that he fought well. Had he lived, he would have made certain the trespassers paid a high price for their audacity in seeking to colonize Spanish territory." *All true*, thought Bruce.

The official secretary stepped to the side of the king's chair and whispered something. Philip looked toward a side door, lifted a hand, and the guard opened it to admit Viceroy Maximus, Don Favian, and Doña Sybella. They entered, kneeling and bowing low before the monarch. Bruce heard the secretary say to the king, "The viceroy has brought this letter from the governor at Saint Augustine. It arrived this morning, sire, brought to the viceroy by a nobleman arriving on the *Maria* from Florida." He handed King Philip a rolled parchment sewn in an envelope of silk. "The letter, sire, is from Governor Sanchez of Saint Augustine."

Bruce dare not show his alarm. *A letter from the Spanish governor!* His fingers tightened about the handle of his sword. He glanced from the sealed letter toward his father, but Maximus was as immobile. The rugged face with thick brows and strong jaw matched the six feet of hardened muscle. Only a slight roundness to his stomach revealed the mounting years. He was dressed splendidly in the uniform of the viceroy, with a hint of gold braid and crimson.

What had the Florida governor written to the king? wondered Bruce. Was Tobias right after all? Had his brother Favian suspected the truth and gone to the governor with a detrimental report?

A look at Favian's darkly handsome face with its sullen mouth and flashing black eyes revealed nothing, for Favian avoided eye contact. But Sybella did not — her mellow eyes were warmly upon him, and a vague smile softly touched the corners of her full mouth as she cast her glance downward when Favian turned his head to look at her.

It was no secret to Bruce that the Spanish governor who had been left behind to govern Saint Augustine was suspicious of Commander Demetrio's death. Before Bruce had sailed from there to come to Madrid, he had filed a report with the governor. Even in the best of times, the governor had not approved of him, complaining to Commander Demetrio that Bruce was too lenient on the Seminole Indians attacking the small Spanish town there.

Philip motioned for his secretary to open the silk cover that sealed the letter. The moments passed dangerously slow. Bruce glanced in the direction of the window. If he should need to make an escape — *impossible*. Whatever information the letter contained, he was as trapped as a fowl in a snare. It would be his sword against the guards, and no doubt against Maximus and Favian as well.

Philip took an agonizingly long time to read through the official letter before glancing sharply at Bruce. "You amaze me, Don Valentin."

Bruce's steady gaze remained fixed on the king.

"This report — it confirms the royal decision to have you knighted this day."

Bruce did not move. He felt the eyes of Maximus and Favian swerve toward him. Favian moved uncomfortably, looking bewildered. He glanced at Maximus, who had turned a hard glance upon him.

"Two English ships sunk in four months!" said King Philip. "And this done, besides the removal of the trespassers from the unauthorized colony in Florida! Governor Sanchez also writes of how you fought gallantly to save Commander Demetrio from a sudden attack by Seminole Indians on the beach."

Bruce remained as smooth as butter. He bowed. "Your servant, sire." But to himself he thought, *What? Governor Sanchez could not have written these words! The letter was forged. Who could have sent it, and in so careful a diplomatic manner that all were deceived by it except myself?* Not Tobias, surely, for he would have told him he had done so. Anyway, Tobias had been concerned that a letter from the governor may have arrived.

"Don Nicklas, certain tales questioning your allegiance have circulated, but I see now they have been hatched from jealous tongues. Your future and Spain's are wrapped up together with great acclaim. And so . . . we shall proceed without further

59

delay." He leaned forward and tossed the letter on the table to be taken away by the secretary. Bruce saw the eyes of Favian follow it suspiciously.

"You have no doubt heard of how certain English governors in the Caribbean secretly defend the pirates in their attacks against Spanish shipping," said Philip.

"A vile treachery, sire," agreed Bruce.

"These buccaneering thieves in the guise of privateers operate from an island of robbers called Tortuga. They persist, despite my orders to Viceroy Maximus Valentin to stop these attacks on the holy treasure fleet of God's chosen Spain."

So Maximus was under pressure from the king. If anything, it would make his father more ruthless.

"I want this robbery on the seas stopped, Don Nicklas, at whatever cost. Your service so pleases me, that your request to serve in the garrison at Grenada has not only been accepted, but I have decided to expand it."

"I am most honored, sire!"

"You will insure the security of the silver from the Peruvian mines as it is transported down the mountain to the treasure galleons at Cartagena on the Main. There, Viceroy Maximus is to make certain the treasure fleet sails unmolested to Veracruz, and home to Spain."

The viceroy bowed. Bruce sought to calm his heart. His plans were coming together as though borne along by the trade winds themselves.

"It is my prayer, Your Majesty, that the valuable treasure be brought safely to its worthy destination," said Bruce. "And to that end, I do hereby vow both my strength and my sword."

The king stood. "Remove your sword, Don Valentin."

He did so, handing it to Philip. He took it, passed it for blessing to the bishop, and Bruce went down on one knee for the second time. The benediction was given in Latin, then the sword was returned to the king, who placed the tip upon Bruce's right shoulder. Bruce stood, received it back, and taking the handle with both hands, brought the blade to his lips and kissed it as was the custom. But in gazing at the Spanish monarch, Bruce envisioned the English Union Jack. "Death to our enemies," he said.

Silence filled the throne room as the moment was considered by all, then Philip said, "One thing, Don Nicklas. Of late, the production of silver from the mines has decreased."

Bruce suspected some conquistadors of manipulation for personal gain. There was even reason to think the new English ambassador, Earl Robert Radburn, may be involved with Maximus. This, he thought, might hold some future possibility to see the end of the Valentin rule on the Main.

"I want this matter looked into and remedied with all good speed. If necessary, you will acquire more slaves, but see to it the silver production is doubled. It is no secret even to you that the war debts of Spain, as we fight the holy cause, continue to mount. The bankers must receive their pay; the lending merchants as well. The populace of Madrid also suffers want, for the soldiers of the Holy Inquisition must be fed, clothed, and supplied with weapons and ships, at whatever the cost."

Bruce looked on as though in total agreement, thinking contrarily that matters were falling into his hands like ripe, sweet figs!

"Viceroy Maximus will journey ahead to Cartagena. You will sail to Grenada with a letter for the governor to provide you with troops before you continue to Lima. You will also bring a shipload of slaves with you to work the mines, and all other necessary goods."

"I am humbly honored, sire. It is a great

satisfaction to me that I shall be provided with all that is needed for the success of this mission."

King Philip's humorless face stared back languidly. "Ah, Don Nicklas, you indeed will succeed. I hold you responsible, and the viceroy," and he turned to Maximus. Maximus strode forward and bowed low at the waist.

"You will see that my orders are carried through with all speed, granting what is necessary in the way of supplies, ships, and men."

"Yes, Excellency."

He handed him a paper. "Send copies of this order to the governors at Cartagena, Portobello, Havana, and Veracruz."

"Yes, Excellency."

King Philip dismissed them with a raise of his pale hand. "I will join you later in the plaza."

A moment later, wondering that the meeting had progressed so well — almost too well — Bruce bowed himself out of the king's cabinet.

Now, back at the guest chamber that Bruce had been given to prepare to meet the monarch, his half brother Favian filled a Venetian wine glass from a bottle that was delivered by a servant, along with a silver platter of fruits and nuts. Favian was tall and slim, and though not ruggedly built as Bruce, Favian was nevertheless wiry and strong. Ofttimes he carried the languid airs of unbearable conceit and dressed with ostentatious grandeur. Unlike the robust features of Maximus, his fine structure gave him a boyish handsomeness that the Señoritas found attractive: his sensuous mouth, his large eyes appearing like liquid pools the color of cinnamon looked out with cynical boredom upon a world he found not to his liking, yet did not care to change. A feather protruded stylishly from his flat red-velvet hat arranged at an angle on the side above his long, dark, wavy hair. His ruff was edged with Venetian lace, and he carried a white rose in his jacket that he now and then lifted to his nose. Far from being timid, however, Bruce knew his half brother had a reputation with the sword that was respected by the best.

"Valdepenas from Morena," said Favian, sniffing the wine, satisfied. "One thing I have missed in the cold climate of Lima is grapevines, my father. We ought to build an hacienda in the warmer regions and cultivate a vineyard." He lounged against the marble pillar and sipped, the dozen gold rings on his slim fingers winking.

Maximus turned to him with dark eyes that churned with internal restlessness. "Does that mean you will rise early to tend the vines, my son?"

"There is no need when we have slaves," he retorted. "Would you have me ruin my sword hand, Father? You have so many enemies."

"Your insolent tongue serves you better than your lazy wit," Maximus replied and turned toward Bruce.

Bruce lounged on the divan, consumed with thoughts of his own, for he was yet disturbed over who had sent the forged letter from the governor in Florida.

"Nicklas, have you no more enthusiasm for your success than to lounge there indolently eating grapes!" snapped Maximus. "You have won the favor of Philip. You have done the Valentin name honor. And yet you sit there."

Bruce plucked a purple grape and studied it while Favian remarked with a sneer in his voice, "Perhaps my brother thinks more of winning the favor of Sybella."

"If I do, my grinning peacock of a brother, you will be the first to know — and to languish in your disappointment."

"Bah!" Maximus strode to the balcony and looked below impatiently. "Sybella will hardly have time to mourn the loss of her husband with the two of you already drawing swords over her. Forget her — listen!" and he gestured below the balcony. "The name of Valentin is on the soldiers' tongues. I thought I would never hear a word that drips with such sweetness. Come, Nicklas — come and salute them!"

Bruce glanced at Favian. "What is Sybella doing here? She ought to be in Cordova mourning the death of Cousin Marcos."

Favian shrugged. "Ask Father. For all his words to the contrary, it was he who brought her with us. Sybella mourns for but one man," and from the look he gave Bruce, it was clear whom he meant. Bruce resisted the dart of fleshly pleasure. He wished to stay far removed from her, and yet he had been the first to ask of her welfare.

Favian walked to the marble table and poured himself more wine.

Maximus came and stood, strong hands on his hips, looking from one son to the other, his impatience growing. "I might as well have sired two women for all the good this success does either of you. A Valentin of another generation would have risen to seize his opportunity today. He would be out there among the soldiers on horseback receiving their praise. You lounge like a lapdog eating grapes, while Favian sops up the wine."

"Nicklas is tired," mocked Favian. "He has been up all night forging a letter from the grandee at Saint Augustine."

Bruce's eyes darted to his brother. The two measured each other.

"Forging?"

Favian shrugged. "What else could it be? We both know Governor Sanchez was displeased with you. I heard a rumor circulating this morning that the governor's correspondent had arrived last night. What could have possibly happened to his letter?"

"Enough speculation, Favian," said Maximus shortly. "Rumors are the work of jealous tongues."

Then the governor from Florida had written a letter to the king, probably telling of the death of the commander as well as the mild treatment given English colonists, thought Nicholas. *What had happened to it? Who had intervened to aid him?*

"I wonder what was written in the letter the governor sent," continued Favian, his pensive gaze on Bruce.

Bruce lifted a brow. "You should know, my brother. You were there to have heard firsthand from Governor Sanchez. No doubt you had a few suggestions to offer."

"Are you accusing me of questioning your allegiance to General Demetrio?"

Maximus banged his silver goblet down on the marble table. "I said, 'Enough,' Favian! Will you seek to undermine Nicklas to bolster your own reputation? You hang around the foolish courtiers picking up gossip like an old woman! Why are you not out making a name for yourself? You have the courage of a rabbit!"

Favian flushed and glared at his father, then walked over to the balcony. Bruce stood and snatched up his cloak and hat. Favian's suspicions troubled him, but his father's shameless insults attacking Favian's worth as a man angered him even more. Bruce had taken too much from Maximus when young to enjoy seeing more of the same ruthlessness.

"I must go," he said. "I have much to do before I ready the ships to sail for Grenada."

"You cannot leave!" Maximus's eyes burned with emotion. "The parade — you need to make your appearance."

Bruce's jaw set, but his voice was calm. "You mount the horse and ride among them for the applause, my father. The acclaim suits you far better than me."

He flung open the door and walked out, heedless of Maximus's shout: "Nicklas!"

Bruce went swiftly down the polished stairs into the receiving hall and was on his way out to the plaza where his horse waited out of sight, when another door to a smaller chamber already open a few inches, opened wide. Bruce stopped, surprised. Doña Sybella was there, a finger to her lips for silence, her eyes sparkling. She beckoned.

Bruce hesitated, glancing behind him. Seeing no one had followed him, he entered the dusky chamber with heavy velvet drapes and rug, all in red.

She closed the door quietly and moved toward him as though she owned him, her arms entwining about his neck and her lips seeking his. She smelled of heady musk, and the black lace of her mourning dress was stiff beneath his palms.

"I have dreamed of you constantly," she breathed. "You did not come to me! I waited and waited! Did you not receive my message in Saint Augustine?"

"Yes," he said quietly, looking into the luxuriant, creamy face that he remembered so well.

Her eyes widened. "And you did not come?"

"You were a married woman, Sybella." He unloosed her hands from behind his neck and held them tightly together in front of him. Her nearness brought temptation that he did not want.

"But married no longer," she whispered heatedly. "Marcos is dead."

"I see your grief has overwhelmed you," he remarked, knowing she had not loved her husband.

"I always loved you. It was Maximus who made me marry him. Maximus that —"

"Do not tell me of Maximus." He walked away from her, moving the thick drape aside to look out the arched window. It was beginning to rain, and Madrid looked drab and somber, the way a sorrowing widow should look. He looked at her, unsmiling. "Why are you here in Madrid?"

"Maximus brought me. But I would have come on my own in a carriage once I knew your ship docked."

"I will not be here in Madrid longer than a few weeks. I sail for Grenada." He knew this would not hold her off, but he hoped she might reconsider her feelings.

"I am going to Cartagena," she stated. "Maximus has arranged it with Doña Sevilla, my aunt. He has convinced her my grief is such for Marcos that I must get away and return home to the Casa Valentin." She lifted her chin. "I have a baby. Maximus —"

"Yes," he said rather abruptly. "Let me

guess. Uncle Maximus wants this boy to grow up under his thumb."

She gripped her hands together. "He is Marcos's son, and Maximus thought well of Marcos."

Well enough to see that Sybella married him instead of me. He looked at her, showing no emotion that might encourage her to think the flames between them could be rekindled.

"There is nothing in Cartagena for a woman of your upbringing. You belong to Spain," he tried to convince her.

She shrugged and came to him, laying her palms against his velvet jacket. "Though I am supposed to be in mourning, he has already made plans for my remarriage in a year." Her eyes looked into his. "To your brother Favian."

He could understand why Maximus would want a match between Sybella and Favian; she came from a wealthy and powerful family, with lands in Spain. Still, it made him wonder why Maximus had not chosen him — not that he would ever allow Maximus to control his future again, or the woman he married.

"I do not want Favian. It has always been you, Bruce."

The memory of her lips had all but faded

from his heart in the intervening years since her unexpected marriage to Cousin Marcos. Bruce intended to keep it that way. She was a beautiful woman, and the temptation to give in was strong. But he would not permit her to overwhelm him.

"Do not go to Cartagena," he said, steeling his emotions against her. "There can be nothing more between us, Sybella. I am a different man from what I was a few years ago. I have a calling — one that is dangerous. I do not know where it will end, but it may not end well. Marriage . . . love — it is all out of the question now."

Her eyes rebelled. "Is it? That is not what I have heard!"

He smiled, cynicism showing in his eyes. "I do not know what you have heard, but there is no one I care about enough to marry."

"It wasn't from Maximus I heard it, but Favian."

"Ah, Favian, of course. And what did he tell you?"

She shrugged. "He picks things up among the sons of the dons."

Bruce folded his arms and leaned his shoulder into the door. "I am curious about this gossip that is circulating about my marriageable intentions. Especially since I know nothing of them!"

"Then it isn't true," she breathed, satisfied. "I was so afraid you did not want me anymore."

"Sybella —"

"Favian says you will marry an Englishwoman from one of the Caribbean islands. Already there are plans being discussed between Maximus and the English lord."

Bruce laughed, for the idea was preposterous. "Favian savors too much wine, and sniffs too many white roses. There is no Englishwoman. But if there were, I would need to disappoint her and her conniving father dealing behind my back with Maximus. I am in no state to wed her or anyone else."

Sybella looked pleased that there was no other marriage arrangement. "I have no choice but to sail to Cartagena. I will change your mind about us when you get there, Bruce."

"You are sure of this?" he asked. His mouth tipped downward with a smile.

"I can make you change your mind," she murmured.

He took the long black lace on her mantilla and wrapped it around her neck, briefly touching the side of her face with the back of his hand.

"I promise you nothing," he said softly.

"And once there, Sybella, you will be unhappy. You remember how it was in Lima. There is nothing there. Not like Madrid or Cordova. You will quickly grow bored."

"I will never grow bored if you are there."

"I will be busy and gone much of the time. Do not come."

He reached behind him, found the door latch and opened it, letting in the daylight. She grabbed his arm, her eyes flaring. "I saved your life this day!"

He came alert, studying her face.

"I have friends in powerful places," she whispered. "I am a Ferdinand, or have you forgotten?"

"I have not forgotten," he said wearily.

She lifted her chin again. "I had the letter from Governor Sanchez intercepted. I destroyed it and had another drawn up in your favor. Had I not done so, you would be languishing in the dungeons below right now. And will you dare refuse my love?"

He watched her, his gray-green eyes turning hard.

"I will come," she insisted in a low, heated whisper. "And you will come to me. And if not . . ." her voice trailed off.

He looked at her evenly, his handsome face unrelenting, then turned and left, his boots sounding on the marble floor.

4

"And Thy Right Hand Shall Hold Me"

The night air was humid, as though it had blown over a steaming kettle, and the yard was thick with orange honeysuckle and blue peridots growing on a wide path between some storage sheds and barns and a large pepper tree. Skirting the edge of the tree, Devora was making for the back-porch steps when a snapping branch drew her attention. In the tree were two thatch-roofed beehives belonging to the overseer. Tad, the ten-year-old waif who had sailed with his brother on a buccaneering vessel until his brother was killed in a duel, had been rescued from the wharf by Barnabas and brought to stay at Ashby Hall. It appeared to her as if he were hoping to rob the beehive.

"Tad, climb down at once. Do you wish to be stung?"

He turned to look at her through the leaves, a sheepish expression on his face. "Weren't going to be a thief."

"No? Why aren't you inside with the other children helping Emily with supper?"

"They be not liking me none, Miss Devora."

He quickly changed the subject as he scooted down, his eyes bright as he turned on bare feet to look at her.

"Guess what I seen, miss, coming in nigh to an hour ago."

She folded her arms. "A pirate ship. And you best stay away from it."

"How'd ye know? 'Bout the ship, I mean?"

"Percy mentioned it. And the buccaneers are men to stay away from."

The wistful gleam in his eyes suggested otherwise, and she knew it would be hard for Barnabas to keep him at Ashby Hall, especially after her departure. Her uncle's health was declining with age, and he had depended upon her for help, especially with Tad. A sadness filled her heart, and she feared to mention to the boy that she was leaving, knowing it would feed his own desire to find some vessel he could serve on as cabin boy. She must remember to pray daily for Tad, not allowing her own problems to narrow her concerns.

"I seen Captain Bruce Hawkins at Tortuga before," said Tad, a gleam in his eye. "Seen him duel a Dutchie an' lay him low."

"That sounds quite revolting, if you ask me."

"It waren't his fault, miss. The Dutchman forced the fight. I seen some of Hawkins's crew, too, all carrying boarding pistols and cutlasses. He were friends with my brother, but Hawkins? He's sunk more galleons than even James did."

He told her wistfully how he had sailed on pirating ventures with his brother and how it was a cabin boy's duty to set the ship "afire."

"After we takes an enemy ship, they's real careful how they divvy it all up. 'A very exact and equal dividend is made,' is how they puts it. Captain, he receives five or six shares, master's mate two, other officers as their work goes. A crewman gets one share. A cabin boy like me, a half share." He grinned proudly. " 'Tis risky bein' a boy, miss, because when captain and crew leaves a ship to ruin, it's me who has to stay alone and set her afire. 'Tis dangerous work, miss. An' after we sets it afire we has to scurry off with the fleein' rats before she blows. Heard one cabin boy sailin' with Captain Jean le Testu who were blown to bits. Sharks came later and ate him."

Devora frowned. "There will be no more of that, Tad. You don't want to grow up a pirate —"

"Buccaneer, miss. A freebooter."

"Buccaneer, pirate — there's little difference to me."

"Nay, but there is, Miss Devora!"

"You want to be like Barnabas. Remember how he said he'll teach you medicine? When you get older he may send you to Boston to learn. And when you graduate, you can come home to Ashby Hall and be the best doctor in Barbados."

"What about you, Miss Devora? Will you be one, too, and Mister Edward?"

A melancholy smile tugged at her lip. "I'll do what I can with the learning Barnabas gave me. As for Edward —" she paused. His plan had been to voyage to England to study for his medical degree. They planned to marry when he returned. . . .

"I'm sure Edward will do fine enough with the Lord's good plans. Has he arrived yet? He was to have supper here."

"My shame, Miss Devora, I was to tell ye sooner. He's in Bridgetown, at the governor's house. Miss Sarah called him to a ball. Everyone gets to wear a mask."

Governor Huxley's daughter invited Edward to a ball? Why hadn't he mentioned it to her on Sunday? She knew that there was talk that Sarah Huxley had noticed him, but she hadn't considered the information seriously.

She lifted her chin. Nevertheless, she must see him. If he would not come here tonight, then she would ride into Bridgetown. Tomorrow would be too late.

"I guess Edward had forgotten about the ball. . . . By now Miss Emily is wondering where we're both at. Come along. We'll have some sweet tea before I ride into Bridgetown."

"You still going to call on Mister Edward? Can I come with you? I can bring your message while you wait outside proper-like."

She hesitated, then decided his presence may provide the assistance she needed. She could see Tad was anxious to visit the governor's mansion.

"All right, but we'll tell Emily where we're going. Maybe Clyde can bring me instead."

Tad beamed. "He can't. He ain't here. He's down at the boiling house. They got a new contraption today on that ship comin' in from Boston. Clyde says Mister Barnabas will produce twice as much sugar now."

They neared the door that opened into the kitchen of Emily's bungalow. The familiar homey smells of baking bread and fresh-boiled coffee met Devora with a pleasant welcome. Twelve-year-old Agnes and 14-year-old Libby, the two daughters of Emily and Clyde, were busy with food preparation, and Emily was removing a hot urn of coffee from the oven built into the wall beside the hearth. All three turned to Devora with ready smiles, and Emily ushered Tad back out to the porch to wash his face and hands in a barrel of water.

"Edward was called into Bridgetown," called Emily. "Did Tad tell you?"

"Yes. I'll be riding in to see him. It's important" was all she said when Emily stopped to look at her with raised brows.

"I'm bringing Tad," added Devora.

Now that she was here to pour out all her grief on Emily's sturdy shoulders, she couldn't bring herself to ruin their last hour together by bringing on everyone else's tears to mingle with her own. In the five years that Devora had been at Ashby Hall, she had come to look upon Emily as an older aunt or sister, and the good-bye would be too painful. Emily seemed to read her face and know at once that something was wrong.

"I heard your mother arrived today."

"The news is all over Bridgetown that Countess Radburn has come for her daughter," added the older Libby, and from the glow on her cheeks, anyone could see she at least thought the idea thrilling.

"Yes," said Devora. "I was the last to know, about an hour ago." And she took the chair at the round table that Emily drew out for her. "I'm going — away."

"Where? To the estate of your grandmother?" Emily's eyes searched hers.

Devora reached for the cup of tea. "No. Cartagena."

Emily stared at her, then sank onto the opposite chair.

"Spain?" whispered Libby gravely.

The smaller girl, Agnes, came in from the stone cook room carrying a large black steel pan, her eyes bright and the freckles standing out on her nose.

"Mama's baked a wild plum cobbler!"

"Careful with that," hollered Libby. "It's burning hot and if you drop it —"

"I won't." The girl set it down carefully on the stone hot plate on the table and looked at her older sister proudly.

"You still shouldn't have picked it up. Isn't that right, Mama?" said Libby.

Devora and Emily were still looking at each other, their gaze telling all that ached in their hearts.

Devora blinked hard and smiled as Tad

returned washed and pink of face.

"I'll get the plates," cried Libby.

As the smell of the cobbler filled the kitchen and the chatter and laughter of the girls and Tad sounded in her ears, Devora could almost believe that her life wasn't going to change after all, and that the arrival of the countess had been a bad dream.

5

Mysterious Stranger

Outside Governor Huxley's residency in Bridgetown, Barbados, Bruce stood hidden beneath palm trees lining the walk, making certain the way was clear. He was here for a covert meeting with Lord Arlen Anthony, a confidant of King Charles II of England, and a friend of Governor Thomas Modyford of Jamaica.

The white building with a red roof was overflowing with important political guests, many of them planters, when he arrived for the masked ball. The rooms were bright with chandeliers, and the windows radiated a golden glow that fell outward upon the front veranda. On the green, the big shade trees and the trellis-lined walkway were also glowing with small lanterns made of colored glass that hung from branches and tossed hypnotically in the trade wind. Music came lazily to him, unhurried voices rose and fell, and laughter drifted with the sultry heat.

The masked affair afforded Bruce the cover he needed, for even in Barbados there were certain political figures, such as the new English ambassador to Spain, who would instantly recognize him as Don Nicklas Valentin. Bruce would meet with Lord Anthony upstairs in the listening gallery overlooking Governor Huxley's hearing room. Lord Anthony, who had learned some of the details of a friend's disappearance, had arranged for a serving man to bring a secret message to Bruce at Grenada. While Bruce was a careful man, though deliberately daring at times, he had felt that he had no choice but to come to Barbados.

Tonight, however, was not one of those times that prompted him to excitement and danger. He was already concerned he had been followed, and was therefore late in coming to the meeting.

He entered the house as previously arranged by Lord Anthony's serving man by way of a little-used entrance near the side of the house which Anthony had made certain would be unlocked. He stood, glancing about, only vaguely curious. The parlor was hung with ivory-and-green damask. There were French tables and chairs of walnut, some of them gilt, and a long walnut divan with thick green cushions fringed with ivory silk. He noted that many of the more expensive items in the governor's house were from Madrid and Malaga. His eyes swerved toward an anteroom that he knew from a past visit led up to a small listening gallery that overlooked the official hearing room of Governor Huxley. Swiftly he went up the steps, his polished black boots with silver buckles making no sound. His hand rested on his scabbard, making certain no clink of steel alerted anyone.

From farther back in the house he heard muffled waltz music coming from the ballroom. The governor's lady was entertaining. This ball was the perfect situation for his arrival. He adjusted his mask. Although the notion of Don Nicklas Valentin waltzing with English ladies did tempt his sense of irony enough to risk it, he had glimpsed the women in attendance, and there was no one that interested him enough to extend his stay. And he must avoid seeing Lord Robert Radburn at all costs. He would keep his meeting with Lord Arlen Anthony, then return secretly to Grenada. Had it not been that Sir Arlen had important information, it would have been madness to have come here.

Lord Anthony was a powerful British lord serving the Duke of Abermarle, a cousin of

Sir Thomas Modyford of Jamaica, the English governor there who was a secret supporter of the buccaneers. For the last two years while Bruce had been serving King Philip in the region of Florida, Bruce's buccaneering vessel *Revenge* had been captained by his friend and buccaneering ally, Captain Kitt Bonnor. His Spanish galleon *Our Lady of Madrid* was anchored at Grenada, but within two months he would be on his way to Cartagena to oversee the mule train from Lima to Cartagena. A sardonic smile touched his lips.

Reaching the top of the steps, he entered the upper gallery, a sparsely furnished room with some listening benches near a rail overlooking the governor's hearing room. A curtain was drawn closed, and Bruce removed his dark cloak and wide-brimmed hat with white plume and set them on a bench. He was late, and he would have expected Lord Anthony to have been here by now. Then he heard him below, followed by the curt voice of the English ambassador Earl Robert Radburn — a man he had long disliked while in Madrid, but who thought well of Don Nicklas Valentin. Curious as to why Radburn was in an argument, Bruce went to the curtain and eased it aside to peer down.

Lord Anthony and the governor of Barbados, Winthrop Huxley, were lounging in cane chairs with Jamaican rum toddies, and while the ambassador vented his frustrations, they were devouring heaps of boiled crabs and oysters. Lord Robert reminded Bruce of an ancient Viking with glacier-blue eyes and cropped golden hair. A deep scar ran from above his right eyebrow all the way down to below his ear — a scar that Bruce had been told in Madrid had come from a death fight with an angry Inca Indian in Cuzco. Bruce didn't blame the Indians of Peru for anger over the stealing of their great hoards of gold and silver.

Robert continued his fiery discourse on the need to capture —

"That bloodthirsty pirate Hawkins!"

Amusement flickered in Bruce's smile. Kitt had put the *Revenge* to good use during Bruce's absence in order to maintain the Hawkins reputation. His tanned fingers drummed his leather baldric with impatience. If Robert knew who Hawkins actually was, he would be astounded to realize how he had sipped refreshment with the "bloodthirsty pirate" on several occasions in Madrid in the aristocratic homes of the best and wealthiest dons. After Bruce had recently returned from the perpetual wars that Spain declared in Europe, it was Lord Robert, the new ambassador sent by the king of England to the court of Castile, who had hailed him to His Most Catholic Majesty as a fine and heroic soldier of the Spanish crown. At the present, Lord Robert believed him to be commanding the galleons in Grenada, preparing troops to bring with him to Cartagena.

His amusement faded. If Robert saw him here, he would certainly recognize him, though donned in English garb. He came alert as Robert continued.

"Yes, Governor Huxley, a warning, unfortunately, from the esteemed Spanish viceroy Maximus Valentin of Lima, no less."

At the mention of his father, Bruce's interest intensified. A warning from Maximus?

"Either catch this diabolical pirate Hawkins preying mercilessly on Spanish shipping and hang him or send him to Jamaica to Execution Dock, or Viceroy Valentin will not be held responsible for the consequences to the citizens of Barbados."

Father would not dare attack Barbados, thought Bruce.

At last the feisty governor, who had listened in agitation while he devoured his oysters and washed them down with rum, was on his gouty feet, wincing his discomfort.

"I'll not be intimidated by Spanish threats! You know as well as anyone I've no taste for buccaneers. This isn't Jamaica. How was I to know Doctor Kitt Bonnor was sailing the *Revenge* under the name of Hawkins? Kitt was a doctor, coming and going, aiding my gout better than Barnabas Ashby. I didn't even know Kitt could sail a ship."

Lord Robert gave a short laugh. "He can sail all right. There isn't a better scoundrel in the Caribbean except Hawkins himself. The two make a bloodthirsty pair of pirates."

"One hardly credits Kitt with such a reputation," argued Governor Huxley. "As I say, Ambassador, he's a doctor."

"A doctor, perhaps, and I've heard he has a medical degree from London. But he has also been attacking Spanish shipping under the Hawkins name. You will forgive us, Governor, if we don't believe his terror on the Caribbean was a secret to those in your parliament."

"Drivel. Do you mean to accuse me of harboring a pirate?"

"There is no question but that Kitt Bonnor is a pirate; unfortunately, when he was brought as a prisoner to the Main we learned that he was not the real Bruce Hawkins."

"And you thought he was?"

"The governor of the Isle of Pearls was so convinced."

"And you think I know where the real Hawkins is?"

"Whether you do or do not at the moment is inconsequential. We are almost certain he has been away. We think that Hawkins will come to Barbados for Kitt Bonnor. There's little chance he knows that the Spanish governor of the Isle of Pearls has him in the dungeon where he belongs. But Hawkins will want to return to his ship, and he'll probably seek out Bonnor."

"Then why not put a guard of soldiers around the ship? Why plague me about it?"

"If it were so easy, do you think we would come to you? We have no idea where his ship is —"

"It is not here in Carlisle Bay, I can assure you, Ambassador."

"And if he sets foot on Barbados, Viceroy Valentin is holding you responsible to see him captured and turned over to the Spanish government."

"Now you listen to me, Ambassador. I have nothing but regard for your daughter.

She has a pristine reputation in Bridgetown. But I don't know where Hawkins is, and Kitt Bonnor came and went as a physician — I didn't know him as a pirate. But regardless! I'll not be buffeted about by snarling threats coming from the Spanish viceroy."

"Then the viceroy cannot promise the safety of Carlisle Bay."

"Our safety is not dependent upon the viceroy. And if any Spanish warship comes within an inch of Carlisle Bay, I'll provide a welcome for the buccaneers from Tortuga with my blessing! I'll order 'em to blow your Castilian ship from here back to Madrid! You tell Viceroy Maximus that!"

Bruce smiled.

"Now, now, gentlemen," drawled Lord Anthony, speaking for the first time. "May cooler heads prevail. Look, Ambassador, this isn't Port Royal. You know that. So do the buccaneers. Barbados doesn't shelter the vessels of the Tortuga Brotherhood. The parliament can assure the viceroy that neither the real Captain Hawkins nor the *Revenge* will be tolerated in Barbados."

"That is not the information coming secretly to me, Arlen," came the cool warning voice of Lord Robert, but Anthony waved a calm hand.

"The buccaneers already know they're

not wanted here. We're doing everything we can to urge Chevalier de Fontenay of Tortuga to clean out that rat's nest he has inherited from the French pirate Jean Le Vasseur, but to no avail. Let's not blame Governor Huxley here. We thought the young Kitt Bonnor a fine gentleman, knowing the ways of medicine."

The tired governor sank back into his rosewood chair of bright claret velvet, and snatching his black periwig off his head, threw it on the table. "Blazes, Ambassador, d'ye think Hawkins is a fool? He won't set a sail near Carlisle Bay. He knows I would land him like an overstuffed fish. Barbados is civilized. D'ye think we're called Little England for naught? Surely it's Port Royal he'll be setting his anchor for. And if you're looking for the *Revenge*, that's likely where you'll find it — and Bruce Hawkins. Why d'ye not go weary the bones of Governor Modyford with your words instead of me? I tell you Hawkins won't show his face anywhere near here."

Bruce allowed the curtain to fall gently back into place, covering a smile. As he did, he heard a movement from the door.

Danger prickled the air and he came alert, unsheathing his blade and moving cautiously toward the faintly moving drapes on the other side of the chamber. Swiftly he drew the drape to one side and stepped back, sword lifted, certain he would face the man who had followed him from Grenada.

Bruce snatched a slight breath of surprise.

A woman stood there. . . .

In the shadows of the gallery he was unable to see her face clearly. She wore a ball mask, which appeared to be hastily cut from unadorned calico cloth. A deep-hooded black cloak concealed her hair, but it was her hand that brought a cool glitter to his eyes. She held a dagger. She sucked in her breath, turned, and fled.

It took him a moment to recover his surprise at seeing her there. Her light footsteps were hasting to escape down the corridor — no doubt into the dark night where an accomplice waited. He flung the drapes aside in pursuit, coming to the end of the corridor in time to catch a glimpse of black cloak swirling around the corner.

He knew the arrangement of the immediate rooms since he seldom risked a meeting in enemy territory without knowing several possible exits. He pursued to see her race through a heavily draped archway.

Bruce smiled. He had trapped the quavering little rabbit! If he were right, there was no exit in that chamber, for it led to a stairless balcony.

Now at his leisure, he drew aside the drape with one hand, his sword still in the other, and glanced about. The converging shadows on the carved wainscoting momentarily concealed her. Her back was toward him, and she gripped the iron railing, staring below.

He contemplated her, tapping the point of his blade against a carved wooden post. "So you carry a dagger and are now ready to swing down from a balcony. You are a woman of interesting talents, madam. However, I wouldn't try going out that window. The jump is very steep." He sheathed his sword.

She turned to bolt past him. He leaned both palms into the doorjamb and stood blocking her path. A brow lifted.

Seeing she could not get past, she said breathlessly, "Sir, this is a mistake, the dagger is not mine. I — I did not intend to use it!"

He scanned her, seeing silken flounces, jade velvet ribbons, and an inch of white lace petticoats as a strong gust of wind blew in from the sea. Again, she looked below the balcony, then back at him.

"Now surely, madam, you must be the

offspring of Ann Bonny," came his sly remark.

She looked bewildered. "I do not know Lady Ann Bonny!"

He laughed. "If you would call her a lady, then I've no choice but to believe you, for a lady she is not, but a wench — a nasty little pirate on Tortuga."

"Pirate! I beg your pardon, sir!"

"Indeed? Then remove your mask and state your name and cause."

It was obvious that she was not a wench. Bruce recognized fine manners, and there was something in the lift of her head and the way she drew back from him that betrayed a finishing-school demeanor, but she was obviously wishing to disguise her face.

"I've half a mind to believe you," he admitted. "A young woman in petticoats is somehow not my idea of an assassin. Suppose you explain. I'm in a hurry. Or were you a decoy?"

She drew in a breath as though that idea had not entered her mind.

"An accomplice could also hang," he said smoothly, enjoying himself.

At the word *hang,* instead of fainting in a heap of ribbons and lace, she appeared to freeze, then said tartly, "I do not find your grim humor entertaining, sir."

"Oh! Pardon! Nor do I. Hanging is quite humorless except for the rabble that enjoy such spectacles. Come now, Señorita —" He stopped, catching what might have been a fatal error in giving himself away. With an impatient wave of his hand to distract her, he said, "Madam, do state your name and cause. I've no time to waste on pretty games."

He could see that despite her attempt at affected calm, she was alarmed.

"While you hold me here, sir, the man you seek is no doubt escaping."

"Precisely the reason I am detaining you. You will tell me everything. Come, come, out with it. Who are you and what do you want?"

"I had nothing to do with it! You must believe me!"

"You've given me little reason to believe you. Come now, remove the mask."

Her frustration was evident.

"I tell you I must not be seen."

He lifted a brow again. "If I were in your slippers, I would not wish to be identified either — sneaking about the good English governor's residence carrying a dagger. Nonetheless, my dear, I'm afraid I must insist," and he smiled, took a step toward her, knowing she would try to dart past again. He caught her, and with swift, deft fingers snatched the dagger, then snapped the ribbon that held the handmade mask. It fluttered helplessly to the hardwood floor.

He paused. Her hood had fallen back, displaying silky honey-colored hair that was swept back and pinned up becomingly with pearl combs. His eyes narrowed when he caught sight of them; there was something familiar about the pearl combs. . . . But it was not the pearls that held the unexpected interest of Bruce Valentin. He encountered a lovely pair of violet-blue eyes with thick, dark lashes. He had seen but one pair of eyes like these before, and they had belonged to the viscountess Catherina Ashby Radburn, wife of Lord Robert. But unlike the viscountess, an older vamp, as untrustworthy as a snarling cat, the eyes of this young woman and her facial features were not simply alluring, but they also spoke undefilement. He was moved against his will. He rejected the sudden rise of his heartbeat — something he had never felt as keenly before upon seeing a lovely woman, and he had seen many lovely and even beautiful woman in Spain and across Europe. With wonder, yet a goading sense of unease as well, he knew that hers would be a face he would not quickly forget, nor perhaps want to dismiss.

He looked critically, noting her schooled quietness with cool, meditative interest. A faint flush of color rose into her pale cheeks. He said in a low voice absent any amusement, "You are definitely not related to Ann Bonny."

Despite the pounding of her heart, Devora struggled to hold onto the proper demeanor taught all young women of quality as she stared into smoldering gray-green eyes that favorably contrasted with dark hair, worn in cavalier length. His bronzed features were decidedly striking, with dark, slashing brows and lashes, and a masculine cleft in his chin. The slim mustache gave an air of boldness, as did his somber cut of black velvet without a hint of either gem or lace, as though he had almost wished to go unnoticed at the ball. But who was that other man at the door with the dagger? Why had he strangely dropped it when he saw her coming up the steps? Had he wanted her to pick it up, to distract this man from pursuing him?

Irritation at herself grew. She should not have picked it up nor run!

"The dagger is not mine," she whispered

and pulled to release her wrist from his hand.

He held firmly, however, a faint smirk on his mouth. "Nay, madam, not yours — but if true, you should at least be able to tell me its owner. Surely your fair hand belongs to the most cunning of female assassins." And he released her right hand and lifted her left, casually inspecting.

Devora's eyes narrowed, for she suspected he was searching for a wedding ring. So then . . . Her fingers tightened into a balled fist. She drew in a breath and, pulling her wrist from his hand, stepped back as if insulted by his effrontery.

He was not in the least put off by her behavior, and his arrogance increased as he barred the doorway, leaning there, scanning her thoughtfully.

"In all my travels, madam, it is not often I meet a damsel with so hard and cruel a nature as to hope to plunge a dagger into my tender and valorous heart. And why would you wish to harm me — an important guest of the governor?"

Devora tore her eyes from his to stare at the gleaming silver dagger that he was turning over in his hand, studying it with an immobile face. A shiver ran down her back as she looked at it.

"I am innocent — sir — sir — ?" and she groped for a name.

He looked at her with humor. "Sir Bruce will do," he said, too simply.

"Bruce? Sir — Bruce, I beg of you!"

"Indeed?" The color of his eyes seemed to dance.

"Oh please, I —"

Devora stopped abruptly. Something in his half-smothered smile told her that his severity was a ruse. Her eyes left the dagger.

"I perceive, Sir Bruce, that you find this horrendous situation somewhat amusing."

"Is an attack on my life deemed amusing?" he asked gravely, scowling. "Tell me, who taught you to use this weapon?"

Again Devora shivered, but was determined not to show the sickening sensation that churned in her stomach. She had glimpsed the man who had dropped it, but she had not seen his face. If she admitted to being an eyewitness, it would require an appearance before the magistrate and the necessity of admitting she was Lady Devora Ashby. The earl and countess would be furious with her for coming here uninvited to see Edward, whom Tad had been unable to find. He had asked the doorman, who insisted he had never heard of a guest named Edward, and that Lady Sarah, Governor

Huxley's daughter, was not in Bridgetown but visiting a cousin in Jamaica.

Devora had been certain that the doorman had been mistaken, and so the clever Tad had come up with an idea so that she could go to the ball to look for Edward herself.

"All ye need, Miss Devora, is a mask — and I kin make one for ye easy with me knife. This piece of cloth from ye under-skirt, and two holes cut like so — and ye can go and nosey about and who's to know?" He had grinned, and Devora, amused, had smiled wryly. "You do come in quite handy, Tad, but I fear neither of us is a very good in-fluence on the other right now. All right. Make me a mask!" And she had turned her back, lifted her top skirt, and managed to slice off a section of white underskirt.

Devora looked down at the cloth mask on the floor, and with a surreptitious glance at Sir Bruce, stepped over it to conceal it, hoping he would forget.

He did indeed appear preoccupied now. He was standing deep in thought as he turned the dagger over in his hand, walking toward the anteroom. He stopped, looking at it.

All the while Devora was watching his every move. She stood very still so as not to distract him from his thoughts. At the moment they served her well. He moved farther away from her, toward the balcony where the wind swept in with a gust that stirred the hems of the cream-colored lace curtains. She held her breath with hope and, when he had taken his last boot step, her eye darted to the unguarded doorway where the drape had fallen back into its place, judging the distance. When his shoulder was momentarily toward her, as the balcony curtain swept out again softly like inviting fingers, she stooped and snatched up her mask, then rushed madly for the drape and out into the corridor, racing as fast as her feet would carry her.

She heard him coming behind, but she had reached the salon that branched off in two directions: the side door, which she had used to come in earlier unnoticed, and on the other side of the salon a wide double door that stood open, leading into the bright ballroom where a crystal chandelier winked with a myriad of lights that seemed to beckon her forward.

She looked back at him. He was still on the steps watching her, as though he hoped she would not go into the ballroom. Then that's exactly where she would flee!

Devora rushed toward the ballroom, tying

on her mask as she went. Her instincts told her that he had not come for the ball, nor did he wish to be seen any more than she did. It was a bold move on her part — one that might yet see her standing rebuked before the countess. She could not imagine how she would adequately explain her audacious behavior of appearing uninvited at the governor's elite ball. But as Sir Bruce's maliciously amused eyes flashed across her mind, she preferred even a confrontation with her mother.

She was not dressed for a ball, but could she get by with it? She would have to. For she found herself in the ballroom, her feet on the glossy floor, the strains of the waltz filling her ears, while all about her satins and velvets and camlin and taffeta swirled like so many gracious wings in a world of butterflies. She expected every head to turn and look toward her with surprise, but hardly anyone noticed her — except the African serving man with a heavy silver tray in his hands filled with Venetian glasses of who-knew-what-sort-of wicked concoctions. Devora murmured her thanks and took the tray and began to move away from the entrance and along the rim of the ballroom floor as though a servant.

"Thank you, m'dear, just what I needed,"

said the blustering old planter Mr. Hiram. "The West Indian climate. Treacherous! Ah, but treacherous!"

"Sadly so, sir, yes, sadly so —" She glanced back. Her heart sank. If she had thought herself bold to come in here, then the man was bolder still. He had put on his black mask and also entered. He stood by the double doors scanning the floor until he saw her. Devora's steps quickened. She skirted the perimeter of the room, still holding the tray, intending to escape out the door on the other side. But when she arrived he was already there.

If her entry had gone without notice, his had not. Women's heads turned, and some ladies seated in chairs along one wide wall lifted their fans and whispered behind them.

Devora found herself standing before him. He took the tray with a smile, set it aside on the table, and taking her elbow firmly steered her onto the floor.

"You are making us the center of attention," she whispered, staring straight ahead.

"A risk far greater to me than to you. Is your father here tonight?"

"My father?"

"You are the daughter of Lord Robert Radburn, aren't you?"

She hesitated, for in truth he was her stepfather, but she didn't think it wise to tell him this. However, the Earl of Radburn was politically powerful and might discourage him from pursuing the dagger incident — unless he expected to use it as a means of extortion.

"You're mistaken," she said truthfully. "The earl is not my father."

"I was almost certain. You bear a resemblance to the countess."

She said nothing and glanced about uneasily. "This is madness, Sir Bruce. Let me go."

"Not until you tell me who you are."

Since she did not have the name Radburn she was safe. "Oh, very well. I'm Lady Devora Ashby," she said stiffly. "My uncle owns Ashby Hall plantation here in Barbados."

"Why did you come here? Not for the ball. Your dress is plain and your hem is dusty. And your mask is laughable."

Under his brief smile she flushed. "I think you're a cad."

He laughed. "Maybe I am, madam, but you're hardly better, traipsing about with a dagger in hand, crashing the governor's ball in a ragpicker's dress."

"How dare you. It so happens I was working on my uncle's plantation before I came — tending sick children, if you must know."

The devastating smile continued. "And you decided to drop everything and come to waltz with Sir Bruce. Your daring boldness has me entranced."

She gritted her dislike of the man and stiffened, trying to pull away.

"Easy, my little charmer, we wouldn't want to make more of a scene now than we already have, would we?"

"Are you afraid to be discovered?" she hissed. "You can't deceive me, sir. You hadn't planned on being seen any more than I. And why was that man spying on you? What have you done?"

"You're very intimidating. Alas! Should I tell you who I am?"

She gave him a belittling glance that was far from what she felt. "You need not explain. You're a pirate! A thief, and who knows what all else!"

He laughed. "You're right," he said, trying to restrain his amusement, and drew her a trifle closer as she stiffened, trying to resist without drawing attention to the fact.

Her heart seemed to flip-flop. Her eyes looked into his questioningly.

"If you think to scream, beware. I am known to take prisoners aboard my ship. I confess, one so lovely would be a first. Now," he stated firmly, his arm tightening about her waist, the other holding her hand as he drew her toward him, looking down at her. "Why did you come here, not wishing to be seen?"

She swallowed. "To find Edward Townsend."

"Sounds a much-boring fellow. But perhaps not if he has troubled to lure you here."

"He did not lure me here. I am not lured by anyone, thank you."

"My pardon, madam. Then?"

"That, sir, is a personal matter between him and me."

His teeth showed beneath his mustache. "A woman with a dagger? I am making it mine also."

"All right. I — I am being sent away from Barbados. He is in training to become a doctor," she said flatly, "and my uncle has also schooled me in such matters. There is sickness breaking out on Townsend plantation among new slaves recently brought in, and I had information I wished to pass on to him before I set sail. I had no intention of crashing Governor Huxley's ball tonight, except that the child I sent here to ask for Edward was told he wasn't here. Speaking with him before I left was well worth the embarrassing risk of coming inside. I didn't want to be recognized so I wore a mask — one created momentarily on a whim."

"A very creative whim. From a petticoat, I gather from the lace. Most intriguing. And the dagger? We must not forget that most interesting part of your adventure."

She began to think he believed her, but did she believe him? Was he a pirate? He certainly had the arrogance of one! She briefly explained to him what had happened with the dagger. "And now, you surely waste time. While you accuse me of a despicable act, the real villain escapes."

"Had there been a chance of overtaking him, I would have done so. He was cunning enough to have disappeared into the throng on the green. You were my best hope for information."

She followed his glance toward the open windows to the green where guests were gathered talking and enjoying Governor Huxley's refreshments.

"Then you *do* believe I am innocent!"

He smiled.

She gave a sigh of relief. "I assure you I never saw him before. He was standing by the drape when I came up the steps. I saw the dagger in his hand, saw him draw aside the drape, but before I could cry out, he heard me coming. When he saw me on the stairs, he dropped the dagger, threw himself over the banister, and swung down. I unwisely picked up the dagger."

"So instead of telling me what happened, you ran — allowing me to chase you and become diverted."

Devora felt her face turn hot. "I admit I behaved unwisely. I thought only of saving myself from being discovered."

"No longer worry yourself. What did he look like? You must have seen his face."

"He wore a mask," she said lamely.

"Anything at all memorable in the brief moment you saw him?"

"No, I am sorry. It seems I've made a pretty mess of things." She looked at him, the moment giving her the first chance to wonder why anyone would wish to kill him.

"You have determined enemies, so it seems. Why would he wish to harm you?"

He studied her face for a moment, his answer offering too little to be taken at face value. "Perhaps it was a mistake in identity."

Somehow she felt it went deeper than that.

A weighty silence settled between them as they waltzed. She had an uneasy notion that he was risking even more by being seen on the ballroom floor than she. He was a daring and reckless adventurer, she thought, one whose company she would never seek on her own. Yet, in his arms, she was drawn against her will. They stared at each other for only a moment, but that moment seemed to Devora to be transfixed.

"I must go," she whispered breathlessly.

"As must I. I've an appointment I cannot miss. I would appreciate it if you would say nothing of this meeting to anyone."

She smiled ruefully. "I was about to request the same thing of you, Sir Bruce."

He smiled. "Your secret is safe —"

"Ah, Governor Huxley!" someone was saying.

"Hello, James, you've met the Earl of Radburn?"

She saw him glance toward the doorway that led from another room.

So her father was here. Panic gripped her heart. Bruce's hand dropped from her waist, and he said in a swift, low whisper, "There is a door in the hall. Take it. It will bring you to the side of the house." He caught up her hand. "Your beauty is such that it sorely pains a man to say good-bye." He lifted her hand, almost in a courtly style reminiscent of Spain, and pressed his lips to it. "But the winds of chance come between us, even as they have momentarily brought us together.

I bid you my leave." He bowed and was gone as quickly as he had come. Nothing remained but the fading touch of his lips, the feel of his hand on her waist.

Devora, troubled, her heart questioning, went to the veranda and saw him disappear smoothly over its railing and fade into the fragrant night.

The steady beat of her heart sounded in her ears.

She came awake from her emotions, her back straightening. Then he was a pirate! A rogue, after all! And no doubt on the slippery edge of finding himself being arrested and hanged if either the governor or her father had known who he was. Would they have recognized him? Most assuredly. Else why would he have escaped so swiftly?

For a moment she forgot her own plight, for she was in no more state to be seen than he. Quickly she slipped away, having all but forgotten the cause for which she had come. It wasn't until she and Tad were riding the mare back to Ashby Hall, a sprinkle of tropical rain wetting her face, that she even thought again of Edward.

6

An English Uncle

The drape between the listening gallery and Governor Huxley's hearing room parted. Bruce turned to see the man he had come to the governor's residence tonight to meet. His mother's brother, Lord Anthony, came in from keeping his earlier meeting with the Barbados governor and Lord Robert, the English ambassador. Lord Anthony, garbed in a gold taffeta coat with lace, saw his nephew Bruce, and the gray-haired man grinned and came toward him, grasping his shoulders. There was a vague resemblance between them, though the eyes of Arlen were lighter, like Bruce's Grandmother Lillian.

"You're looking more as I remember Lady Marian each time I see you. So! What's this cunning news I hear, that you've been knighted by King Philip?"

"With the sword you gave me," Bruce said with a brief smile.

Lord Anthony threw back his head with

pleasure. "The effrontery of it all! But I'm afraid your wit will bring about your hanging yet, and don't laugh — this is no matter for your malicious humor!"

Bruce drew aside the curtain and glanced below, making certain the governor of Barbados and the English ambassador were gone. Satisfied, he shot his uncle a curious glance. "I heard what Lord Robert warned about Maximus. How long will he be in Barbados?"

"Robert?" he asked with a frown. "Not long, fortunately. The man is a weariness and a goad. He leaves tonight for the Isle of Pearls to be joined there by the countess in several weeks. The island's Spanish governor, Don Luis Toledo, is the cause for which I deemed it important enough to ask you to risk coming here." Lord Anthony's eyes turned sober. "It's about Kitt."

Captain Kitt Bonnor was a physician, but he was also a buccaneer and close ally of Bruce. He considered Kitt to be essential if he were to carry out the plans he would make once in Lima to divert the treasure of the Spanish fleet sailing from Cartagena to Veracruz.

"Kitt is being held with ten others from your old crew on the *Revenge* in the dungeon on the Isle of Pearls. But that is not the worst news. You heard how Viceroy Maximus is going to Governor Toledo to bring Kitt to Cartagena for trial. You know what he expects to get from Kitt," he warned in a low voice.

Bruce regarded him tensely. He could not allow Kitt to stand trial. "Yes, I know what Maximus wants: the true identity of Bruce Hawkins."

"Knowing Kitt, he'll never betray you."

"No, and it would be unfair of me to expect him to pay the horrible price to be true to our friendship. I cannot leave him to Maximus." He paced.

His uncle watched him with growing concern. "There is no way to break him out of that dungeon, Bruce. I've seen it. We know the prison is beneath the ballroom of the governor's hacienda."

Bruce gave no response and continued to muse to himself. He was not due in Cartagena to serve King Philip for two months. That would certainly give him more than enough time to accomplish his buccaneering expedition to the Isle of Pearls.

"I will find ready support among the Brotherhood at Tortuga."

His uncle's frown deepened. "An expedition? So soon before your due arrival at Cartagena? If something goes wrong and word reaches Maximus —"

"It won't," said Bruce with cool confidence. "I've deceived Spain before, and I'll do it again."

"But I've heard from Modyford at Jamaica that Henry Morgan is cruising elsewhere."

"I don't need Morgan," Bruce said lazily. "And I don't need Governor Modyford." Bruce walked again to the drape and looked below. Empty. "I shall sail my own expedition. It is safer to me that way. I can pick my own buccaneers. If Captain Jean le Testu is on Tortuga, I shall have some of the best fighting men."

He had heard that Captain Jago Quinn was also back from a raid on Grenada. While there, Bruce had undergone days of listening to lamentation from the Spanish governor telling him about a recent raid by Quinn and his vessel, the *Top Gallant*. Bruce did not like Quinn. The man was a fiend. Unfortunately, Quinn had one of the best armed vessels in the Brotherhood: an 18-gun frigate.

"You'll never get the governor of Jamaica to grant you a commission against Governor Toledo under an English flag, and Barbados is out of the question. If you go as an outright pirate, you'll have the High Admiralty onto you."

Bruce looked at him with a hint of sardonic smile. "Is not the new governor of Tortuga French? With a worthy gift I shall seek to bait him to the cause."

Lord Anthony scratched his beard thoughtfully, but his frown only deepened. "What does Friar Tobias say to this?"

Bruce waved a hand and affected indifference. "When he hears about Kitt, he will be as concerned as I. If anyone knows the dangers Kitt faces in the hands of Maximus, it is Tobias. He'll be afraid Kitt will crack under interrogation and betray me."

Lord Anthony paced, pulling at his beard. He looked at him. "Will he?"

"Kitt? Betray me as Hawkins?" Bruce considered in a moment of silence. "No."

Lord Anthony appeared not as confident. "It would mean Kitt's death — in a most horrible fashion, I fear."

Bruce smoldered with internal dismay. "Yes. And so the risk I take is deemed worthy. Not just for Kitt, but for us all. Your identity would also be unveiled, and King Charles would as likely call you home to the Tower. And Tobias, too, would be known to King Philip as a traitor to the holy cause of Spain. You see," said Bruce firmly, "rescuing Kitt is essential. Too much of value is at risk." He flashed a smile, his green eyes dancing. "I want that treasure fleet for Holland, Uncle Anthony, and to accomplish it my identity must remain secret. When I return to Cartagena with Spanish flags flying for King Philip, there must not be a question in the viceroy's mind as to the loyalty of Don 'Nicklas' Valentin."

Lord Anthony's eyes snapped with kindled excitement. "By jove, you've got me as riled as the king at a cockfight! You're sure you can do it, Bruce?"

"Do or die, my uncle. But first — Kitt. And with the right buccaneers from Tortuga and a legal commission from its governor, I should be nearing the Isle of Pearls in three to four weeks. By doing so, I will save us all from the wrath of kings!"

Lord Anthony removed a cigar, bit off the end, and lit it from the candle burning on the stone bench. "You walk a precipice between two pits, both of which, if you slip, will bring you to your death. If either King Philip or Maximus discovers who Hawkins really is, I shall lose you as well as having lost your mother."

"Ah, that too, but my plans for the silver mines near Lima are well worth the risk! I have friends among the Incas who will prove great warriors if I can arrange matters my way. It will take time once I'm there — perhaps six months. But if matters go as I have so long intended, the mule train over the mountain will bring silver not to Madrid but to Holland."

Anthony's face was lined with concern, but a wistful smile tugged at his mouth. "If I weren't so ruddy old, my boy, I would join you on this venture. This one, above all others, I would delight to see."

Bruce gave his shoulder an affectionate tug. "You continue to convince King Charles that Hawkins is a friend to his cause. That is battle enough."

"You're sure then you wish to risk so much?"

Bruce watched him with a smile. "And miss the opportunity of a lifetime? Uncle! It is not often I shall have opportunity to emulate Sir Francis Drake and plunder the very mule train that brings hundreds of thousands of bars of silver to my beloved King Philip." He laughed softly. "For this moment I have long dreamed —" and his smile faded, "since a water boy at the Peruvian mines. I will not turn back now."

Lord Anthony nodded and thoughtfully puffed his cigar, his face pensive. "And how is Lillian?" came his quiet question.

Mention of his grandmother in Lima at

118

the Valentin hacienda also brought a sober moment to Bruce. He did not want her to know his plans, for it would mean a great loss of life. Lillian was Arlen's mother — he had not seen her in 25 years.

"She grows old," said Bruce softly, "but she is at peace. She knows my mother rests safely with the Lord. And she has confidence in my knowledge of the faith, including a hearty appreciation of Calvin and Luther." Bruce would not think about how any of his plans might conflict with what he knew. There was a small flame in the back of his conscience that burned brightly, and if he was quiet long enough, it revealed that his anger and bitterness for Maximus were dangerous and dark. Until dealt with alone before his God, there would be no peace.

Bruce told himself he would have peace and satisfaction once he destroyed Maximus, but no matter how often he stubbornly thought this, the tiny flame seemed to burn even brighter.

"God's truth is more persistent than your unrelenting will," Tobias had told him with a smile.

"Lillian is content to be buried where her daughter died," Bruce told Lord Anthony. "Returning her to England would do more harm than good. She speaks the Spanish language as well as I, but she has not forgotten the past, nor her Reformed faith, though she worships in secret. There is no choice in Lima. The Dominicans are everywhere."

Anthony nodded silently, his face sad, and walked to the drape and the steps that led downward. "Then we will leave matters as they are. Be careful, Bruce. And if I learn anything more about Kitt, I'll send word again through Digges," he said of his serving man.

"You leave without me," Bruce told him. "We must not be seen together."

7

Voyage to the Isle of Pearls

The brightly lit core of the Great House facing windward loomed ahead in the evening shadows as Devora left Tad at the overseer's bungalow and rode back to the stables. Percy, snoozing in the doorway, awoke to greet her with a lantern.

"Careful, miss, the countess be askin' round fer ye."

He led Honey away to water and feed, and Devora ran toward the house, hoping her mother had given up waiting for her and had retired to her chamber. Did she know that Robert was meeting with the governor at the ball? Why hadn't her mother gone? Odd that she had not seen Edward there either, she mused. Perhaps he had been called away for some medical emergency on the wharf. While Barbados was not as wild as Port Royal, there were duels at the bawdy houses nearly every night. But there was always the possibility she could write him later even from the Spanish stronghold of Cartagena. Her uncertain future was left to the wise and good counsels of God. There was no time to muse over the merciful dullness that encased her heart. Tomorrow would hold new problems of its own.

The breeze billowed her skirts as she came up the walkway toward the house. The lanterns were still aglow in the sitting room and on both floors of the big white house. With good fortune she might slip up the stairs to her room before anyone saw her. She wished to see Uncle Barnabas and discuss the changes in her life. *But not tonight,* she thought wearily. She was afraid the meeting might bring on her tears, and she didn't want to add to his despondency.

Devora paused near the front hedge, then darted down the path toward the back of the house where an arched lattice overgrown with honeysuckle led to the back porch. She passed the small garden of sweet peas, hollyhocks, and lavender that wove their blending fragrances into the night air.

Inside the back porch, slippers in hand, she peered toward the kitchen and saw the house slaves preparing the next day's bread. The smell of barbecue beef and hens, usually her favorites, was now offensive to her. The slaves cast her curious glances. By now they, too, would have heard that she was being taken away by Countess Radburn. No one spoke as she sped through the wide cook room, through an anteroom that adjoined two wings of the house, and into the wider front hall.

She reached the stairway unseen, rushed upward, then across the hall and into her chamber. She shed her stockings and began to climb out of her dress, her hands shaking. Spain . . .

A tap on the door alerted her, and she turned quickly. The door opened and a tall, olive-toned woman with high cheekbones and still, black eyes stood there. Devora had never seen her before and assumed she must be one of the serving women that the countess had brought with her from the Main.

"Countess Catherina wishes you to come to her chamber, Señorita Devora."

So her mother intended to tell her about Cartagena tonight. It would do no good to plead to stay with Uncle Barnabas. The more Catherina knew she wished to stay in Barbados, the firmer would be her opposition. She couldn't believe that her mother really cared about her welfare. Her concern had come 17 years too late. No, there was something of greater importance on Catherina's mind — something that had brought her all the way from London to Barbados. But what?

Devora fixed her dress and walked slowly down the hall to Catherina's room.

The room was near the end of the corridor, and when she was allowed inside by the maid, she saw her mother pacing the floor like a brooding hen. Did her mother think she would resist her?

The furniture was of carved, dark wood, polished and opulent. The walls were covered with pale-blue damask and painted with delicate gilded doves. Devora had never liked this room, for the birds appeared trapped, and she too felt as though she were meant for little more than decoration for some palace which kept her from the fullness of life. Blue cloth covered the chairs and a footstool, with an inch of yellow fringe. Catherina, wearing yards of loose-fitting red satin, sank into the chair and snapped her fingers at the maid to prop her feet more comfortably on the stool.

"And to think I once waltzed the night away in St. James palace in gilded slippers! Your mother grows old and ill."

Her remark was meant to bring a smile to

Devora, but there was no laughter residing in her heart tonight.

"Bring me a glass of Madeira," she told the house slave.

"Yes, countess."

"And my chocolates too. I don't sleep well on an empty stomach."

"Yes, countess."

Catherina snatched her feather fan of wispy, bright-pink ostrich feathers. "This wretched tropical heat! It's as wicked as Cartagena. I shall wither if I do not get back to Spain soon. We've an enchanting place on the Mediterranean, Dear." She glanced about impatiently. "Taffy!"

"Comin', countess."

Catherina's face settled into bored lines. "That lazy African child. Slaves! Such indolent and sullen creatures. Why your father bothers to invest in the Royal African Company is beyond my understanding. I wouldn't have African slaves. Give me an Indian or Spanish girl any day."

Devora's schooled expression successfully concealed the fires smoldering in her bosom. She remained silent under the coldly analyzing blandness of her mother's eyes. They were a violet-blue — not like the warm shades of the Caribbean, but chill and empty, like a frozen pond in January.

"Well, you're certainly a little beauty, I must say. Almost as pretty as I was at your delightful age, but you'll do well enough. Spaniards like fair women, you know. Yet," and she sighed as though an earthshaking event had her in its grip, "I do not know if I can get the man for you I have in mind. He is sought after by many eligible and wealthy women from the families of the dons."

Devora just stared at her, listening.

"Well! Don't stand there gaping, Devora — say something. This religion of yours that Barnabas tells me is so important to you — has it taught you any manners? I *am* your mother!"

Devora curtsied. "Welcome to Barbados, countess."

Catherina's lips parted slightly, then her eyes snapped. She threw her fan into the folds of her lush crimson skirt and leaned forward. "So you wish to be cold and indifferent, do you? Do you think to hurt me, to punish me for five years of absence?"

Not five, seventeen, she could have quipped, but she held back her sarcasm. The Lord would not have her behave so. Still, she could not lie and behave as if she were not deeply hurt and resentful. She looked down at the carpet and studied the outline of a strutting peacock.

Catherina sighed and leaned back into the softness of the velvet chair. "This looks to be a hopeless case, does it not?"

Hope sprang to life. "I wish to stay here at Ashby Hall."

"No," Catherina said curtly. "You will not. Regardless of how you feel about me and Robert, the plans for your marriage will proceed." She fanned herself, her mouth thinning. She scanned her daughter. "The Spaniards are known for passion, Dear — fires that kindle and burn in their Latin bones. I fear Don Nicklas Valentin will find you a tightly buttoned little mouse."

Devora's eyes narrowed. She said nothing. Her mother didn't appear to notice.

"The mealy-mouthed Puritans are a plague in England," Catherina carried on. "I'm aggrieved you've been influenced by them."

"I am not, madam, I —"

"Not now. I'm in no mood for religious chatter. Thank God, Cromwell is dead and buried!"

It seemed not to dawn upon her mother that thanking God was inconsistent with her philosophy that foolishly considered God to be somewhere on the other side of His heaven, bored by His creation and indifferent to its rebellion. While she did not care to discuss "Him," she nonetheless could breathe His name for vain purposes.

"At least Robert has been able to reclaim some of the family jewels from Radburn Hall. It shall be so delightful to make a trip to England to get them and meet King Charles again. I'll do so, as soon as this marriage of yours is arranged with the Valentin family."

The countess leaned her dark head back against the blue velvet chair and rolled her eyes toward the ceiling. It was painted with flying cherubs with trailing green ribbons strung with wee red rosebuds.

"You have so much to learn, Devora. I could wish now we had brought you to Madrid with us, though having a child on my hands would have been exacting upon my fragile health." She reached for the box of French chocolates, already half-empty.

Devora's stepfather, Robert, who was the second Earl of Radburn, an ally of the Stuart king, and loyal to the Church of Rome, had fled England when Parliament arrested Charles I. Her father took refuge with a cousin in Madrid who had served as English ambassador for the Spanish court and married into the powerful Valentin family. Don Maximus Valentin was now head of the vice royalty of Lima, perhaps the most powerful representative of King Philip in the Spanish Main.

When Oliver Cromwell came to power with the Roundheads — men whom Cromwell called "God-fearing" and who sang psalms when entering into battle against the Royalists — her father had feared for Catherina and smuggled her into Spain to join him. But Devora was deemed too much trouble to have on her mother's hands, and was instead placed on a ship with her governess to voyage to the Indies to take up temporary residence in Barbados at the sugar plantation belonging to an uncle. It was not known to her father and mother that the uncle was at that time a Roundhead. Devora's "temporary" residence had lasted five years.

"As I told Barnabas earlier, it was a dreadful mistake to send you to the accursed Indies. My cousin Barnabas has proved himself a Dissenter, a strict and pompous man. He had the audacity to tell me I enjoyed my Madeira too much."

"He is loyal to the new king and to God. Oh, madam, he is a very generous and warmhearted man!"

Catherina's sweeping black brows shot up. "So you can bestir yourself after all. I was beginning to fear Barnabas had so overlaced your emotions with the fear of 'sin' that I had no red-blooded daughter left."

Again, Devora felt the heat rise into her face. She loved Barnabas and considered him even more dear than the distant memory of the earl and countess, but she was leery to say this, knowing her mother was jealous enough to tear her away from Barnabas — never to let her see him again. Catherina was an odd sort of woman. She had lightly esteemed Devora's love these five years, and before that in London. Yet she expected her daughter's undivided loyalty and devotion the moment she showed up looking more like a stranger than a mother. Devora could hardly reach into her heart and bring out the word *mother,* for speaking it with any meaning at this time in her life proved as difficult as swallowing Yasmin's lime juice and liniment when in bed with a sore throat.

"Barnabas may yet lose this plantation if the king learns he was disloyal during his exile in France."

Devora noted the satisfied look in her mother's eyes. "That must not happen. He has worked so hard to make Ashby Hall what it is."

The countess shrugged her white, plump shoulders. "I have nothing to do with it. Robert may intercede with the king. I know that titles will be given out to the Royalists here in Barbados for their loyalty, and land will be awarded as fit payment. But Barnabas is such a cantankerous fellow, I doubt he'll bow his stiff knee to the king even to save Ashby Hall."

But he bows willingly to the Lord Jesus, thought Devora. *How quickly men will get their tongues black from licking the shoe leather of kings who are but men, while refusing the Lord of mercy and grace.*

She would not dare say this to her mother, lest she find herself harshly slapped. It wouldn't be the first time, for the countess had a temper that could flare like a brushfire among the dry sugarcane. Her father, too, was far from being warm and lovable like Uncle Barnabas.

Her parents didn't understand him, she thought. They mistook his devotion to Scripture reading and prayers for narrowness. Devora could not agree. Her faith in Jesus was due to her uncle's interest in teaching her Christian doctrine when she arrived from London, ignorant of things religious except the rituals at church.

"Never mind about Barnabas," announced the countess in the manner in which she dismissed any subject that no longer interested her. "I've called you here to discuss your future. You must not think that years of running wildly about a savage plantation in any way frees you from your responsibility as my daughter. Do sit down," and she gestured a pale hand, heavy with gold and silver adornments.

Devora sat obediently, tightening her cold hands in her lap and watching the woman who was her mother. She looked the same as she had five years ago, like the large portrait that hung ponderously in Devora's bedchamber along with the autocratic portrait of her father, the Earl of Radburn. Catherina, though she had gained at the waist, remained a beautiful woman in an opulent sort of way. Her hair was black and drawn away from an oval face into curls and waves and braids so elaborately done that Devora couldn't keep her eyes from straying there, wondering what her own honey-colored hair would look like if arranged in the newest fashion. The countess retained white skin, and she had unusual eyes which Devora had been fortunate to inherit — the rare color of almost violet. Catherina's mouth was full, and a bright red. Devora had glanced curiously at a silver Peruvian box full of pots and tiny bottles of paint, oils, and powders.

"You'll use these to enhance your beauty when we go to Spain," the countess had informed her when she had followed her glance. "Despite the pomposity of Barnabas, I find no wickedness in face paint, and neither will you."

Devora watched her mother lift the glass of Madeira and empty it, then extend it outward toward the maid who had traveled with her. The older woman looked to be part Indian. She took the glass and skillfully refilled it.

"I left orders with the governess that you were to learn French and Spanish. As it turns out, Spanish has become all-important to us. How well can you speak it?"

"Well enough, madam," replied Devora in Castilian.

"Then we shall converse so. If you need future lessons, I shall see you have them. I will not have you stammering with a weak tongue and causing us embarrassment."

"Rise," she said in Spanish. "Turn around. Let me see you."

Devora did so, feeling foolish, longing to escape back to her chamber.

"No, no, *no!* That dreadful frock looks like a childish pinafore. One would hardly guess you're 17. Nicklas Valentin is the man we need to impress, but I'm not certain even I can arrange it. He has gained quite a reputation recently, and His Majesty King Philip has called for him in Madrid — and Nicklas . . . he's devastating. If I were younger, ah well . . ." She waved a resigned hand, picked up her gilded hand mirror, sighed, and tossed it aside on the divan. "Robert says Nicklas will have a horrendous inheritance when old Duke Anthony dies."

Devora's curiosity was pricked for the first time. Duke Anthony was English.

"How is it that a Spaniard would inherit from the duke?"

"Nicklas's mother, my pet, was the old duke's granddaughter. It is a long tale, fraught with tragedy, and it will do you no good to hear it now. I want your visit to Cartagena to be pleasant. Bright with festivities! Let us not lament the past. And now —" she went on as though the matter were settled, but Devora was more curious than ever. *What tragedy? The duke's granddaughter?* Yet she set it aside as her mother rambled on. Devora was worried about tragedy enough of her own. Marriage to a Spaniard!

"But of course Nicklas is not a full-blooded Valentin, since his mother was the duke's granddaughter. . . .

"The duke is bedridden now, and another dank London winter will probably bring on the hearse. Nicklas will inherit everything. It's his ties to the Valentin family that have pleased your father. . . ."

Devora tried to keep her face in peaceful lines, trying to recall snatches of Scripture she had memorized to bolster her courage. The Lord would intervene. He would not allow her to be sent there.

"As for Nicklas's interests in women, you may do, but the man is arrogant, hardly attainable. It is so important you please him on your first meeting." Her mother stood and began to walk about, analyzing Devora as though she were a questionable breed of lapdog the countess was considering purchasing.

"Your hair is memorable, and you have my eyes, but you are entirely too shy. You'll need lessons on how to look at a man. The dimple is good — provocative. And you have good lashes — what can a woman do without them?"

Devora's anger was churning. "I have told you, I do not wish to leave Barbados, nor go to Spain to marry this stranger!"

"And I have told you that Robert will not reconsider. It is important you marry

Nicklas — if only he'll have you. You will at least go and meet him. And since your father will become the new Spanish ambassador, you will return to Madrid with us!"

Devora felt sick, but retained her poise. There was one hope: that the son of Don Maximus Valentin would find her unsuitable. He must, of course, once he discovered her true allegiances.

"I can see you're overwhelmed," Catherina said wearily. "You may go to your room now. And Devora, Robert will make that alliance with the Valentin family one way or another." As though exhausted, she sank onto the lush sofa. "Close the door softly as you go out, Dear. I've illness coming on."

※ ※ ※

Lord Robert had left Barbados for the Isle of Pearls a week earlier to prepare for their arrival. Due to Catherina's health, two weeks passed before Devora boarded the *Trade Wind*. Now was her opportunity to arrange a secret meeting with Edward! But the countess was clever, and even in her illness she had outguessed Devora's plans. One of the mute-faced servingmen who had accompanied the countess from Madrid had been waiting to intercept the written message Devora had managed to send to old

Percy, the groom. Percy, riding the mare Honey, had gotten only a short distance down the road toward the Townsend plantation before he was halted and the intercepted message brought duty-bound to the countess. Devora was immediately summoned to her mother's chamber and upbraided in a spirit of betrayal.

"How could you trouble me so and disregard my wishes? I only want the best for you. You have no appreciation for all I've gone through. I am not so old and unromantic, my dear, as to not suspect such action on your part. You'd naturally be foolish enough to want to run away with Edward Townsend and thus ruin your life. Henceforth you shall be kept under watchful eye until we sail. And if the ungainly fellow dare set his cloddish foot on this property again, I shall need to use some harsher method against the Townsend plantation. I am sure you don't want to see the end of Edward's medical studies in England?"

"But Countess — you wouldn't hurt him so. I mean, Mother, I —"

"Tsk! Enough lamenting!" she moaned from her silken pillows. "If you were any manner of loving daughter, you'd show some vexation over my suffering. Yet you selfishly inflict me with more undue anguish by disregarding my wishes. Wishes for *your* future well-being in Madrid. No —" she held up a weak, bejeweled hand dripping with red and black lace, "I'll not hear your excuses, Devora. Run along to your chamber.

"Therese!" she called to her maid. "Therese, quickly, you lazy creature. My medication. Where is it? I feel a new attack — bring the Madeira wine."

On Monday, August 15, Devora, with Catherina and her handful of grim-faced attendees, set sail from Carlisle Bay for the Spanish Main. Devora had swallowed her disappointment and resentment, and told herself she would be free to write Edward once at the Isle of Pearls. Taking solace in the King James Bible carefully concealed in her trunk, along with a book of Puritan prayers that Barnabas had given her, she braced herself for the unknown future.

✳ ✳ ✳

With tears in her eyes, Devora watched the shore of the island slip away until a haze concealed it from view. Her old life was gone; a new one was beginning. Her one foundation was the faithfulness of the Lord. In the unknown, His truth remained steadfast. His purposes were secure, even though they remained in a haze in her mind, as hidden to her heart as Barbados was now. She was tempted to believe He had failed her, had permitted the strong will of the countess and earl to bypass His plans for her. It was then, reaching her hands into her cloak, that she found a piece of paper. She blinked through her tears and read the words in the childish hand of Tad. The words were misspelled and misshapen, but their truth warmed her heart and brought a smile and new peace: "Jesus loves ye. Tad."

Yes, she thought, amazed at what profound theology was contained in only three words. They embraced the finished suffering of redemption, and her eternal joy and security. If all that were true, then she could also trust Him with tomorrow's uncertainties and the mysteries that surrounded her future.

Perfect love casts out fear, she thought, remembering the verse in 1 John.

He loves me. I can trust Him.

8

A Bribe for the Chevalier de Fontenay

Tortuga, Buccaneering Stronghold

Captain Bruce Anthony Hawkins stood on the quarterdeck of his buccaneering vessel the *Revenge*, leveling his telescope toward the Caribbean island off the northwest coast of Hispaniola. The trade wind ruffled his dark hair as his tanned face, chiseled by the best features of the two opposing races of England and Spain, wore a reflective mood. His eyes, an unusually striking gray-green, surveyed the familiar island appropriately named by Columbus on his first voyage to the West Indies for its shape and for the many turtles on its shore: "Tortuga." It had been two years since he had left the Brotherhood of buccaneers, while supposedly serving King Philip off the coast of Florida.

Tortuga's fair harbor and the island's

proximity to the larger Hispaniola made the humpbacked sliver of rock 25 miles long a natural stronghold. At its best, Tortuga was home to nearly a thousand buccaneers and pirates — a host of men with a wide range of backgrounds who had formed an alliance as the Brethren of the Coast, sharing one common cause: a vow of vengeance upon Spain.

Tortuga was a natural islet for the buccaneers and pirates, for it offered them easy access to the hunting grounds on the other Windward Islands, and to wild cattle and pigs, which were flushed out of the underbrush on Hispaniola by the buccaneers to be slow-roasted over boucan fires into dried strips, then sold to smugglers and merchants anchoring offshore. Perhaps more importantly, Tortuga lay athwart important Spanish shipping routes through the Windward Passage and along the coast of Havana, where the galleons of the Spanish treasure fleet made a stop before sailing on to Madrid. Tortuga was also defensible against the attacks of the hated and feared coast guard, the "guarda costa," since there were only a few places where the Spaniards could land in force. The north shore of the island was pounded by the Atlantic surf, and except for Cayona Bay, most of the south shore consisted of shallow bays and flats covered with dense mangrove tangles.

Since 1660, the white and golden lily-dotted banner of Louis XIV, king of France, had been flying not only over Tortuga but above ports Margot and de Paix on Hispaniola. Receiving a percentage of all the buccaneer's *purchase,* which was the term used for booty from a Spanish ship or town, the French governors in their turn exacted a hefty share for their own pockets as well as for the king of France.

"I hear the rapscallion Jean Le Vasseur is no longer the self-appointed governor," said Friar Tobias as he stood beside his nephew Bruce at the rail. "You'll be dealing with the new French governor, but he's hardly better than Le Vasseur. Sagacious and debonair, I hear."

"You speak of Chevalier de Fontenay?" mused Bruce. "He's a sly fox in crimson silk."

"Hah. So then you've heard of him. Can we trust him then with plans to rescue Kitt? If I were in your boots, I would worry much. Fontenay could easily send a boat to the Isle of Pearls to warn Governor Toledo of our coming. Anything for a bag of gold doubloons. And if he guesses how badly Maximus wishes to capture the pirate

Hawkins, he may secretly wish to strike a deal with him. We'll land to find every Spaniard who can rally a blade or a musket awaiting you at the Castillo La Gloria."

Bruce understood the risk in letting Fontenay know of his plans to attack the Spanish Isle of Pearls, also called Margarita. But without Fontenay issuing him a legal marque to harry Spain, he wouldn't gain the men and ships he needed on Tortuga to sign articles with him. There had been a number of hangings recently of outright pirates, and one of the most feared — Captain Zajac — was being held for questioning by French officials at Martinique. Nearly half of Bruce's old crew, along with Captain Kitt Bonnor, was, as Lord Anthony had told him in Barbados, being held prisoner in the dungeon on the Isle of Pearls.

"We've no choice but to deal with the man," said Bruce, leveling his telescope toward Tortuga. "Don't worry, I bring our honorable Frenchman a worthy gift to whet his appetite."

"This is one case where you're tempting the devil, rather than the devil tempting you. One look at what you bring and the chevalier's appetite will become a bottomless pit for more and more."

Bruce steadied his telescope toward the

French fortress. "As long as it comes from our 'beloved' King Philip, I will not grieve the loss." He couldn't resist the opportunity to tease his uncle. "Better watch your own temptations, Friar."

"Me! Since when have I received a singular piece of eight from all the chests of treasure we've taken?"

Bruce's mouth showed amusement beneath a sliver of dark mustache. "Never mind fat pieces of eight. I was thinking of that silver platter holding the roast goose last night — I found the platter empty of all but bones this morning. Your appetite worries old Githens. The cook complains of long hours, and wishes a half share more in the next purchase we take for all his work before the cooking fire."

Tobias's mouth curled downward. "Githens, that mutinous cur. He's riled because I dumped his secret hoard of Kill Devil rum over the side of the *Revenge*. The poison all but eliminated the sharks following in our wake."

Bruce enjoyed each Sunday morning when his crew found themselves being preached to by Tobias, who warned them of the fiery, gaping jaws of Hades, if they did not repent of their "infamous greed, rum guzzling, and all manner of impieties."

Having Tobias along freed Bruce from being the one who needed to crack the whip of moral discipline. Although Bruce's crew knew him to keep a Bible and read it on Sunday, it was Tobias who received their grumbling.

"Better remove that habit and cross again. If the Tortuga welcoming committee spots a Spanish friar from Peru, I'll be rescuing you from a pirate's stew pot — or maybe they'll roast you over a boucan fire."

Tobias removed his long brown robe, and grimaced as he glanced down at his pirate's calico shirt and drawers. The act of removal of the religious garb was not new. Bruce had seen him do the same on every voyage they took together on the *Revenge*. A voyage that turned Nicklas Valentin into the English buccaneer Captain Bruce Hawkins also saw Friar Tobias become his trusty Lieutenant Tobias.

For Tobias to become a buccaneer enlarged Bruce's problems. While the friar had become an expert in throwing a dagger, he was as clumsy as a bear when it came to handling a Toledo sword. During the times in which they had sailed the Caribbean with Kitt, there had been several near-fatalities for Tobias. Still, the friar refused to let Bruce sail without him. "Should worse

145

come to worse and the Spaniards catch you, having a friar aboard to intercede will do more for your freedom than even a sword, unless," he warned, "it is your father, Maximus, who discovers who you are."

Tobias looked at his nephew. "One day I shall surely see myself either abandoned to the Dominicans at Cadiz, or to the English dogs at Execution Dock," and he groaned as he folded his frock and handed it to the Inca Indian from Lima. The Inca named Tupac had been Bruce's friend since they were children near the Peruvian silver mines.

"Take them away and hide them in their usual place, Tupac. And hand me my Tortuga hat."

The tall and lean Inca, who claimed to be the last son in a line of Inca princes, handed Tobias a new, fancy wide-brimmed green velvet hat.

Tobias grimaced. "What is this monstrosity?"

"Your new buccaneer hat, Tobias. I have made it with my own hands," said Tupac gravely, but the corner of his lip twitched.

Tobias pointed at a bright-red parrot feather sticking from the brim. "So that's what poor Sunbird was cackling about this morning."

"I did not harm parrot. He is greedy and

prideful, Friar. Should he not look upon a donation to your new hat as a privilege to serve you?" Tupac's black eyes sparkled mischievously. "You know how he struts before the looking glass."

"Like someone else I know," murmured Tobias good-naturedly, for the Inca took great pride in his sleek-muscled olive-brown body and his warrior-like abilities, many of them shared with Bruce when they were growing up.

Bruce had smiled, but turned his attention back to thinking of Chevalier de Fontenay. He was, as Tobias had warned, as merciless with his soldiers on Tortuga as Jean Le Vasseur, and he must be cautious when he met with him on arrival.

"Tupac, have the crew bring up the chests for the governor. Hakewell!" he called to his true lieutenant. "Ready to dip colors!"

"Aye, Capt'n!"

Bruce looked past Cayona Bay's blue-green water to the mountaintop fortress dominating the Harbor that at one time had been an old Spanish castle. Years earlier it had been blown up in a battle with the English General Venables, but it had been rebuilt and enlarged by the Le Vasseur family to govern the buccaneering stronghold.

Bruce signaled his quartermaster to hoist the tattered Union Jack and send a volley of greeting toward the lookout manning the French fort's six cannons. The *Revenge*'s heavy culverin belched a shot that splashed harmlessly into Cayona Bay.

✳ ✳ ✳

At Tortuga's fortress battery, the gun captain — a brawny Englishman — came out the guardroom door in a faded blue head scarf and yellow calico drawers, sweat-stained and ragged at the knee. He lifted the telescope.

"Sink me sails, it's the *Revenge* and Capt'n Bruce Hawkins."

"Hawkins? Ain't seen him for two years. Last I heard he sank hisself a Spanish galleon off Saint Croix. The fancy captain swore to see him swayin' as barracuda bait on the gallows." The gunner snorted a gleeful chuckle. "The Spanish governor from Riohacha were on the ship, too. And Hawkins makes the two of 'em walk the plank. 'Ye can swim to shore,' he tells 'em. An' all the while he fires shot to keep the jackanapes a'swimmin. A fine sight. I could'a wished they had sharks on their papist tails all the way."

"Too bad they didn't get eat'n, since what happened to Capt'n Kitt Bonnor. Probably send the poor feller to Cadiz so them holy inquisitors can practice more of their inquisitin'."

"Aye," he said darkly. "I be knowin' what that is." And he shoved out a mangled hand, showing stubs for fingers. "Took 'em one at a time. An' I still ain't no papist," he said proudly.

The chief gunner watched the *Revenge* negotiate skillfully the narrowest part of the one practical channel into Cayona Bay. He took a final swig of Port Royal's Kill Devil rum before replenishing the charcoal fire kept burning to ignite the slow-burning matches. "You ready with the breechin'?" he asked the gunner.

The gunner, shirtless, as brown as a sun-baked coconut and just as tough-skinned, lit a slow match from the charcoal.

A third man joined them: a lank, lean Dutchman with yellow hair fringing his black scarf. He spat. "Always did say thar was somethin' odd 'bout Hawkins."

The gunner, blowing hard on the match, pressed it lightly against a pinch of priming powder graying the saluting pieces touchhole. "Why ye say that, Hans?"

A finger-thin line of flame spurted vertically. Then the deni-saker boomed and gave birth to a small ring of powder smoke, which clung lazily about the little cannon's embrasure.

"Heard him speaking like a Spaniard once to his half-caste, that man from Brazil. Spoke it as fancy-tongued as one of them dons."

"Means nothing. Some o' the others speak it, too. Hawkins went to a university, they say. Probably learned it there."

The Dutchman shrugged. The gun captain turned and looked at him with a grin. "Heard you speakin' a bit of French to that half-caste girl at the Sweet Turtle. Does that mean you is French?"

The Dutchman spat again. "French is one thing, but the language of the rat-toothed dons is another matter. I'm careful of any man who can speak it as smooth as honey."

"Yeah, well yer always was the suspicious sort, Hans. Better watch yer step when it comes to Hawkins. Saw him in a duel once at the Turtle, and the man he kilt were good with the blade, but Hawkins left him sprawled dead across the floor."

The Dutchman mused with a dour face. "That were Tom Bingham, the cousin of Capt'n Quinn. Quinn is saying Hawkins didn't fight fair."

"He were fair all right. One thing about Bruce Hawkins: He don't look for no duel.

Tom goaded him into it."

"Hawkins has his enemies and his friends. Me? I'm neither. Aim to stay alive that way."

✳ ✳ ✳

Once the *Revenge* had maneuvered prettily through the reefs protecting Tortuga's harbor, Bruce observed the other various vessels in port. The typical buccaneer longboats were at port, lateen-rigged and lying low in the water, suited for cunning and swift attacks from out of river mouths or coves. Propelled by either sweeps or sails, the longboats could easily pounce upon an unsuspecting Spanish vessel. There were brigantines as well, and frigates, with a few bigger-tonnage vessels such as his own, some with as much as ten guns.

No sooner had the *Revenge*'s anchor plunged splashing and seething down into the harbor's translucent green depths than her crew commenced eagerly to swing out the boats and load them with bundles of hard-won booty and treasure.

Ashore, Tortuga's greedy merchants — every bit as cutthroat as the pirates — who stole through their outrageous prices for goods and drink, rushed to welcome the new crew. Fresh kegs of Jamaican rum were rolled down to the sand as the governor's treasurer, Monsieur LeBrette, came strolling toward the beach to welcome the captain of the *Revenge*. The Frenchman wore salmon-pink pantaloons and a claret satin jacket, his black periwig elaborately curled and draping across his shoulders. He wore a big silk hat with a feather, and was followed by two castle soldiers in cut-off calico drawers carrying the treasury book.

Bruce masked a brief smile as his keen eyes darted over the treasurer, who was all smiles of anticipation. His snapping eyes swerved to Tobias wearing dark hose and a forest-green tunic that fell loosely over his wide waist to his thighs, his green velvet hat with the red parrot feather flopping in the breeze. Tobias patted his leather scabbard where a sword was slung.

"Whatever you do, my uncle," said Bruce wearily, "do not unsheath it." He said in a low voice to Jorge, the half-Portuguese ex-slave from Brazil, "Keep an eye on Tobias."

Jorge flashed a smile, showing white teeth against his walnut skin. "Aye, Capt'n. Last time his preaching riled the men in the Sweet Turtle and they booted him out."

Jorge and the Inca, Tupac, both garbed in leather, came behind their formidable captain, their muscles rippling as they hoisted the two chests upon their bare shoulders and strode up the white sandy incline.

"Ah, Monsieur le Capitaine Hawkins! Welcome to Tortuga!"

Bruce doffed his hat, his panther-like strength restrained beneath silken gentility. "*Bon jour,* Monsieur LeBrette."

LeBrette rubbed his palms together as he eyed the chests, but sobered when he met the gaze of Tobias, who wore a look of exhausted boredom.

"And where, Monsieur Hawkins, have you made your famous raid this time, eh?"

Bruce replaced his hat, smiling smoothly. "Oh, various interesting places," came the evasive tone, and he glanced ahead to where the sloping sand hill was beginning to crowd with pirates. They stood in slouching stances, their coats or shirtwaists unloosened, and brown, hairy chests showing. Cold eyes and unsmiling faces with rattailed mustaches stared in silence, measuring his haul, silently comparing it to their own recently meager hauls. Some smoked from long clay pipes, as tiny puffs of whitish smoke spiraled. Others lifted their flasks of Jamaican rum, and still others fingered their big silver-butted boarding pistols.

Bruce did not recognize any of these particular men. He sought for Captain le Testu, but the leader of a fearless crew of French buccaneers was not in view. What if he had already sailed on a voyage of his own? Bruce needed the best of sea rovers, and while le Testu's men were rank pirates, Jean himself controlled them with an iron fist. These men before him were as scurrilous a haggle of pirates as he had yet seen. Yet many of the well-known ships were in the harbor, including Testu's *Le Defenseur*. Perhaps Jean was in the Sweet Turtle, and Bruce glanced up the beach past the palm trees to the meeting tavern — a two-story building constructed from sections retrieved from a Spanish galleon. A carved sign read "Sweet Turtle" in French.

Chevalier de Fontenay came down the steps of the fortress adorned in satin and silver lace. He swung his gold pomander ball, which reflected in the sunlight, and lifted it to his long nose to whiff the astringent lavender. With his other hand he held an exceedingly long pipe to his narrow, ascetic mouth. A squad of appointed soldiers from the fortress guard escorted him to where a red canopy was set up over a long, scarred mahogany table that was, like most everything in the fortress, pirated from Spanish ships.

A short time later, nearing sunset, they met beneath the fortress on the wide, palm-tree-fringed beach. "Captain Hawkins, *bon jour,* ah, but you are notably a man of good fortune and strong fortitude, monsieur." The red-gold sun seemed to sit like a floating orb on the blue-black Caribbean, scattering colored jewel-like flecks across the water, like tiny boat sails. A warm, moist breeze gave a jaunty snap to the yellow-fringed canopy.

"The other captains — they have not been so competent in their purchases lately," explained Fontenay. "It is a distinction to have as a guest the scourge of the Spanish Main under the immunity of the flag of the king of France."

Bruce offered a bow as though he appreciated the flowery compliment, but cast it aside as dangerous.

"Sit, monsieur, and we shall talk."

A secretary pulled out a cane chair for the governor, who sat himself, crossing his long legs at the knee. One foot swung thoughtfully, housed in the stylish, high-heeled polished shoe of the French court, its yellow buckle shining. He rested his elbow on the arm of the chair and drew in on his clay pipe, his shrewd, deep-set eyes weighing Bruce in the balance.

Bruce took all this straight-faced, and gestured for Tupac to come forward with the chests of booty and set them upon the long, heavy table. Tobias stepped forward to open the latch. Bruce watched the chevalier's eyes as the jewels spilled onto the table — a scintillating mound of finger rings, earrings, chains of gold, brooches, emerald- and ruby-studded silver crosses, snuff-boxes, and pomanders.

"A gift for you, Excellency," said Bruce. "A token of appreciation for your fair and just rule on Tortuga," and he smiled, ignoring the dubious glance that came from Tobias. Bruce gestured for Jorge to proceed. The Portuguese man stooped into the still-warm sand and opened the largest of the chests. Goblets, plates, and altar ornaments were heaped into a sun-drenched pile that flashed.

Bruce removed a bag of gold doubloons and pieces of eight and set them on the table. "In honor of His Majesty, King Louis of France," he stated smoothly, and offered another small bow as a toast, his green eyes showing malicious humor. "Monsieur Governor, you will see that he has this — a gift from the king of Spain!"

Fontenay's pasty features were slightly flushed with inner excitement. He gave a wheezy laugh. "Monsieur Philip is most thoughtful, Captain." And he turned to his bulging-eyed treasurer, LeBrette. "Transfer these goods to my private storage chamber."

Once the purchase had been hauled across the sand into the fortress, Fontenay stood cheerfully. "It is my pleasure to ask you to the fortress to dine later tonight, Monsieur Hawkins. And you also, Monsieur Tobias. We shall talk then."

It was the invitation Bruce had hoped for. He doffed his hat, and Tobias followed suit. The governor was escorted back across the beach to the residence.

"You have won his hearing at least," said Tobias. "Even so, it won't be easy to convince him to give you a marque against the Isle of Pearls."

Bruce looked at his uncle, showing more confidence than was the case. "You forget that many captains on Tortuga still hold old Portugal marques. Captain Jean le Testu, for one. If Fontenay should refuse me, then I will hold a meeting with Jean."

Tobias looked at him. "Just remember what Hakewell told you the other night. Le Testu and Quinn have signed articles. Any agreement with Jean may of necessity include Quinn."

Captain Jago Quinn was little better than the feared and hated pirate L'Ollonais. "I need fighting men, Tobias," said Bruce. He sighed, and a light tone of mockery reflected in his voice. "And to think I have a hundred soldiers from Madrid under my command at Grenada."

"A misfortune you cannot use them now." Tobias turned serious. "Caution, my son; you have heard of Quinn's devilish behavior at Campeche when he sailed with Henry Morgan."

Bruce frowned. He also knew that Captain Quinn held him responsible for the death of his cousin in a duel some years earlier. Although Quinn had never confronted him, word had circulated that the incident was not forgotten.

9

"Monsieurs les Boucaniers"

The governor's residence had been furnished beyond the modest decor which had housed the first governors of Tortuga. The long table was set with gold eating utensils and goblets and an array of foods not seen by the pirates, much of it slipped in on French frigates from Saint Kitts, Saint Croix, and Saint Martinique. The walls were draped with new French tapestries of red, and a painting of King Louis XIV stared down with cool disdain. Fontenay had the fine taste of an aristocrat, despite ruling one of the most lawless and wicked ports in the Caribbean. Tortuga was even a greater conglomerate of dangerous renegades than was Jamaica. Jamaica at least had a militia made up for the most part of planters and merchants, but there were no planters on Tortuga, and the governor's militia was virtually nonexistent since it was made up of pirates who gave lip-service to the French governor. The governors were mainly to issue commissions and to see that the king of France received his share of the purchase.

"My apologies, Monsieur Hawkins," the Chevalier de Fontenay was commenting as they walked into the dining room. "The table is set for we three alone. I did not invite the other captains to dine with us, thinking a discreet discourse over our meal was wise. While the other buccaneer captains are, of course, trustworthy, I have heard you do not speak of your plans in public. It is wise."

Wise, indeed, and if I hadn't needed Fontenay, he would not be learning my plans now, thought Bruce.

Behind each chair, a mulatto maidservant waited to attend. They were dressed in flowered skirts and white shirtwaists set off by red sashes, but Bruce noticed the usual iron slave rings on their ankles. He glanced at Tobias, but he was careful not to convey his displeasure. It was Friar Tobias who had first introduced Bruce to the cruelties heaped upon the Inca Indians in Peru by the Spaniards. Tobias had once journeyed to see King Philip about the evils of the conquistadors but had not been received into audience.

"It is because of Maximus," he had told

him darkly. "The man has gotten rich on the Incas. And will become richer and more powerful still if his plans to work with Lord Robert Radburn proceed."

Bruce knew there were laws in the Church forbidding cruelty to slaves; however, such laws drawn up in the quiet cloister halls of the palace in Madrid were all but ignored in the West Indies by the Spanish colonial governments, or if not ignored, then gotten around in clever ways that even offered a cloak to cover their sins. When Bruce was a boy, Tobias had told him about a "missionary" trip to the Inca Indians that he had made with Maximus and a group of soldiers to Cuzco.

"First the priest made a declaration that the Incas were heathen Indians to be converted, and that they could not be said to be enemies of the gospel until they had 'heard' the gospel and rejected Christ. Maximus and the conquistadors, however, did not want converts, but slaves to work their plantations and dig the mines. And because they feared my teaching of the mercy of Jesus Christ might actually bring some Incas to bow the knee, do you know what these sons of Belial did? They deliberately refused me the right to speak the gospel in their native tongue. They told me I could only talk to them in Spanish! Needless to say, Bruce, they could not understand. Therefore, Maximus and the other grandees with him had rounded up a large group of new slaves to work the fields." Tobias's eyes had sparked with righteous indignation. "So I sailed to Madrid to report them. And then Philip did not receive me!" He banged his big fist on the table, making the cups and saucers rattle. "Many died, either from overwork or sickness brought from Spain. Thereafter, I turned into a Reformer — not that we do not have our sins as well. Oh, that I could have met Luther!"

"You are a brave man, Tobias," Bruce had told his uncle. "Together, one day we will change things on the Valentin hacienda and in the silver mines."

Bruce, having been the child of a woman enslaved for a short time by Don Maximus, felt no sympathy for the cause of the grandees and their need for laborers in the sugar and tobacco plantations.

But the grandee he saw now at the dinner table on Tortuga also had his sins, as did all men, and he seemed to have donned every last pirated ring he could cram onto his slender, brown fingers. About Fontenay's neck hung a huge golden chain supporting a frame of gold filigree with a sizable pear-shaped emerald from Brazil.

Bruce now dressed as he did among buccaneers, for there were times enough that he was forced by protocol to wear velvet and lace when in Madrid as the son of Don Maximus Valentin. He wore a clean, white Holland shirt, tight about the wrists, and black trousers, a simple gold chain about his throat. His scabbard and baldric were noticeably present. On Tortuga a man was a fool not to be armed to the teeth.

He saw that Tobias was enjoying the meal of roasted beef, marrow bones, broiled crab, and sautéed fish in plantain leaves sprinkled with ground nutmeg. Bruce, who loathed fish and crab, took a hefty slice of the buccaneers' wild cattle, surprised that it was tender.

"Is it so, monsieur, that you have all but disappeared from the Caribbean these past two years?"

Careful, thought Bruce. Tobias, too, hesitated, while a large marrow bone dripped from the end of a glittering gold fork in hand.

Fontenay sipped his wine, his face showing nothing but curiosity. *He could not possibly know whose son I actually am,* thought Bruce. No one on Tortuga knew. Nor could Fontenay have discovered that for the last two years he had been serving King Philip out of necessity as a soldier of growing renown . . . all an integral part of his plan to ultimately deal a staggering blow to the viceroy.

"I assure you, Governor, I have been fully occupied in dealing with the Spaniards," said Bruce truthfully, and smiled. "But it is not my expeditions of the past two years that bring me to Tortuga, but the need of a new marque. I have heard you will issue this with the blessing of the King of France, seeing as how the English governor at Port Royal is under strict forbiddance. King Charles, so newly installed back in Whitehall, has speedily negotiated a treaty with the Escurial," he said of Spain's palace 27 miles from Madrid.

"And with my king withholding commissions, I turn to the king of France."

"And what, monsieur, do you have in mind this time? Where do you expect to cruise? For what opportunity do you search?"

Bruce hesitated, but had no choice, and could feel the reptilian eyes upon him. "The Isle of Pearls, or as you may know it, Margarita, on the Main."

The Chevalier de Fontenay sucked in a quick breath, saying something in French, his wine goblet poised. "Monsieur, you are as I have heard — and as your bounty proved this afternoon — a buccaneer of daring. A notable guest is soon to call at the Isle of Pearls!"

"It is imperative I make such a cruise. I have word on good confidence that a friend of mine is being held there a prisoner. I will not leave him to the interrogators, for they seek not only a cause of death against him, but desire to trap me and my crew also."

"In some astonishment, my friend, I can only believe this friend of yours must be the English physician, also known as Captain Kitt Bonnor."

Bruce studied him with a sharp gaze. "May I be so bold as to inquire how you knew this?"

Fontenay shrugged and smiled. "You have your spies. I, of equal necessity, monsieur, must needs have mine. I had heard a notable prisoner was taken, and my curiosity provoked a search for information from the friendly governor in Hispaniola, thinking the prisoner on the Isle of Pearls might be a French cousin of mine from Paris who was to have arrived last month. I have not heard from him." And he made a hissing sound and sadly shook his head. "The Spanish governor assured me the prisoner was the famous pirate Hawkins. But alas, since this prisoner was also said to be a physician of some reputation, I guessed it was not you, but Monsieur Kitt. I must say, your presence here now proves me right."

"Kitt's reputation is established more with the sword than with his medicines, but that is of no matter at the moment. He cannot be left to rot in Governor Toledo's dungeons, nor my crew. I am sure you understand me, Chevalier."

"Such a loss to you is grievous. One wonders how it happened, seeing that your fame is such that you lose no friend to the 'guarda costa.' "

Again, he must move cautiously, as he felt the probing gaze. He did not want Fontenay to know he had not captained the *Revenge* these past two years. Bruce had not lost Kitt, but Kitt's love for medicine and investigating herbs in Spanish territory, sometimes while visiting the native Indians, ofttimes outweighed his wiser judgment. He had heard that Kitt and a handful of the crew had taken a pinnace to shore at Panama to seek a cure for tropical fever from some Panamanian Indians who used the Abuana leaf. While there, an attack by Spanish soldiers took Kitt and the others captive. His lieutenant, Hakewell, had rushed men to rescue them, but the guarda costa had been spotted coming from farther down the inlet, and Hakewell had no option but to save the ship and the rest of the crew.

"The boy Tommy was with them," Hakewell had later told Bruce, and there were tears in his eyes. Tommy was a mere lad of 13.

Of course, it was not in keeping with Bruce's interest to explain all this to the chevalier, for it would also mean explaining his own absence until now.

"And you seek a marque to cruise in the sea of Margarita? And what is my share in the purchase in this expedition? To grant you such a marque when a notable Spanish visitor is due to arrive there from Cartagena demands much risk on my part, monsieur," and he gestured his slim hand to the slaves to bring in sweet cakes and fruit. "It is true that while I fly the flag of His Majesty Louis XIV," and he lifted his glass and sipped a toast, "France is not at war with Spain. Like your English governor, to offer a marque is a great risk."

Bruce leaned back in the high-backed chair and watched the chevalier carefully. "A risk, true; but one that may fill your personal coffers to overflowing. The share you received this afternoon is but little of what you may likely receive."

Fontenay mused, tapping his nose, his rings sparkling, as with the other hand he lifted his golden pomander and sniffed his lavender, all the while considering. Bruce feared the wily Frenchman would refuse him. In the end, he lifted a slim finger in a salute.

"I will grant your marque, Captain Hawkins. You and I shall draw up papers to insure my fair share."

Bruce, calm, toasted him. "The Isle of Pearls, Monsieur Fontenay."

"Doctor Kitt Bonnor should be most thankful of your abiding friendship," said Fontenay.

Bruce would not admit that there was more involved in the need for Kitt's rescue than a personal liking for the physician. Friar Tobias, who had recently come from Cartagena, had also informed Bruce about the plans of Maximus. It was his father, the viceroy, who was the notable official due to arrive to see Governor Toledo. Maximus was growing uncomfortably curious about the English devil named Captain Hawkins and was on his way from Cartagena to interrogate Kitt. Bruce owed it to Kitt to get him off the Isle of Pearls be-

168

fore Maximus arrived.

Bruce's jaw tightened. He knew his father. There was little he would not accomplish when determined. More disturbing than even this was why his father was growing curious about Hawkins. There were few people who knew who he really was.

Bruce stood from the table. "I am anxious for the marque, monsieur. I must also meet with some trusted captains at the Sweet Turtle. Let us draw up the paper now."

Fontenay seemed to have expected it. Had he already somehow guessed Bruce had returned for this expedition? Fontenay gestured to his secretary to bring him a sheaf of papers sitting on a hard, glossy table.

A short time later, seated in the drawing room with the governor, Bruce watched Fontenay select a sheet of foolscap and a pen from a shot glass bristling with white goose quills. The granting of commissions proved a lengthy business transaction, because the governor's share must be agreed upon, as well as the amount of stores, canvas, powder, shot, and small arms. The governor usually always supplied what was needed to the other vessels sailing, but Bruce needed none of this. The *Revenge* was well-provisioned for he had seen to the need at Barbados before sailing to Tortuga.

Fontenay scribbled a few lines, then signed and sealed the document and handed it to Bruce, a smile on his pasty face. "Fortune and fair trade winds, Captain, and a rich and speedy return to Tortuga with Doctor Kitt Bonnor."

Outside the governor's residence, Bruce stood with Tobias, and in the bright moonlight shining through the palm trees, he read that his commission was good for three months. He was free to operate against the crown of Spain wherever he wished. The way was open to sail to the Isle of Pearls.

"It will mean your end, my son, if you are recognized," said Tobias in a low voice. "You are no stranger to the homes of the grandees there."

"I will make certain that I am not. What color periwigs do you have?"

"All colors, just as you ordered, and French clothes as well — as gaudy and colorful as anything Fontenay wore tonight."

"Let us hope I will not need them," Bruce said dourly. "Then, Monsieur Tobias," he said in smooth French accent, "I think the trade winds blow softly in our favor. It is imperative you arrive before me to arrange my entry into Governor Toledo's hacienda. Find the location of the dungeon below the rooms, and learn how many soldiers man the cannons of the Castillo La Gloria."

"That will be the least risk. What if Maximus arrives before you? What if he is there when you arrive?"

Bruce looked at him. "It will be up to you, my dear Friar, to distract him. Somehow speak with Kitt in the dungeon and let him know what our plans are. It will bring him and the crew cheer."

"I shall try, but while you may have your marque, what of the other captains? You will need at least a hundred men to take the Isle of Pearls."

Bruce looked up the sandy slope toward the Sweet Turtle. "It is time to meet with Jean le Testu. You best return to the *Revenge* and wait for me."

❊ ❊ ❊

Alone, Bruce entered the meeting hall and tavern. The large room below the top floor was filled with wooden tables and chairs, and a heavy link chain was looped across the ceiling holding chandeliers. A gilt-edged portrait of the king of France hung on one wall, and on the other, a painted portrait of the Stuart king in velvet and pearls. Not to be left out, the Dutch buccaneers had placed a painting of their admired naval admiral with sword in hand above one of the tables.

The buccaneers were made up primarily of French, English, and Dutch, but there were a handful of escaped African and Indian slaves as well, and even a few Spanish prisoners who had joined the Brotherhood and sailed as secondary crew. These afforded the buccaneers handy sources of information on the Spanish language and customs that aided their attacks on the Main.

As Bruce entered, the sea rovers were gathered, drinking and gambling, wearing head scarves or wide-brimmed hats, and sporting gold or silver jewelry. Their garb was a mixture of Spanish and French livery, all pirated, displaying the gaudy colors of purple and yellow taffetas, and red and green satin. They were all a dangerous and quarrelsome band, whose friendships could easily explode into vicious quarrels leading to a duel. Although a system of law called "the orders and articles of the Brethren of the Coast" prevailed, seldom did the quarrels end peaceably.

As rum poured and dice clicked, Bruce glanced about for Captain Jean le Testu. He saw him with two of his officers and walked up. The Frenchman was a tall, sprightly man with a fair sense of humor. His black eyes matched the color of his rattailed mustache. When he saw Bruce, he stood with a pleased smile.

"Mon ami, it is you. Sit! I have heard good things of you since we last sailed together. And what prize do you think to make your own that brings you to Tortuga?"

Bruce greeted the other Frenchmen, then sat down, but he noticed Captain Jago Quinn at one of the other tables watching him — a man of raffish reputation, an experienced swordsman, physically strong, and as swarthy as a Spaniard. Bruce wished no trouble over the duel he had had years earlier with Quinn's hot-tempered cousin, and hoped Quinn's brain was not fired up with rum enough to cause him to foolishly seek a quarrel tonight.

Bruce casually tested the interest of Captain le Testu on a raid to the Isle of Pearls.

"Ah, monsieur, you and I? We together would do well enough, for we see eye to eye. Alas, had I known you would show yourself again on Tortuga, I would not have signed articles with Quinn. But now, whatever I may do, he must be included."

"Jago is treacherous," warned Bruce. "Consider that you have made a mistake where he is concerned."

"Ah, so I have already discovered, but there is little to be done now. This expedition of yours — has it to do with Kitt?"

Bruce explained, keeping matters as simple as he could until he was certain what help he would receive.

"Kitt is a rare swordsman, one I highly regard," said Jean le Testu, sighing. "It is an insult to the Tortuga Brotherhood to leave such a gallant man pining in the wicked Spanish dungeon, yes? I will join you; we will sign articles. But Captain Quinn must sail with us. Will you agree to this if I vow to keep him from his cruel and evil ways?"

Because Bruce disliked Quinn, he would not commit himself at once, but because he needed Jean for the success of the mission, there was little recourse. He agreed to consider the matter and let him know the next morning.

"I will speak to Quinn," said Testu.

"He must agree to follow my orders as captain," insisted Bruce, and not wishing to remain long, he left the Sweet Turtle before trouble could ignite.

By the next morning when Captain le Testu rowed out to the *Revenge* in a cockboat, bringing Quinn with him, the matter appeared to have been judiciously settled, with Jago Quinn agreeing to follow Bruce Hawkins as lead captain of the expedition.

That morning, with the sunlight dappling the blue-green water of the rockbound Cayona Bay, the three captains met in full buccaneering regalia on the quarterdeck of the *Revenge* to sign the articles binding them together. The plumes in their hats ruffled in the breeze, and their leather baldrics boasted boarding pistols.

The articles contained all the clauses that were common, among which was one that Bruce added: Any man found guilty of concealing any part of the purchase would be hanged from the yardarm.

Captain Quinn leered.

"You understand, Jago? And agree?"

"Aye, Hawkins, let's get on with the signing."

With the matter seemingly settled, they signed their names to the articles and made ready to leave from Tortuga within the week. They would sail southwest toward Trinidad, through Dragon's Mouth, and rendezvous in the bay east of the Main not far from the Isle of Pearls.

"Plans for how the expedition will be fought will be made clear once we rendezvous," said Bruce. "No more will be discussed now. The less said of our plans, the less chance they will find their way to Governor Toledo."

When le Testu and Quinn rowed back to shore, Friar Tobias came up to Bruce, a frown between his wide, silvery brows. "Having Jago along means trouble."

Bruce stood with hands on hips looking after the cockboat. "You're right, my uncle. Though he didn't mention the past, I could see he has not forgotten the duel with Tom Bingham. But I don't think I will need to concern myself with the matter until our purpose on the Isle of Pearls is completed. By then, if his greedy pockets swell with pearls, it may be enough to part in peace. I should hate to match swords with him."

10

On the Isle of Pearls

Governor Toledo's private coach was waiting for Countess Catherina Radburn and her daughter, Lady Devora Ashby, when they landed at the Isle of Pearls by ship from Carlisle Bay. Devora saw a castle-fortress with cannon overlooking the Caribbean and was told by Catherina that it was the Castillo La Gloria, manned by a Spanish garrison of soldiers which protected the island from pirates.

Devora had never seen such a stylish coach. It was carved of quebracho wood and decorated with gilt work and metal fittings of silver, and pulled by two white horses. The coachman and footmen were African slaves who wore the stylish red Toledo livery, and they brought Devora and the countess along the palm-lined beach via a narrow cobbled roadway that appeared to run for miles along the shore. Soon they arrived at an iron gate within an adobe wall, and the horses trotted through into a large Spanish plaza facing the official governor's hacienda. There were more palm trees, and a large garden that connected from the outer adobe wall to a patio.

Lord Robert came down the outer steps to meet Catherina, with the governor, serving men, and maiden house slaves trailing behind. Devora's stomach tightened. This was the first time she had seen her father since the night he had slipped away from the country estate in London to cross the border into France and then Spain, fleeing the Roundheads. Lord Robert was a striking man in his forties with thick, light-brown hair that sparkled in the sunlight. His Norman ancestry showed itself in his height, broad shoulders, and pale-blue eyes. Dressed in fine black camlin and blue silk, he looked his title as the Earl of Radburn, and more than one woman beside Catherina had thought herself in love with him. But he remained as much a stranger to Devora as did the Spanish governor.

Robert was a skilled swordsman as well as a politician, and tales had drifted to Devora of a duel in Madrid. Sadly, he was willing to use her to open doors of opportunity on the Spanish Main that would grant him trade access with the Royal African Company. He and the British royal family owned ships that sailed to the African coast of Guinea for slaves which were sold in the British-, French-, and Dutch-owned islands. But he also wanted to sell to the Spaniards, who bought most of their slaves from ships owned and operated by King Philip. With Devora the daughter-in-law of the viceroy of the Main, Robert could envision open doors for his business.

Still, Devora's eyes clung to him, hoping to see some spark of warmth or affection for his daughter, even if it was only for appearance, but even that was missing. He went straight to Catherina, helping her down and kissing her forehead, asking of her voyage and comforts.

"I hope your cousin Barnabas was not a problem for you concerning Devora? The man can be a positive bother at times with all his piety."

"He was disappointed, of course, but could do nothing once he knew our minds were made up. Darling, this is Devora."

"Of course. You've grown up, my dear. Don Maximus will not be disappointed." And he kissed her forehead and turned back to the governor to introduce them. *That was all . . . You've grown up, my dear.*

Devora swallowed the dry ache in her

throat. She was schooled in restraining outer emotions from spilling over "rather sloppily," as her mother would have described it. A moment later, Devora gave a brief but perfect little curtsy, and even managed to respond to Governor Toledo in silky-smooth Castilian — a courtesy that brought a glow of approval to his dark eyes.

"When Maximus arrives, he will be impressed with your daughter, Lord Robert. You are most lucky to have such a lovely Señorita to offer the Valentin family in holy matrimony."

Holy . . . Devora was reminded afresh of her impossible situation. For how could she willingly marry out of her faith? Yet she could not resist the will of her father and mother, for she knew that in God's sight she was also to honor them. The dilemma was once again pushed away as too painful to handle, and her wordless prayer was sent winging toward her everlasting Shepherd. He knew. He had not abandoned her to a situation that was ready to swallow her into its dark depths.

As the serving men took the trunks and bags down from the carriage, a husky-looking friar in a brown robe with a cord tied about his wide middle came striding from the back of the residence across the polished stones, his leather sandals clicking with bold confidence.

"Excellency, a moment of your time, please!" It was more of a polite order than a humble request. Devora was both curious and interested in the older man at once, for there was something of an English accent to his voice.

"Ah, Friar Tobias, welcome home, Señor," called Governor Toledo, and the way he turned to him told Devora that she was right. This was no ordinary monk. And — what was the difference between a monk and a friar?

"Good day, friend Carlos," the friar called to the governor. "It is important I interrupt you for a few moments," and he gave a bow of his head toward the countess and Devora.

"Tobias, you have met the Earl and Countess of Radburn? And this is their daughter, Lady Devora Ashby of Barbados."

"Ah yes, assuredly! Welcome to the Isle of Pearls, Lord Robert, Lady Catherina, Lady Devora!" And he turned to the governor. "Señora Toledo regrets she cannot greet your guests."

The governor's countenance altered. "It is Margarita?"

"Your daughter's illness has worsened despite our prayerful vigil. The Señora is with

181

her now and begs you excuse her from the festivity tonight. May I suggest you try a different physician? You know how these from Lima are worthless. They know nothing and seek only more silver for their foolish concoctions."

Devora listened, curious and alert to know why the friar looked so despairingly upon the Lima physicians. Uncle Barnabas had suggested the Jews knew more of medicine than did either Spain or England, and that when the Jews had been driven out of Spain during the reign of King Ferdinand and Queen Isabella, Spain had lost in the field of medicine.

"If I may suggest such a thing, Your Excellency, there is the Englishman, Kitt Bonnor, rogue though he be," said Tobias smoothly.

Devora opened her lace fan and swished it uneasily when she saw the hardened expression on the governor's face.

"You astonish me, Tobias. Call for the Lutheran?"

"If I may be so bold as to suggest it, Señor, what have we to lose in the matter?"

"And what gives you confidence this Englishman will not poison my daughter out of revenge?"

"I shall keep a stern eye upon him. And

the man seems a gentleman."

"A pirate?" he scoffed. "A man who sails with the devil Hawkins?"

"One hardly thinks it of him, Señor, and he can be trusted when practicing his medicine."

The governor looked distraught. "Hah, you may so say, Tobias, but it is a very great risk you ask me to take in releasing him from the chains to attend Margarita. Yet, perhaps — what does the Señora say?"

The Señora, Devora decided, must be the governor's wife.

"I have not dared to mention it to her yet."

"A mistake, Governor," said Lord Robert firmly. "The pirate cannot be trusted out of the dungeon. He is a madman — a devil with the sword."

Devora couldn't keep silent. "If you will permit, Governor Toledo, I know something of the practice of medicine myself. I've worked near my uncle for three years in treating slaves and in midwifery. If there is anything I can do, I should be pleased to look at your daughter Margarita."

Aware of the sharp look coming from Lord Robert and the surprise of her mother, Devora nevertheless kept her eyes on Governor Toledo.

"You, Lady Devora, know something of medicine?" asked Governor Toledo.

"My uncle is a brilliant man, and I have learned much from him. He served General Cromwell in the war and —"

"Devora, my dear, His Excellency will care little to hear of the supposed exploits of the now-dead Lord Protector of England. As for your mother's cousin Barnabas, any physician serving Cromwell was more likely to be a physician of mules than lords. Cromwell, I doubt, could tell the difference."

Despite the concern for his daughter, Governor Toledo laughed. "Words well chosen, Señor Robert. It is good the Chief Mule is dead, yes?"

Devora swallowed her father's rebuke in silence. Insulting Barnabas's medical skills was a rebuke to her abilities as well. Obviously, no one thought she had any.

The governor turned to the friar. "I am sure you are well able to care for this need, Tobias. I have heard from your brother the viceroy you are no average friar when it comes to medicine."

"My brother boasts, Excellency. I know so little compared to the English prisoner. I do think, despite the ambassador's suggestion to the contrary, that we should risk his help — under guard, naturally."

Then Friar Tobias was a Valentin. He would be the uncle of Nicklas Valentin. She found that bit of information interesting, also that he conducted himself with confidence in their presence. Tobias's brother Maximus sat in the seat of the powerful viceroyalty of Lima, which also made him governor over all the Main and the local governors. No wonder her father wished a marriage between her and the viceroy's son; it would aid all Lord Robert's exploits.

"Then speak with him. Judge his heart. He is not to be brought to my daughter's chamber without adequate guards surrounding him at all times."

"As you wish, Señor! At all times."

The friar looked pointedly at Lord Robert, and Devora noticed that her father was watching Tobias with a musing glance. Tobias bowed slightly toward the countess and Devora, then turned and strode back toward the rear section of the hacienda, his sandals clicking.

"An unusual friar," noted Lord Robert. "I did not know he was the viceroy's brother."

"Two strong men, often at odds," the governor sighed. "They clash like bulls. Slavery, the Incas, religion — it matters not. If one pulls one way, the other pulls the other. It was that way over Don Nicklas as well. Recently it has been worse."

Devora was alert with interest but tried to keep it concealed. She swished her lace fan.

"Oh? Trouble between them? Why so?" asked Lord Robert, and Devora could see he was paying particular attention.

"Ah, Maximus demands a greater production from the silver mines, all at the orders of King Philip, which Tobias strongly opposes. He complains of the deaths of the Incas. Nicklas will be the deciding force in this matter once he arrives. It is said he will be placed in charge of the mines. Nicklas wisely agrees with His Majesty."

Devora's muscles tightened. She looked from her father's cool, satisfied face to the hot frown of the governor, who was looking after Friar Tobias Valentin.

And does my father actually expect I would willingly marry this man Nicklas?

She thought of the prisoner. The friar had hinted he was a physician. What was an English physician doing in a dungeon below the governor's residence? What ship had he been taken from, and when? Where was the rest of the crew? Were they in dungeons as well? What of their captain? Why was no mention made of him?

Devora was shown to her chamber — a splendid affair of chairs and divans with minutely carved walnut, and burgundy and gold drapes hung on the tall window-doors that opened onto a balcony overlooking the plaza garden. There would be a ball that night given in their honor, and many important grandees would be there, so Countess Catherina had told her. "You are, my dear, to look your most charming self."

Upon the night of the festivity the governor's daughter was still ailing, and neither she nor the governor's wife made an appearance below in the hall where numerous guests and wealthy hildagos had gathered. Devora had heard that the viceroy was on his way, not only to meet the daughter of Earl and Countess Radburn, but on military business that was in some way connected with the prisoners kept in the dungeon of the governor's castle.

Devora tried not to think about them, nor the dark environs below the tile floor. Everyone waited to see the lovely English Señorita who was to be offered to the viceroy's son. Devora felt nervous and horribly embarrassed. How could this be happening to her?

The countess arrived to see her daughter a good two hours before the festivity to make certain everything connected with her first debut went flawlessly. Two Spanish maids arrived with her mother, each of them carrying numerous boxes and trinkets, "all to make Señorita Devora very beautiful."

Catherina brought her own maid to adorn Devora's honey-colored hair with exquisite waves, curls, and pearls, adding two small, white curling ostrich feathers. Devora had thought to resist until she caught sight of the white satin dress her mother presented her with. It was so stunning that she hadn't the will to refuse it. The dress was 20 yards, all supported gracefully over crinolines.

When mother and daughter were escorted downstairs, the Spanish hacienda was aglow with warm, golden lantern light spilling from elaborately carved bronze lanterns on the stone walls, and a fragrance of spicy red roses wafted in through the terrace windows. Guitar music came from the strolling musicians below in the circular patio as the warm sea breeze drifted to her, smelling of the Caribbean. From the latticed terrace the moonlight reflected on the water and on the canvas of several vessels across the bay.

There were thick crimson-colored carpets, chairs lined with velvet and brocade, candelabras of Peruvian silver, a Toledo clock of rare design, hangings of silk and tapestry. Food and various bottles of wine covered several long tables in the open patio, and servants went about with carved Peruvian silver trays offering Venetian glasses.

"I must tell you, Señor Robert," the governor was saying, "your appointment to the court of Castile has brought the governors on the Main new hope for an end to the English, French, and Dutch pirates. And today we have cause for celebration upon the news that your daughter, Señorita Devora, should become the bride of the viceroy's son."

"Let us hope a wise and peaceful agreement can be reached," said Lord Robert. "So many good things have been attributed to Nicklas by the army of Madrid that my daughter is anxious to meet him."

"And where are Don Maximus and Nicklas?" asked one of the guests. "Should they not be here by now?"

Devora looked up, her interest aroused. Nicklas was coming here tonight? Why had she not been told this sooner?

"The viceroy comes on military business with the governor to interrogate the prisoner, but Nicklas remains in Grenada."

"What prisoner is this?"

"Ah, not the infamous one, Señor. But the friend and confidant of the man the viceroy now seeks with great dedication. Have you not heard of a certain English pirate named Hawkins?"

"Who has not? The rogue has pillaged the coast, I hear, and sunk a galleon."

"Not just any galleon, Señor, but one belonging to the viceroy — one which carried slaves for the silver mines and treasure for the governor of Lima. This Captain Bruce Hawkins turned the slaves loose in Panama and carried off the treasure. If that were not enough, he had the effrontery to set the viceroy's galleon on fire! You can understand the personal animosity the viceroy has for this diablo."

A gentleman standing nearby turned his head and looked keenly. He bowed to the governor, and again to Lord Robert and a silent Devora. "Your pardon, Ambassador, but you spoke of the English pirate. Has that madman been caught yet?"

"Nay, the pirate leads a charmed life, so it appears," said Lord Robert. "I have spoken to both Governor Huxley of Barbados and Chevalier de Fontenay at Tortuga, demanding they do more to stop him, but they make excuses. But I assure you, King Charles will soon clean out those pirates' nests and send them all to the gallows where they belong."

"Perhaps, Señor Robert, we hope so," said the stately gentleman. "As to that, we shall see. Viceroy Maximus Valentin will put an end to Captain Hawkins as soon as Nicklas arrives to strengthen the war fleet at Veracruz."

He bowed slightly, and passed on.

Devora fanned herself languidly, thinking of pirates and Spaniards and Englishmen, her senses alert, stimulated by the rare opportunity that was hers in mingling with the grandees here. She would have so much to tell Uncle Barnabas when she returned home to work with him. Perhaps while she was here she might even learn something of the Spanish techniques for treating tropical fever. Her excitement grew, in spite of the fact that marriage was the least thing on her mind.

She glanced across the room through an archway, where she could just see that dice was being played where a great many young caballeros were gathered, but the game seemed to have more the nature of a cold reception. Watching these darkly handsome young men with unease, she wondered if the soldier Nicklas was like them in their fine black-and-gold suits. Magnificently clothed gentlemen of all ages strolled from group to group; there were ladies among them, and

Devora caught some of her mother's conversation: ". . . and we're not expected to be quite so discreet as were the ladies of Spain in a bygone age. Heavens! If we were, dear, I would never have agreed to come to Madrid — oh!" She noticed some gentleman and gestured with her jeweled fan. "Señor Diaz!"

Serving men dressed in the Toledo livery offered refreshments on heavy silver trays. With the Spanish wines went sweetmeats and fruit: grapes, apricots, and dark-purple plums.

There was an oppressive grandeur overall, thought Devora, who was accustomed to the Puritan surroundings of Uncle Barnabas's Ashby Hall in Barbados. Each Spaniard seemed well aware of his high degree, and there was a somewhat stern satisfaction with opulence, as though they deserved to rule. *It's nearly as treacherous as what Uncle said the nobility were like in London before Cromwell,* thought Devora wryly. And she had heard that King Charles had entered into a reconstruction of the grand and glittering past with wholehearted abandon.

Devora noted that there was a sobriety about the people. The Spaniards engaged in measured, sedate discourses absent of light, carefree laughter. She heard a somewhat commanding soprano voice at her elbow and turned to see a lovely woman of ivory skin. She used her black lace fan for unique expression as her rather cold, unfriendly gaze studied her.

"There are few women either in Madrid or on the Main who have not heard of the two dashing sons of Don Maximus, or who wish to marry them."

Devora did not wish to appear rude, but she felt no need to pretend to wish to marry either of the viceroy's heirs.

"I confess, Señora Sybella, I have not met them."

"They are most gallant. Both! Soldiers for His Majesty King Philip. Heroes against the enemies of our nation."

Just then, Devora heard one of the dons saying, "And now that Nicklas was knighted by the king, he will return to the Main to put an end to the heretics' murderous and thieving ways on the Caribbean."

"What can Nicklas do that the viceroy has not been able to accomplish?"

"He will return with war galleons, and will make the heretics pay for their treachery."

Sybella leaned toward her. "You see? You are favored."

"Perhaps it is so," said Devora. "But from

what I've heard of Nicklas Valentin, he is arrogant enough to make any woman's life miserable."

Sybella looked shocked, then her eyes warmed, and she laughed so loudly that stern, reproving glances were cast her way by men and women alike.

"As you can see, they do not approve of me," Sybella whispered, with a bitter twist to her henna-colored lips. "I should have stayed in Madrid. Someday I shall tell you all I have done. And you do not know, I am sure, that I am related to Nicklas — and he does not know I am here yet."

There was more to Sybella than what Devora was able to glean from the surface, but from the determined glow in her dark eyes it was plain to see that not all that she felt about Nicklas Valentin was in the past. Was the feeling mutual?

"You are related to him?" she asked curiously.

"Doña Sybella Valentin Ferdinand. A distant cousin of his, they say. My husband was killed recently, and I came home to my uncle's house in Lima, my baby with me. Some say I came only because Nicklas is returning. That is not quite true."

Devora moved uneasily and swished her fan. "You might as well know, Doña Sybella, that I have no desire to wed Nicklas. It is my father's wish, but one I hope to counter in the appropriate time and way. I am sure the viceroy will not approve of me anyway. If such could be the case, it would save us all much dissension, would it not?"

Sybella studied her as though she did not believe her. "It would, but Uncle Maximus wishes this alliance with his son and the Earl of Radburn for reasons not yet fully known to me, but I shall find out what they are. And it is well you do not wish to marry Nicklas, because I hope to do everything in my power to prevent it from happening."

Devora stared at Sybella, certain she was quite serious, and wondering what her own reply should be. If Devora were in love with Nicklas, she might clearly rebuke Sybella in no uncertain terms, but since she did not want this marriage, she had no reason to become offended.

Devora remained silent, and Sybella walked away with head high. No sooner had she gone, then the friar she had seen upon her arrival entered the room. She read his expression of sobriety, or was it caution?

It must be the governor's daughter, she thought. Perhaps she's taken a turn for the worse. Devora hadn't seen the governor since speaking with Lord Robert, and neither man was in view now. Wondering if there might be something she could do for the ailing Señorita, Devora made her way through the guests until she came to where the friar had stood a moment ago. He was gone, but she noticed a door that led into a corridor. Going there, Devora found herself in an arched colonnade with large clay pots holding leafy palms. The friar was walking toward the far exit that appeared to be an entrance to a garden patio. He strode purposefully as though in a hurry, and she called, "Friar?"

The big-shouldered man turned at her voice and stopped. His look of caution remained, but he seemed relieved to see her. Whom had he expected? Perhaps he was only worried.

She walked up with a smile and briefly curtsied. "Is the governor's daughter recovering? I do hope she hasn't taken for the worse?"

His eyes searched hers for a moment as if to judge her sincerity, then they softened. "It is gracious of you to inquire, Señorita. I take it you are the daughter of the Earl and Countess of Radburn?"

"Yes, Lady Devora Ashby. I'm — um — visiting temporarily with my parents. My father has been newly appointed ambassador to the court of your king in Madrid."

"Yes, so we — I have heard. But you will remain in Cartagena."

Devora felt a nervous pang at the thought. "Your city is fine indeed, Friar, so you will not take offense if I suggest I will seek to return home to Barbados at the earliest convenience to your viceroy."

Friar Tobias watched her, and Devora wondered why there were such serious musings in his eyes, but she attributed it to his religious calling.

He tapped his smooth chin. "Pardon, my child, but there has been much to occupy my mind recently. I believe you have been brought by Earl Radburn to seek an arrangement in marriage to the house of Valentin?"

"It is the intent, yes," she said briefly, not wishing to offend him by stating her concealed anguish at the thought.

"You see," he said by way of explanation, "the news of the matrimonial arrangement was only recently brought to my attention by way of a brief from Maximus. He comes from Cartagena, perhaps arriving tonight. The news was surprising to me and to others," he said, clearing his throat.

Devora guessed that the "others" chiefly included Doña Sybella. She noted the look of concern in the friar's face and wondered if the news disturbed him because he did not yet know where she stood in the way of her Christian faith. Since he was connected to the Valentin family, he would be naturally most interested in the religious allegiance of the woman to marry Don Nicklas.

Devora, for all that she had heard of the impatience in the Roman Church to seek the recantations of dissenters, somehow did not fear this man. Something about Friar Tobias suggested to her heart that he had no part with the office of the Holy Inquisition. Dare she confess to him her Puritan beliefs? Or was she being foolish to rush to conclusions about the man? Certainly it was wise to wait, to pray, to seek the Lord's guidance first. Feelings could be very deceptive.

Still, she wondered if the Lord had not already come to her aid and provided an unlikely friend in the house of conflict. Perhaps the friar could quietly arrange with the viceroy to send her home to Barbados once her parents sailed to Madrid. But her plans must wait.

"I hope to be returning to Barbados soon, Friar," she said carefully.

"You do not look with particular favor upon this marriage then?"

"I confess it so. It is not my way."

"So! Maximus wishes a bride for Favian, does he? I cannot say it will improve him." He leaned toward her and spoke in a low voice. "Between us, my child, I don't think the brooding rascal is worthy of you."

She smiled. "I don't know about that, but marriage is sought not with Don Favian but his brother Nicklas."

"Nicklas!"

"You are surprised. No doubt he will be, too, since I've only just learned from the countess that the viceroy has not spoken of this to him yet. A rather unusual arrangement, Friar Tobias," she said dryly.

Tobias rubbed his chin, a curious look in his eyes. "Nicklas, you say. An interesting set of circumstances," he said to himself, then looked at her. "He would not know, Señorita, for Nicklas has been away — er at war, fighting for His Majesty — and doing a rare job of it, too." He suddenly gave one brief chuckle, as he mused to himself. "He will be most surprised to hear of his wedding. Perhaps you will meet him sooner than you think." His humor vanished when voices drifted toward them from out of a quiet corner of the patio garden.

"I note you are in a hurry, Sir Friar," she said. "I have kept you too long. I wished only to inquire of Governor Toledo's daughter. Should you think I could be of use, I gladly offer my presence in her chamber."

"Of use?" he asked absently, his attention apparently straying again toward the voices coming from the patio.

She too glanced there, wondering why the voices disturbed him, but saw no one. "Yes, I've studied apothecary at Ashby Hall."

"Ashby Hall?"

"My uncle's home at Barbados. He was a doctor and trained me in certain respects so that I might work at his side. He has great mercy and concern for slave and planter alike. I've delivered babies, tended those struck with typhoid —"

He turned his head, his interest awakened. "Ah? Perhaps — yes, it may be of benefit if you could go up to Margarita's chamber to help the physician who is there. The man doesn't speak Castilian, so he cannot tell the serving maids what to do. If you could help?"

"I should be glad to. You've only to bring me there, or have one of the servants do so."

"Ah! Speak of blessings from above, you are just the answer to my prayers. Your presence will convince the governor — I mean," he corrected himself, "the addition of your medical help in the chamber will be of benefit. I'll call one of the serving men immediately — that is, just as soon as I return from a little meeting in the garden. Er — do you think you might wait in the archway, Señorita Devora?"

Curious, but quite amenable, Devora smiled and walked back toward the hall where the guests were conversing and moving from group to group. She looked back over her shoulder. Rather odd, the friar's behavior. Something had disturbed him from the patio. No matter — it didn't concern her. She looked toward the guests to locate her mother to inform her where she was going, but neither the earl nor the countess was anywhere in view.

She gathered up her white satin skirts and ascended the stairs to the upper corridor and, once on the landing, waited for the friar to return from the patio garden. She had already made up her mind that she liked the brother of Don Maximus.

11

Rendezvous in the Plaza Garden

The chamber of the governor's daughter, Señorita Margarita Toledo, was warm with the vibrant colors of yellows, oranges, and red-brown bricks. Curved, gilded cages with blue, green, and crimson birds swung from the ceiling, alive with fluttering wings. The oversized wood bed with carefully carved posts knobbed with silver was draped with white silk, and the bed was elevated and stood back in an alcove where countless prayer candles gleamed with flames looking like oval golden eyes. Señora Toledo was kneeling with clasped hands beside the bed where her daughter lay in stillness. The older woman's black lace mantilla extended down over her shoulders and touched the polished hardwood floor.

Below the semicircular balcony that extended over the plaza garden, the sounds of pleasure coming from the governor's guests continued to play on the hot night. Señora Toledo stood and pulled the bell cord, summoning her maidservant, and spoke to her in soft Spanish. A few minutes later, Devora looked on while Friar Tobias entered, bringing the English physician — the prisoner from Hawkins's ship, the *Revenge* — Doctor Kitt Bonnor.

Somehow she had pictured him to be older, perhaps because the notion of a physician conjured up images in her mind of her uncle Barnabas Ashby. But Bonnor was a rugged young man with mid-length golden-brown hair, a wide mustache, and a short, pointed beard. His dark eyes were as sharp as the parrot that sat in a gold loop on a table; his skin had been browned from the Caribbean sun. What remained of an exquisitely detailed shirtwaist of blue silk was now tattered from months in the dungeon. His leather breeches were worn, and his calf-length boots, scuffed. All that was missing was a sword scabbard and boarding pistols. She noted the same look to his face that Sir Bruce had worn at the governor's residency in Barbados: a boldness and confidence that set her on guard, but whether for good or evil remained in doubt.

Kitt Bonnor appeared unbeaten, as

though he expected important liberators at any moment. The idea made her glance uneasily toward the balcony.

She saw his alert eyes survey the chamber, taking note of the surroundings, as though conscious of possible routes of escape should the moment arrive. He surveyed the governor's wife, noticed Devora with a hint of surprise — no doubt because she was English — and then turned his attention on the ailing daughter. He neared the bed carrying a small leather satchel and stared down purposefully at Margarita, who lay in a deep sleep.

Curious that the prisoner from the *Revenge* went unguarded except for the friar — a man who also bore an unusual huskiness and virility uncommon to the other clerics she had seen since arriving. Devora studied Friar Tobias. Why would the brother of the viceroy appear to be on friendly terms with Kitt Bonnor?

Her estimation of the prisoner improved when she saw his response to Margarita. He sat down on a stool beside her bed, taking her slim hand, and listened to the pulse, a studious gravity on his face. For the moment at least, he was all physician. He was doing all the proper things that she had seen Uncle Barnabas do a thousand times —

things that he had taught her as well.

"I've heard by way of the Indians in Panama that one can sleep for weeks without dying. It depends on how strong the body, how long it can go without food. The Señorita is already small and thin. I do not know . . . there are things to be done, but risky." He looked at Tobias, who was looking toward the balcony. "I've heard the leaves of the Abuana plant can effect a cure. But who can say for certain? The Indians showed them to me, and I took a few samples. Still, I've no notion how much to give her or for how long." He rested his chin on his brown knuckles and meditatively gazed at the white-faced girl. "I will need to make them into tea — to guess on the strength. And if I'm wrong and the girl dies . . ."

Tobias strode to the balcony and looked out toward the plaza garden where the high adobe wall enclosed the governor's hacienda from the street. In the distance, the moon beamed its halo onto the dark Caribbean.

Devora watched him, wondering what he saw that interested him.

"You may never know the consequences of your medical judgement, my lad. Neither of us will." Then he noticed Devora and seemed to catch himself saying too much.

He smiled in a friendly fashion, and for a moment there was a look of sympathy in his eyes as if he knew she were the pawn of the earl and countess.

Devora held to the carved black bedpost, musing about the strange behavior of both men. "You two know each other?" she asked pointedly.

Bonnor shot Tobias a glance, then grinned when Tobias's mouth tugged downward.

"Come, Friar, not reluctant to admit you know a few rogues," he said, and smiled at Devora, scanning her. "So you've come to marry Don Nicklas Valentin. My sympathy, Lady Ashby."

"Mind your tongue, you educated cocklebur," quipped Tobias. "Tend to the Señorita and leave the fair English damsel be."

"If you will pardon my saying so, Doctor Bonnor," said Devora, undisturbed, "I've heard about the medicinal value of the Abuana leaf myself."

"You've been to Panama?"

She smiled. "No, Barbados."

"So that's it. I knew I had seen you before." He stood, the chains on his feet rattling. He looked down at them with a scowl, then back to her. "You're the niece of Barnabas, aren't you? From Ashby plantation?"

"Yes, I've heard of you as well, through Edward."

"Edward Townsend — yes, a fine gentleman. He'll be a fine doctor one day. Barbados is a fair colony," he added reflectively, as though remembering with a certain wistfulness. "I settled there each year when hurricane season forbade sailing the Indies." His dark eyes showed ironic good humor. "I don't know what Governor Huxley will do about his gout if the Spanish viceroy has his way and ships me off to Cadiz. Let's hope Barnabas Ashby decides my remedy for gout is worthy of his practice."

"My uncle often used Abuana leaves in tea to treat what he calls sleeping sickness on the plantation," she told him. "If he were here, I'm certain he would approve of your using them on the governor's daughter."

Kitt's glance was mingled with a certain amount of respect and pleasure, but Devora pretended not to notice the latter as she walked around to the side of Margarita's bed. "May I see the leaves? To make certain they're indeed the same?"

Kitt bowed, then straightened, handing her the small tin container of crushed, dried leaves. Devora took a whiff, wrinkling her nose and handing it back.

"They are the same. They are very potent,

Doctor. One crumbled in a pot of boiling water is sufficient for several treatments. A small cup, unsweetened, is what my uncle would prescribe."

"I'm certain Barnabas knew what he was doing. We'll prescribe the same, then. Tobias? We need boiling water —" he stopped.

Devora followed his glance across the chamber, but the friar was no longer in the room or on the balcony.

Doctor Bonnor turned to Devora again. Was she mistaken, or was there new excitement in his eyes, as though the disappearance of the friar had brought hope.

"Can you speak to the Señora and her serving maid?"

"Yes, of course," but Devora was still glancing toward the balcony, wondering why Tobias had disappeared, and what it might mean. Had he noted anything earlier when he had been looking out toward the Caribbean that would make him leave the chamber?

"Lady Ashby?" came the questioning voice of Kitt, and she turned, embarrassed. "At once," she breathed, and went to seek the Señora, who had also left the chamber to resume her religious vigil.

The governor had insisted on guards surrounding Doctor Bonnor at all times, but she had noticed that when Friar Tobias came in with him, they had been alone.

There was a curious frown between her brows as she paused before the alcove and looked back at the Englishman. He was grave as he attended Margarita, and she scanned the debonair figure. He must be a pirate. Why else would he be held here on the Isle of Pearls? If so, where were his other crew members? Were they also here, still in the dungeon? He must have felt her deliberating stare, for he lifted his head and glanced her way. Devora flushed, thinking he might have mistaken her curiosity. He smiled a lot, she noticed, and his confidence told her she had much to relearn about what she expected a physician to be — or for that matter, a buccaneer. Who was his captain? Bruce Hawkins? And what was Bruce Hawkins like?

Her mind went flying back to that episode at Governor Huxley's mansion the night of the ball. She had not found Edward, but she had met Sir Bruce. Was it possible the two men were one and the same? He had told her he was a pirate. Had he been speaking the truth to her, or was he only being flippant? But what if he were down in the dungeon? The thought brought an odd, sickening tremor.

She turned quickly and went to seek Margarita's mother.

Devora found her in the small alcove, where an altar was set into a niche in the stone wall, kneeling before a statue that must have been, in the Señora's mind, an image of the Virgin Mary. The flickering candlelight showed on the Señora's face. Devora was distracted by the smell of candles and incense, the lifeless, cold images that stared back from the wall. Obviously, the Señora did not consider the imagery inconsistent, or kneeling before a statue as idolatry.

Devora sadly turned away to seek one of the serving maids to boil the water and steep the leaf into a brew. As she did, the Señora turned her head. There was no peace in the mother's eyes, no confidence that God through the one Mediator, Jesus Christ, had heard her cry for help and forgiveness, for she did not know this truth.

"I am looking for the serving woman," said Devora in Spanish.

"Si, Señorita, she is outside in the garden, I think."

"I will go for her, Señora." She turned, then paused, looking back. "Señora Toledo, God loves us, and He sent us His Son, Jesus, that we can believe in Him and never perish. And He is our Mediator with the Father. He will hear your prayers for mercy if you come in His name because the name of Jesus is above all names in heaven or on earth."

The Señora smiled wanly and nodded her graying head sagely. "Si, Señorita, si," her voice sighed.

Devora smiled at her gently. When she entered the chamber, Kitt Bonnor was standing there. Had he overheard? Did he understand Spanish?

A curious look reflected in his dark eyes. "The slave woman is out in the courtyard. I am not permitted to leave this chamber. Will you go? I need boiling water for the Abuana leaf."

"Yes." She left the chamber, and downstairs found herself once again in the corridor with its arched colonnade and large clay pots holding leafy palms. She passed through the far exit that appeared to be an entrance into a garden patio, looking for the serving maid. She remembered Friar Tobias's interest in the area earlier that evening and wondered if he had come here after unexpectedly disappearing from Margarita's chamber.

Moonlight flooded the garden patio, while the trees cast ink-black shadows on the stone. Gathering up her skirts, she left the lighted entranceway and walked out onto the court, the wind embracing her. In the distance the Caribbean glimmered like a blue-black gem beneath a luminous white moon. The palm trees were black and lacy against the horizon, and she felt a melancholy whim stir across her soul as she thought of this strange land and these Spaniards with whom she was supposed to make a new life. Barbados reached out to her —

"Nicklas Valentin," she breathed suddenly, vehemently, "I hope you remain indefinitely in Madrid!"

"I will convey your wishes to him, madam! But I doubt if he is in an obliging mood."

Devora whirled and glanced about, seeing no one at first, then a slight movement from somewhere above her head caught her eye. Her breath held, and she stepped back.

The moonlight reflected on a wide-brimmed hat with a swirl of feather. A masculine figure crouched on the wide adobe wall, prepared to leap down with sword in hand. He dropped softly to the tile court, the steel blade in his hand glimmering. She caught sight of a leather baldric worn over his head and shoulder, holding boarding pistols. With his left hand he swept off his hat and bowed with expert grace. She had a moment's impression of a sardonic smile.

There was something vaguely familiar about him. . . .

It could not be — the dangerously good-looking rogue she had encountered in Barbados in Governor Huxley's residence! She watched him with surprise and uncertainty, wondering if she had cause to fear, or merely to wonder at their chance meeting. If the Barbados episode had been unnerving, this surprise encounter was even frightening. Obviously, he was a pirate.

"So it's you!" came her half-accusing whisper. "I was right," and she stepped back. "I suspected you were a pirate in Barbados!"

"My, but this is a windfall!" came his smoothly jesting voice. "I didn't realize our illustrious Governor Toledo was in so grand a position as to incur the charming company of Lady Ashby at his fiesta." His gaze flicked over her. "But I will not unfairly judge you. You would hardly be in a position to know your silken slippers have been waltzing to Portuguese guitars atop the polished floor above the governor's dungeon. No doubt the pitiable members of my crew have enjoyed the sound of the castanets as they languish below in chains."

Her breath tensed. His crew?

"Spanish soldiers are everywhere. You'll never get past the front door!"

He looked toward the lighted hacienda, then back to her with a smile. "The upper balcony to that chamber will suffice for now. I understand a captain friend of mine is in there, mercifully attending the governor's daughter. I, too, will need to pay her my respects."

"You are mad to come to the governor's hacienda. An English pirate expecting to enter his daughter's —"

As though offended, he frowned. "Buccaneer, if you please — a man of both gallantry and esteemed wit."

"And insufferable arrogance."

He bowed again. "Perhaps you will reconsider. Captain Bruce Anthony Hawkins. Your servant, Señorita."

"Hawkins!" she breathed. "*You?* You are mad indeed to have dared to come here. Do you not know they seek you with all determination? This very eve they spoke of your capture."

"An early and vain hope on their part. But enough speech, Lady Ashby. There is little time to waste. I would not wish Captain Bonnor to wear out his welcome."

She turned to flee, but he caught her.

"Now that you've seen me, I dare not turn you loose until I've finished what I've come to do." He frowned. "You prove a grave problem, madam."

Had she not been so alarmed, she could have swatted him for the arrogance on his handsome face.

"But perhaps," came the faintly teasing voice, "since you believe I've come for treasure as well as members of my crew, I might take you along as well."

She winced at the suggestion and tried to jerk free, but his hold tightened.

"I — I'll say nothing."

He regarded her, "And you'll keep your vow, of course."

She remained mute, her eyes faltering under a warm gaze.

"As I thought. I could use your assistance."

"It is not my custom to assist pirates who come to steal jewels and pieces of eight."

"I have told you: I come to set my crew free. You may keep your meager jewels, madam."

Meager! She tried to pull away. "Turn me loose! If you won't, I'll scream."

His gaze turned thoughtful. He looked pointedly at her lips. "I should hate to bind and gag you." He looked toward the climbing rosebushes and honeysuckle rambling along an extended lattice. "Then again, I could leave you there until I gather the rest of the treasure. . . ."

Her breath left her, and she saw a malicious glint of humor in his smile.

"Do so, and you'll live to regret it."

"Am I to fear this scoundrel from Madrid — what was his name?" he mused too silkily, "the man you ardently wished to banish forever to Madrid? Ah, Don Nicklas Valentin, was it not?" His smile showed malicious amusement. "He'll hardly come to your aid now."

"You mock, sir, but you won't for long. It is not *he* you will answer to should you dare to abduct me!"

"Oh! Do not say so! Such challenges tempt my daring." He scanned her. "What then am I to fear, if I may ask? Your ravishing charms, or something *less* deadly?"

His smile only infuriated her. She tried to jerk away. "Edward! That's who you should fear. Yes! You best fear *him*."

A brow lifted at this lofty and grave announcement. "Edward," he said as though tasting the name. "Contemplation of this dear Edward surely causes me to shake in my boots. Is he about somewhere? Hiding in the pink sweet peas perhaps? Ah, Edward. A fancy Englishman from the sound of his name. One who likely sniffs his pomander filled with dried lavender and posies, prepared to scat and hide behind the silk curtain in the ladies' parlor at the first glint of my Toledo blade."

Devora grew hot under his gaze. Her fingers clenched. "For your information, sir," she stated with forced dignity, "Edward is *he* whom I intend to marry one day, regardless of the ambitions and schemes to the contrary. Edward is a doctor from Barbados. A noble, upstanding gentleman. A gallant fellow who doesn't brandish wicked swords or wave daggers. Unlike you, sir, he's *not* a bloodthirsty pirate."

He mocked a wince, hand at heart as he bowed his arrogant, dark head. "I stand rebuked, Madame. I cry pardon. Ah, Edward, now I remember. I believe you mentioned him in Barbados at Governor Huxley's ball."

So he did remember their meeting . . .

"If I recall," he was saying, "you came to that ball in a ragpicker's dress with a provocative peep of lace petticoat for a mask, rushing all about in breathless form with a concealed dagger somewhere on you." His gray-green eyes danced as he scanned her, tapping his chin. "I compliment the modification in your appearance, Lady Ashby. Is this change also for sweeting Edward, or may I tantalize my ego by imagining it done for my carefully arranged appearance tonight? Meeting again like this amid the spicy scent of Spanish roses and danger tempts me to hope."

Devora's lashes narrowed. "Your imagination, sir, needs a bit of rude awakening, as your ego needs a good prick of the rose thorn."

He was dangerous. There was no doubt about it. And if he —

"Do I need then inquire whether you have another dagger concealed somewhere within reach, or is my heart safe for the moment?"

Her breath came with restrained temper. "I carry no dagger, Captain Hawkins, but if I had a boarding pistol, I'd use it!"

He smiled. "So," and he offered an affected sigh. "It is as I thought. You are *not* going to be cooperative."

Hurrying footsteps interrupted, coming from the governor's residence. In an instant, his grip tightened, and she found herself with him behind the palm trees, her back pressed against the roughly layered trunk. His hand was over her mouth, his other holding his sword, and she was held in silence by his warm, gray-green gaze.

Devora stood rigidly, feeling the rough bark pressing into her back, her heart leaping to her throat.

The footsteps came closer among the garden trees, slowed, now uncertain. A voice called in Spanish: "Friar Tobias?"

One of the governor's guards!

The shrilling of crickets and the chirping of great bats feeding on insects filled the tense moment.

They heard the soldier walking about, then he must have decided he had been wrong, for his footsteps stopped. She could feel the tension in Bruce's body, see him lift the point of his blade. Her breath slowed . . . then she heard the soldier returning to the hacienda.

Bruce relaxed his grip, but did not turn her loose. Slowly he removed his hand from her mouth. Devora let out a gasp of relief.

"The steps up to Margarita's chamber," he asked in a whisper. "Are there guards waiting?"

"No."

He cocked his head. "You're telling the truth?"

"Yes. Do you think I wish bloodshed?" she rebuked.

His brow lifted. "That, unfortunately,

cannot be stopped. In a short time, this garden will be swarming with buccaneers."

"Thanks to you, Captain Hawkins. After all, they are *your* pirates," she accused. "Whatever happens tonight is your responsibility."

"They are my crew, madam, but I am not to be faulted for all that happens tonight. Had I not come, Kitt would stand trial before the viceroy, who has definite plans to force him to tell all he knows of one certain Captain Hawkins. They have vile ways to make a man talk. So much so, that I would not burden your innocence to explain them. So you see, I feel no qualm of conscience at landing buccaneers to stop the trial. Unfortunately, neither the governor nor the viceroy will surrender Kitt without drawing sword. So, alas! There will be fighting and men will die. What matters to me at the moment is that you are not placed in harm's way."

He did not sound as ruthless as she might have suspected, but she would not admit to him that she thought this.

"How generous of you, Captain Hawkins," she said coolly, and for a moment their eyes met. She saw a spark of green temper in his eyes.

"You have less than five minutes to get

back up the stairs and clear the chamber of the Señora and the serving woman. Tell Kitt to be ready. And if you suddenly decide to err on the side of the Spanish governor and his arrogant caballeros, it will be you and not I who cause the bloodshed. Now," and his face softened perceptibly, "can I trust you to return and behave yourself?"

Devora pulled her arm free and scanned him with a cool rebuke. "I will do as you demand, Captain Hawkins."

"Who is in the room with the girl beside Bonnor?"

"The Señora, and by now perhaps, a serving woman. Maybe the friar as well. He behaves oddly, coming and going secretively."

"If you noticed, I must tell him to improve his technique. He is a friend and waits outside the wall for my signal."

"Your friend?" she asked, surprised.

"Do you think a buccaneer has no allies except a cutlass?" His voice softened. "I could wish you were one right now, Señorita. You could be of valuable help to me."

Wary, yet finding herself responding unwillingly, she scanned his face. "Help? In what way?"

He reached into his baldric and lifted out

a boarding pistol. Hesitating a second, he handed the silver-butted end toward her. He glanced up toward the lighted chamber behind the balcony entwined with blooming lavender and white wisteria. "Bring this to him."

Her eyes fell to the huge pistol, seeing the inlaid silver gleaming. He took her hand, his own warm and strong, and pressed the weapon to her palm. "You said a moment ago if you had a pistol you would use it on me. Perhaps I am a fool, but I have just placed my own life in your hand."

Her throat constricted, she swallowed, looking at it, feeling his touch as well. She resented the strange pounding in her heart that his nearness brought, and looked up at him, managing a noble countenance. Her brow rounded.

"I could, as you say, turn against you. Are you not afraid?"

A vague smile showed on his lips. "If I am afraid, it is not of the pistol you hold, but of your beauty." He stepped back and bowed. "Go ahead. Shoot."

She smiled ruefully, scanning him. "My, how surprised you would be if I did."

His dark brow arched, and he smiled.

She stepped from the palm tree and glanced uneasily toward the balcony to the

Señorita's chamber. She must be mad to help him. She told herself she was doing so to save lives.

"And if I bring your pirate doctor friend this gun, will you then go peaceably?"

His gaze was alert. "If you can see that he has the pistol and climbs down that balcony unnoticed, you have my word as a gentleman."

She looked at him, musing. She did not like to admit it, but there was a gallantry that emanated from his presence, and she could only wonder why it should be so. The tales she had heard of Captain Hawkins and the *Revenge* were frightening indeed.

"Very well."

He studied her, as though her decision surprised him. "Why are you willing to help me?"

She felt the warmth stealing into her cheeks. "A strange question, when you threaten me with bloodshed if I do not."

"I did not threaten. You wish to tell yourself so. Is that not a pistol you hold freely in your hand?"

"Friar Tobias believes you are worth assisting."

"And do you?"

At the moment she wasn't certain what she thought of Bruce Anthony Hawkins.

Tobias must have known Bruce was coming and was trying to arrange his secret entry, as well as get Bonnor up from the dungeon into Margarita's chamber. Quite a task for the friar! Yet he had managed. All so that they might escape at the ripe moment.

"Captain, if I cooperate, it is to save lives, and because Tobias befriends you."

"I will accept that for now. I am a patient man. I can wait the time when you admit that you trust me."

"Will you tell me why it is a man like the friar would befriend you?"

"No. That, too, will need to wait. Tell me, Tobias cannot be certain the viceroy has not arrived. I must not be seen by him. Have you seen him or heard of his arrival to see Governor Toledo? Has the Señora mentioned him perhaps?"

Why was he so concerned that Viceroy Valentin not see him? Why not the governor also? Or the many other officials inside the hacienda?

"I have not heard. I've been up in the chamber waiting for your pirate friend, the so-called 'doctor' to be brought up from the dungeon. The Señorita is very ill."

"She will live," he quipped wryly. "She is too contentious not to."

"So you have met her then," she asked,

surprised. But how was that possible?

He hesitated. "I have heard of her," was all he said. "There is no more time. You must go quickly."

Devora picked up her cumbersome skirts and ran breathlessly through the trees toward the courtyard.

12

Pirate or Buccaneer?

A moment later she came to the clearing where the patio was aglow with flaring torches and colored-glass lanterns. There were strolling guitar players, caballeros, and officials, all wearing fashionable clothes with ruffs. She skirted the edge close to the garden flowers and bushes and, once nearing the steps up to the balcony, climbed breathlessly to the top, entering Margarita's room.

The Señora was still at her prayers in the religious alcove, candles burning; Margarita was asleep. The man standing beside her bed was not Captain Kitt Bonnor, but Lord Robert.

His golden head glinted in the lantern light, his black suit with a frilled white shirt was severely handsome. He turned toward her sharply, his glacier-blue eyes alert, studying her.

Devora wondered if her face had paled to match her fluttering heart.

"Father," she breathed simply, and gripped the pistol behind her skirts, praying he would not notice.

"Where have you been, Devora?"

"I — went into the plaza garden to find the serving lady of Señora Toledo. Unfortunately, I did not see her." All the while her gaze scattered about the chamber. *Where was Kitt?*

"Your mother and I have been searching for you. You must not wander alone. These Spanish dons are strict when it comes to their wives and daughters. Decent women do not display themselves or go about without adequate chaperon."

How thoughtful of the dons, she thought, perturbed, *while they run about doing as they please.*

"Yes, I will remember. The Señorita, did she receive the medicinal tea of Abuana leaves? Where is Doctor Bonnor?"

"Pirate Bonnor is back in the dungeon where he belongs. The man is dangerous and should not have been left here alone with you or the governor's daughter. I am stunned Tobias would go off and leave him unguarded."

Back in the dungeon. Now what?

Lord Robert walked across the chamber and took her shoulders. "You grow pale. I hope this sickness is not something that can spread to the rest of us."

"I am all right. Perhaps if I sit —" And she sank onto the red velvet stool, conveniently allowing her billowing silk skirts to cover her hand and the pistol.

"Viceroy Valentin may yet arrive tonight. I would not have you looking sickly when a good impression is needed."

The hopes and plans of Bruce Hawkins appeared to be swiftly unraveling. He had been very concerned about the possibility of Viceroy Maximus's arrival.

"Were you not with Catherina? Who bade you come up here?"

"No one," she said tonelessly. "I thought I might aid the doctor."

"A pirate. One of crucial importance to Maximus."

She saw her opportunity. "Why would the viceroy of the entire Spanish Main find Captain Bonnor so important?"

His gaze swerved to hers. "He is closely associated with the pirate named Hawkins. If anyone can offer reliable information, it is Bonnor."

"Hawkins must be having exploits similar to Henry Morgan," she suggested to learn his response. She wanted to know more about Bruce's escapades, but her father didn't appear to take up her bait.

"Morgan — that black-hearted fiend. He is another fellow we wish to capture and see dangle. But it is Hawkins's trail we are following at present."

"Indeed, Father, what has this blackguard Hawkins done?"

"He has done his share, my dear," he said wryly, "you can be sure of it. Yet Maximus seeks him for another reason."

Devora picked up her pink feather fan and stirred the humid air about her face. "How curious. I wonder what it could be."

Lord Robert studied her briefly, then walked to the balcony and looked out as the strumming from Portuguese guitars filled the brightly illuminated plaza.

"Maximus is suspicious of the man's identity."

Her head turned in his direction, the fan ceasing; then started up again more rapidly. "I wonder why. You mean he is not Hawkins? That makes no sense."

"He is Captain Bruce Hawkins all right, but when we first captured Bonnor we thought him to be Hawkins. Maximus hasn't entirely explained what troubles him most about the matter." He paused, considering before going on. "You should know that Don Nicklas has been knighted by King

Philip and sent here to not only safeguard the treasure galleons, but also to capture Hawkins and the *Revenge*." He walked back to where she sat, looking down at her. "You do well to be matched with Nicklas. You will have competition from Doña Sybella. Catherina worries you will not do enough to win his heart."

Her fan ceased. "I would prefer to return to Barbados."

"Your mother and I are aware of that, but it cannot be, Devora. Put it from your mind and seek your happiness in the Valentin family. There will be much here and in Lima to interest and entertain you. You will not be bored. Nicklas is far from a boring man."

Her fate appeared all but settled, and there was little she could do. "When does he arrive?" she asked dully.

"Not until the treasure ships are due. Perhaps two months. He is in Grenada preparing his troops and supplies, and will arrive here then."

"What of Captain Bonnor? What will Maximus do with him?"

"He will be interrogated until he confesses all he knows."

Her free hand plucked at her skirt. "Is it ever justified to torture a man, Father? Even if Captain Bonnor is a pirate, he is still a man. It seems cruel and unnecessary."

"Do not concern yourself in such matters. You are not here for that." He looked at her. "Catherina tells me your religion motivates you to unnecessary emotional escapades. Do not misunderstand me, I think religion is fine if it makes you a better person, but whatever your private devotions, see to it you do not speak of them openly. Your marriage into the Valentin family is too important to be put at risk by your personal views. I've plans to accomplish in Lima, and you are a necessary part of them."

The pistol weighed heavily in her hand, but she dared not shift its position. "Father, I think you should have permitted the doctor to practice his medical skills after all. Pirate or no, he seemed to know a great deal," she said boldly.

He looked over at the bed where the governor's daughter lay motionless, impatience at the turn of events visible in the flex of his square jaw. "It is too much of a risk to permit his freedom."

"Even with guards?"

"There were no guards when I arrived. It is madness. I will speak to the friar about this oversight. He might have tried to escape through the balcony."

"There were chains on his feet. He couldn't have gotten far."

"Never underestimate a pirate who wants his freedom. He may have used the governor's daughter as ransom."

"I hadn't thought of that. . . ." She wondered if Bruce had. She decided he would have considered it since he seemed to think of everything else.

Lord Robert walked to the door, glancing toward Señora Toledo, saying something in soft Spanish.

"Sí, Señor Roberto, gracias."

"Come, Devora, I want you downstairs with the countess when Maximus arrives. You are too beautiful to be hiding away up here. I am proud of my daughter and expect to make the most of your good fortune to be born fair."

Now what? What could she do with the pistol?

"I shall be right there, Father. My hair is windblown. Give me a moment."

"Do so, then come down quickly," and he went out.

Devora cast a glance toward Margarita and her mother, then seeing the Señora's shawl of lace, covered the pistol with it, and carrying it on her arm, went out into the corridor. If only she could find Tobias, but the friar was nowhere in sight. Was he with Bruce?

A few minutes later she entered her own chamber. Several chairs of minutely carved walnut were arranged about the room. Burgundy and gold drapes and embroidered tapestries hung on cream-colored walls. There was a Catalan chest with flat pilasters upon its front and sides, and she rushed across the thick Turkish rug and stooped before the chest, lifting its lid. She placed the pistol inside, frowning. There would be no way she could help Kitt Bonnor now. Unless she could somehow have him released from the dungeon. But that was an impossible task. There would be guards there, and who would listen to her? If she had only returned a few minutes sooner! What would she tell Bruce?

She stood, determined. There was simply nothing she could tell him. His plans were foiled. If he were wise, he would go back to wherever his ship was secretly anchored and return to Tortuga. If she risked going to him in the plaza garden, both of them might get caught.

She would do nothing, she decided, her face grim. When she did not return, he would give up and leave. Lives would be saved, and Kitt Bonnor, pitiably, must be left to his dark fate.

Devora went to the vanity and poured water from the pitcher. Wetting a cloth, she cooled her face and throat, then smoothed her hair. When ready once again to leave her chamber and face the guests, some 20 minutes had slipped by.

If she had wondered what Bruce would do when Captain Bonnor did not arrive with the pistol to meet him, the answer became all too frighteningly clear. A brazen-voiced horn blasted its signal. Pistol shots followed, with crackling in the tropical night.

Devora stood unable to move, then, rushing to her window and parting the heavy magenta drapes, she stepped out onto her balcony. More shouting and pounding pirate drums sprang up with feverish clamor, accosting her eardrums. She gripped the rail, her eyes straining toward the trees along the adobe wall where she had last seen Bruce. Was he still there?

Below the balcony, the guitars had ceased. In the blazing torchlight, she could see the governor's guests taken in the snare. The handsomely dressed caballeros and hildagos and their women and daughters in lace and satin lapsed into sudden, tense silence. The women drew back, beginning to cluster together. A terrible silence fell; then an eruption of startled voices overflowed.

Devora looked off toward the fortress tower looming darkly against the moonlit Caribbean sky to where the governor's soldiers were on guard. Bruce's men were already onshore and among the trees. She did not know how many soldiers the governor had at his disposal, but tried to convince herself there would be enough to protect the hacienda from being overrun by pirates.

As she continued peering intently ahead, a dark figure astride a horse came galloping from Castillo La Gloria, shouting for Governor Toledo. The people in the plaza scattered as the rider on horseback drew up. As the torchlight fell upon him, she recognized the castellan of the fortress. His yellow-and-black sleeves flashed above his breastplate, his long cloak fluttering, sword in hand.

"Santiago! Death to the pirates!" he shouted to the governor. "Ole ariba! Pirates! Pirates!"

Governor Toledo, Lord Robert, and other officials surged to the side of the snorting horse asking questions, demanding answers.

"They are inside the fortress walls, Excellency! They have the cannon!"

"How, you fools?"

"They had a friend inside who opened the gate!"

The governor shouted angrily, "I will not hear such foolishness! Defend the fortress La Gloria at all costs! The viceroy will be here tomorrow! Will you have us all hanged from the wall?"

He had hardly gotten the warning out before the buccaneers from the *Revenge* began their attack from the direction of the fortress. The cannon boomed, belching smoke, and Devora covered her ears and looked toward the Castillo, seeing debris flying.

"What good are cannons now? The buccaneers are ashore," called Lord Robert. "In my opinion, it is a ruse. Hawkins does not want the fort, nor the town! He does not hold captives for booty as does Henry Morgan. Hawkins wants Captain Kitt Bonnor."

Devora tensed. Her father was right.

"If I were you, governor, I would call your soldiers from La Gloria and bring them here to defend the hacienda at all costs!"

"And surrender the Castillo?"

"Blast the Castillo!"

"Ah, Señor Robert, nay, the flag of Spain flies! When the viceroy arrives tomorrow, will he see the mocking skull and crossbones of the devil Hawkins over the Castillo? An unforgivable insult for Maximus! He will hang me, Señor, not you! It is easy for you to say, 'Surrender the Castillo!' "

The governor turned on his heel and shouted orders to the castellan astride the horse. "Defend La Gloria!"

Bruce understood the mind of Spain very well, Devora thought curiously. He seemed to have known the governor would react this way.

Governor Toledo continued shouting his orders as the noise grew louder, and soon Devora watched the soldiers in yellow-and-red garb come surging over the plaza, their feet pounding the stone squares. They ran in the direction of the tower to make a stand.

Pistol shots split the night; swords clashed, cutting, thrusting. Shouting voices, fiendish clamor, the eerie beating of pirate drums came sweeping in like the rush of hurricane winds.

Her heart wanted to stop beating as cold fear gripped her in its claws. She did not fear Bruce, but what of the rogues he commanded?

The Spanish grandees and officials were rushing inside the hacienda for weapons; women's voices rose into hysterics. "Pirates!"

But pirates would not enter the hacienda. The thought brought a moment of terror. Bruce wouldn't permit them. Would he? She could hear the vines rustling below the rail, or was it her imagination enlivened by the wind? She backed into her chamber, flung both doors closed and bolted them into place, and in her haste yanked the magenta drapes closed.

What if they did enter? As far as she knew, the soldiers were all making a fighting stand outdoors. And her own mother — where was Countess Catherina?

Trying to calm her shaking and to think wisely, she believed that despite Bruce's arrogance, neither she nor the other women would have anything to fear from him or his immediate crew under his command. But what if there were other pirates sailing with him under another captain? She had heard that Brethren of the Coast often attacked the Main that way. When Henry Morgan sailed on an expedition, there were many captains from different ships, and while they answered to him as lead commander, they also ravaged, looted, and killed on their own!

Devora ran across the carpeted floor and knelt again before the trunk, lifting the lid. With shaking hand she retrieved the pistol that Bruce had given to her. In the lantern light the silver-inlaid handle glinted. But in her haste and fear, she hardly noticed the initials that were carefully engraved, barely making out in the flickering candle flames the daring lettering *B.A.V.* on the handle. "Bruce Anthony." But why the *V?* Should it not be *H?*

A woman's scream sounded from the chamber of the governor's daughter. Startled, Devora jumped to her feet, looking at the heavy carved door that opened onto the corridor. What if the governor's wife and daughter were under attack? And her mother — she had not seen her below in the plaza with Lord Robert.

She rushed to her heavy door, drew back the bolt, and opened it, looking down the corridor. The royal serving women were running with the wives and daughters of the other grandees to hide in the secret chamber which was often built for the governors and their families in the towns along the Caribbean shoreline. Ofttimes the people of the town would flee into the countryside or woods and remain there until the pirates looted the town and Catholic churches of silver, statues of saints, and altar cups and candle holders made of gold.

She did not see the governor's wife among

the women who were all dressed in mantillas. She noticed that all the women, including the dozen female slaves, were carrying satchels of precious belongings, and some carried jewelry boxes. Devora imagined what would befall these women and their belongings if they were set upon by the pirates! One carried a painting from Madrid, another lugged a great crimson silk quilt embroidered with gold.

Devora's anger began to burn, as in the background she could hear the fighting and shouting. Her anger reached out to Bruce Anthony Hawkins and blamed him for this sight of the scurrying women, young and old, and crying children roused from their sleep to be hustled off, hopefully to security.

"Hurry, Señorita, there is an underground tunnel on the other side of the Casa Toledo. It will bring us to the woods where others in the town have fled!"

"My mother, the countess — I cannot leave her behind. And Señora Toledo and her daughter, where are they? And Doña Sybella?"

One of them pointed down the corridor. "I saw the countess running out there. I think she was trying to find you. Doña Sybella has already departed. Hurry, we will leave the hatch open for a few minutes more

— all others have escaped through the tunnel!"

"Go. I will catch up. If I see the countess, I will bring her."

As they rushed ahead toward the great and wide stairway, Devora struggled with her guilt. Her mother had not left without her as she would have supposed she might do. The act was unusual, and tugged at her heart. How little they knew each other! Mother and daughter were strangers. Yet all it took for Devora to feel the deep need to be loved was a simple act on her mother's part to search for her before escaping.

But why then had she not come first to her chamber? Why had she run to Señora Toledo's?

Devora, holding the heavy pistol belonging to Bruce and struggling to lift her white satin skirts, ran down the corridor. If she hadn't wasted time earlier that evening in the garden with Bruce, her mother may not have needed to come searching for her.

Perhaps by now Catherina was with Robert and they were both escaping with Sybella, but her father had always been a fighter — a man who had battled for King Charles, and who had fought a number of personal duels with enemies. He was not likely to run away but make a stand here at the hacienda. Even now he may be trying to muster some of the others to defend the dungeon where Captain Bonnor was held. The man appeared to be very important to her father and the viceroy. Odd. Why did the viceroy think there was something suspicious about Bruce's identity?

Madness reigned in the warm, steamy night. The silvery moon reflected its glow through the dark-fringed palm trees on the beach and on the perimeter of the hacienda's adobe walls.

Her heart was pulsating in her throat as she neared Margarita's chamber. "Mother?" she called urgently. Foreboding silence confronted her with secrecy. *Had Señora Toledo managed to escape with her daughter? Am I the only woman left in the house now?* wondered Devora. What if they had all left? If she could reach Bruce, she would be safe, but she had no notion of where he might be!

Gripping the pistol, she opened the door. The Señorita's great bed was empty. Then they must have escaped in time to hide, she thought, and the countess must be with them. Perhaps they thought she had already gone to the tunnel. Still, she entered the room and cast a quick glance about to make certain that her mother, hardly a woman of valor in time of emergency, had not fainted on the floor. There was no evidence of a struggle.

A breeze blowing in from the balcony lifted the hem of her billowing skirts. She went there, looking below. They must have taken the steps, with one of the servants carrying Margarita. Her pity went out to the governor's wife and daughter, roused from her sickbed. Bruce was to blame for this shameless attack!

Below the balcony she could see men running.

"Come in. Close the doors," ordered Bruce from behind her.

Her back went rigid but she made no sound, closing the long windows, bolting them, and drawing the drapes. She turned and looked at him. Neither spoke.

His face was unsmiling, his eyes like green stone. His jacket was gone. He stood with blade lowered, his buccaneer shirt open at the throat, the billowing sleeves damp with sweat. His dark hair was drawn back and tied.

"I trusted you," he hissed softly. "I should have known you would go straight to Lord Robert."

Her gaze swerved to his, seeing his eyes sparking like heated lava.

"Is that what you think of me?"

"I am still thinking of you, trying to make up my mind."

"Do not trouble yourself, Captain Hawkins."

"Where is Bonner?"

"Down in the dungeon."

"The dungeon!"

He stared at her, and she saw a look of anger and something else. Disappointment?

"I thought your heart finer than to do anything like that. Perhaps you have the cold heart of the countess after all. Many will die now because you did not keep your vow to me. Now I must attack with all the buccaneers and pirates."

Devora grasped the bedpost, staring at him, breathless and angry. A faint scowl darkened his brow.

"Go to your chamber, madam. Bolt the door and stay there. I will now need to make a raid on the dungeon. Soon this place will be turned into a battlefield!"

When she only looked at him, wondering why his disappointment in her stung so deeply when she had insisted his estimation of her did not matter, Bruce took hold of her arm and led her across the chamber to the door, opened it, peered out, and seeing the corridor was empty, drew her out.

He steered her down the hall. Devora felt as though her emotions had received a heavy blow.

"Where are the others?" he asked in a low voice. "Your mother and the governor's wife and daughter?"

She found her voice at last. She jerked her arm away and walked stiffly beside him to her chamber door.

"Do you think I would tell you? So you can send your nasty pirates to chase them down and rob them?" She didn't think he would, but she was furious with him, and saying so helped to release her corralled emotions.

"If I wanted to rob and plunder, Señorita, I would not need to ask your permission. Do you think I don't know about the secret tunnels out of the Spanish governor's hacienda? They all have them. And huts in the woods to hide in. By now they have carried great wealth to bury, like dogs with their favorite bones."

"You sound so superior, Captain. If it isn't jewels and plunder your bloodthirsty men seek, I should like to know what it is you want."

"Do not pretend injured feelings or false innocence, Lady Ashby. You know clearly that I have come for Kitt Bonnor and members of my crew. I will yet free them, but at what a cost!" He threw open her chamber door and, though she resisted, he drew her inside, closing the door and leaning there a moment, watching her with moody intensity.

"I am sorely disappointed in you."

"In *me!*" she whispered, flabbergasted. "What unheard-of arrogance! Oh, what conceit! And you — *you,* Señor —"

"Ooh," he winced, "how delectably a woman of Spain you sound!"

"*Captain,* then! *You* attack the poor Spanish governor. *You* send his feeble household fleeing into the windy night frightened out of their wits! *You* and your band of Tortuga jackanapes —"

"Jackanapes, is it!"

"— blow up the gate of Castillo La Gloria," she continued, "and then — the audacity of your accusation against me — *you* dare suggest I betrayed you to Lord Robert. And *you* are 'disappointed'?"

Having run out of breath, and still angry because he leaned there, taking in all her words with grave deliberation, though a spark of cynical humor had returned, Devora turned her back toward him and folded her arms. Tears prickled her eyes. Why should she allow this cur to upset her so? Why should a woman of her station even care what a man like Bruce Hawkins thought of her?

"Yes," he said calmly, as though having never been interrupted, "I am sorely disappointed. When I first met you I thought, 'Ah, at last, Bruce! You have met a breed of young woman whose high qualities excite you. Yes, her eyes and lips are most memorable, but more importantly, she is intelligent, noble, and entertains moral convictions.'"

"And so you accuse me of betraying you."

"But now I see you are only pretty. A matter of my appreciation, true, but not nearly as interesting as when such physical traits are mingled with other more noble convictions."

"Get out, sir, before I shoot you!"

"Ah yes, my pistol —" he snatched it from her hand, was about to place it in his belt, then on second thought seemed to change his mind. He scowled, and taking her limp hand into his, pressed it there again. "One never knows. You may need it." He flung open the door and looked back. "Bolt it."

As the door began to close, loss gripped her heart.

"Bruce, wait —"

She turned, her eyes searching his. They

were enigmatic, yet they sent her heart pounding.

A moment of silence held them bound together.

"How could you think I would tell Lord Robert?" she whispered.

His eyes held hers, searching for something that he must have found, for a slight breath escaped his lips, and he came back into the room, closing the door.

"You did not?"

"No. Lord Robert was in Margarita's chamber when I returned. There was nothing I could do —"

One arm went around her waist, the other hand lifted her chin. "Why didn't you say something sooner?"

"You wouldn't let me. The earl had already ordered Doctor Bonnor brought below. It was all I could do to make an excuse for where I had been and conceal your pistol."

Bruce frowned slightly and touched her cheek. "I am quick to beg your forgiveness." He bent toward her lips, but Devora, growing languid under his warm gaze, managed to turn her face away just in time.

"Please don't," she whispered.

"Let me show you how I truly feel."

"If you feel anything noble, let me go."

"You test my will to the breaking point." Slowly, his arm released her, and he stepped back with a bow. Devora walked to the table where the lantern was lit. It was wise to keep the physical distance. *I cannot be in love with this man so soon. It is all physical,* she warned herself. *It is that for both of us. It is dangerous.* She turned her head and glanced at him. She saw his mouth tip downward. Quickly she changed the subject to a matter equally dangerous.

"I think Lord Robert is also somewhat suspicious of Friar Tobias. You best warn him to have ready answers when he returns as to why he brought Doctor Bonnor to Margarita's chamber without guards." She faced him now, curiously scanning him.

"He also said that Viceroy Maximus is suspicious of your identity."

He said nothing and merely raised a questioning brow, as if as much at a loss as she. She wondered if his behavior was genuine.

"Are you not curious, Captain?"

He leaned against the door as if deep in thought. He watched her. "Did Lord Robert tell you why that is so?"

"He said the viceroy believes you have another identity."

Bruce watched her. His eyes fell to the boarding pistol still in her hand. He straightened from the door as though just remembering something, and looked at her searchingly. She wondered why.

"Why would he think so?" she asked in a low voice. "About another identity, I mean?"

Bruce walked up to her and casually relit a candle that was going out. "Curious, is it not?" was all he said. "That pistol, on second thought, madam, is too heavy, too cumbersome. Allow me to leave this with you in its place." And he removed a small French pistol from a shoulder holster inside his shirt. He smiled when she frowned.

"In my risky ventures, a man cannot have too many weapons. Here. A better exchange. You can keep that one. I should have thought of it before. And now — what else did the earl tell you about this viceroy from Cartagena?"

"He is to be here tomorrow. And he wishes Doctor Bonnor to be brought to Cadiz for interrogation. But you already know that. Oh, Bruce, is there any way you can get him out?"

"Not without much loss of life. I am sorry it must be so — and sorrier still I blamed you. You are noble, Señorita."

She looked at him over the glow of the candle and noted how dark and rich was his hair held back with the cord. She walked away, pacing. "Do you have another identity? Is Hawkins really your birth name?"

"What a question."

"You have not answered," she said softly.

He smiled and bowed. "I have already introduced myself. "Bruce Anthony!"

"Why is it that I think there is more?"

"A woman is always suspicious," he said lightly with a smile. "All right, my name is not Hawkins."

"So I thought. What is it?"

He spread his hands. "I have no last name."

"I don't believe you."

"It is true. My father disowned me. And my mother died the eve of my birth. I have taken the last name of my mother — 'Bruce' — and the name of an uncle I respect in London — 'Anthony.' "

As she watched him, mostly satisfied, he walked to the door. "You are dangerous," he said. "You keep me occupied when I should have already been about the task at hand. Perhaps — but, no, I refuse to think your doing so is deliberate." He threw open the door, sword drawn again.

Their eyes held; without another word, he slipped away and was gone.

Devora stared at the door.

13

The Buccaneers Attack

Hysteria sounded in the woman's voice as she pounded upon Devora's chamber door. Devora hurried to unbolt the lock and throw it open. An old serving woman stood with lacerations on her face, and other bruises and scratches. She was clutching a crucifix to her bosom as she rushed in, weeping, her dark head scarf dirty and torn.

Devora felt a surge of indignation that the woman would need to undergo such indignities and took hold of her gently, leading her to the green-satin covered chair. She lowered her into it, and the woman's grasping fingers refused to relinquish the gold cross studded with pearls. Tears ran down her wrinkled cheeks from stricken brown eyes.

Devora knelt beside her, trying to soothe her, laying a calming hand on her gray head. "Peace, Señora, fear not! I will not let them harm you," she spoke in Spanish, and went on to ask what had befallen her. The woman, between her tears, poured out an ugly tale.

She had gone to the church to pray to El Niño. The words meant simply "the little boy," but in this instance, "the Christ Child." She had gone with the nuns and priests, that the town might be saved miraculously from the "devil Lutherans" coming in from the sea like fiery dragons. But no sooner had she knelt before the altar with its statues of saints and the Virgin, than these evil pirates had come storming into the church with swords dripping blood from murdering noble and brave Spanish soldiers trying to protect the church.

"They stole everything, Señorita," she sobbed, "even the holy crosses from the necks of the priests. I thought to myself that surely fire from the saints would come down from above and strike them dead, but they did as they pleased."

"No, they did not get away with evil," said Devora. "Perhaps for this life, but everyone — both great and small — will answer to Christ one day."

"A great devil with long, black curly hair struck the priests through with his sword, even the nuns! And he laughed like the voice of Hades when he did it, Señorita."

Horrified, Devora winced at the thought. "Surely the Lord helped you to escape. How did you do it?"

"In the madness, I crawled under a pew. They did not see me, so intent were they in their butchery. There I hid until they had set the church on fire and left the wounded to die crying for mercy! I tried to help Sister Theresa but — but — she was too heavy. She pressed this blessed relic into my hands and bade me save myself and it. Outside the burning building was madness! I saw women in town running from the pirates, and children crying. I — I saw Friar Tobias and he brought me here to the governor's house and told me to come to you."

At least one man has decency still in his heart, thought Devora. *How could Tobias sail with a pirate like Bruce Hawkins?*

The woman lifted a solid-gold crucifix with its image of the Savior still nailed in place, and kissed it.

Her Puritan upbringing stirred within, and it was all Devora could do to keep from taking it away, but she rebuked herself as well. How easy to sit in harsh judgment on one who may never have even heard the Scriptures explained!

From outside the balcony she could hear the fighting growing closer to the governor's hacienda. Imagining all the unrighteous deeds that might now be happening in the town, Devora was aghast and growing angry.

She stood and paced, struggling to understand the conflicting behavior of Bruce Anthony. At times he appeared so gallant! And had he not been offended with her when he thought that she had compromised her character values? How could he then look the other direction when his men behaved vilely?

So! These were the courageous crewmen of the *Revenge*! Not "pirates," as Bruce had so firmly told her in the garden earlier, but "buccaneers."

"There is a difference, madam," he had told her.

Was there? Her violet-blue eyes flared with heated indignation as she looked toward the drapes covering the balcony windows. The fighting was growing closer. She could hear voices and the clash of cutlass and pistol shots in the plaza garden. Bruce Anthony Hawkins was a pirate after all! And his men were vicious and cruel, with little on their minds but stealing treasure and taking revenge on ordinary priests and nuns because of the evil work of the office of the Holy Inquisition. The evil revenge of the pirates could not be justified!

Devora went swiftly down the corridor to Margarita's chamber to get the medical satchel that Kitt Bonnor had left when he was brought back to the dungeon. She carried the bag to the chair where the old woman sat rocking to and fro in emotional shock. "The brutes," Devora said. "Could they not even take pity on the old and helpless?"

Devora spoke soothingly and treated the woman's lacerations with ointment, then brought her to the bed to lie down, and covered her with Señora Toledo's gilded shawl.

"You will be safe here," she told her, but wondered now if she could be all that confident of anything Bruce told her. The woman continued to clutch the crucifix. Devora thought it wise to hide it, but was afraid that if she tried to take it from the woman's clutching fingers, she would grow hysterical again. Little if anything good would be accomplished by forcing the issue, especially in the mental state the woman was in. Her religious faith was bound to the material objects she could see, feel, and hold. The immutable Christ of whom the apostle Paul had written, "We know Him no longer after the flesh," was now inseparable from a piece of gold dug from the mountains of Peru and shaped by the hands of men. She would have liked to comfort her, to tell her that Christ was victoriously alive forevermore, and seated in great power and glory at His Father's right hand, but the woman could not receive it now.

"Did you see, could you tell if Governor Toledo's soldiers are holding out against the pirates?" she asked the Señora.

"No, no, they are falling back, Señorita! The attack is most relentless! Women are yelling and running blindly in all directions. The grandees were rushing wives and children into the churches, then calling for more weapons to fight with. There is no hope, Señorita."

There is hope, Devora thought suddenly. If she could reason with Bruce! If she could get him to stop the rampage of his crew.

Devora hurried to the window facing the courtyard and peered out. In the light of torches and fires that had sprung up here and there, she could make out the pirates fighting with cutlass and pistols. Soldiers were rushing from the tower to confront them. The pistol shots split the air with small, bright flashes. Shouts and curses lashed the night, swords were ringing, slashing and cutting, torches were flaring. Dazed, she watched as the ruthless men in faded head scarves and calico shirts came rushing forward as bold as lions, as savage as wolves, their blades glimmering in the torchlight, cutting and slashing a pathway toward the governor's house.

Her mother she assumed to have escaped to safety earlier, but what of her father? Where was he? Though he was an Englishman, the pirates would soon turn their weapons against him once they knew he had sent Kitt Bonnor to the dungeon to be turned over to Viceroy Maximus.

Devora whirled from the window, distraught. "When you entered the hacienda, did you see the governor anywhere, or an Englishman with blond hair? He is my father, and the Ambassador of King Charles."

"Si, Señorita, both were downstairs with swords. Some soldiers were with them, making a final stand, all courageous."

Then Bruce had not been able to gain control of the dungeon yet, she told herself. If that were so, and if Lord Robert refused to surrender Kitt Bonnor, her father's life could be endangered. Devora paced, still clutching the French pistol. If nothing else, her presence with her father might mean the difference in his managing to live through this night of horror. Listening to the noise of fighting on the patio, she could hear it growing louder.

Devora ran to the chamber door and opened it, determined her father would not die by the blood-splattered cutlass of a pirate.

The corridor was empty, and she rushed to the entrance of the grand staircase.

When she arrived at the wide mahogany stairway beneath a Venetian chandelier, she looked across the arched salon with its rust-colored tile floor running the length of the hacienda. Through the arched windows dressed with orange drapery, she gazed onto the plaza garden, where pirates were converging on the hacienda.

Governor Toledo and her father, Lord Robert, came rushing in through a side door with a handful of guards. Her father's coat was removed, and a blood stain soaked through his white frilled shirt as he gripped his blade.

Devora winced. "Father!" she called, and started down the stairs toward him. He took hold of her. "Devora! What are you doing here? I thought you had escaped to safety with Catherina!"

"Father, let us go now," she urged, giving his arms a gentle shake. "There is still time. There is a tunnel that will bring us into the woods."

"That is our intention, but Kitt Bonnor must be brought with us."

"He isn't worth your life or the governor's! Let Bruce have him!"

"Bruce?" His ice-blue eyes tested her gaze with sharp inquiry.

"Captain Hawkins," she stated, refusing to be sidetracked into explanation. "Let us go now."

"Captain Bonnor is too important a prisoner to surrender. He comes with us. Go to the tunnel entrance and wait for me. Here — take this pistol."

"I have one," she said hurriedly. "Father! They're coming now — there's no time —"

A soldier came running, a pained look on his sweating face. "Excellency! The dogs are inside the hacienda! We cannot hold them back! Shall we not surrender?"

"Make for the tunnel. Quickly, bring the jewels!"

Lord Robert, holding a bloodied sword, turned indignantly to the governor. "Señor! Where is your honor? Will you let these murdering thieves rampage the hacienda?"

"My good ambassador! Have you another idea? We have done all we could! Shall we die for the king of Spain? One would think *you* were his governor!"

"I'll not run like a coward, Toledo, because of a pack of savage pirates!"

"Then you have not entertained these savages for company, Ambassador. You have been too long in Madrid sipping wine with Philip! It is we colonial governors who must bear the angry brunt of their wrath while His Majesty sits in safety in the palace!"

"Ho! You speak treason, Toledo. And what will Maximus say when he arrives tomorrow?"

"Do you wish all these men to be killed to keep one pirate from being set free? We have already lost the Castillo. Now what?"

"Father, the governor is right," cried Devora. "Set aside your pride. Let us escape while we have the moment!"

"Silence, Daughter! Go then, and take our illustrious governor with you. I shall confront Hawkins!"

"Father!"

The governor mopped his profusely perspiring brow and nodded. "No, Señor Robert," he sighed. "If you stay, it is my dutiful honor to stay with you." He gestured to the handful of grim soldiers. "Do as the ambassador says! Captain Bonnor must not be taken by Hawkins! Diego — downstairs! Guard the dungeon at all costs!"

The soldiers swallowed and glanced at

their companions. Just then, the castellan Don Carlos appeared in the doorway, bloodied and fatigued. Devora recognized him as the captain who had first ridden up to warn of the pirates.

"Go, you cowards! Or you will fall upon your own swords now! The English Ambassador speaks courageously. Defend the dungeon! Go! Or I shall kill you myself!"

The soldiers saluted and rushed down the hall and across an inner patio to stone steps that led to the prison house below. Devora tensed. Bruce had been right about "dancing on the polished floor above Spain's prisoners."

Lord Robert and the panting, heavyset governor followed with the castellan.

She heard their bootsteps fade away as she stood gripping the banister. They seemed to have forgotten her.

Kitt Bonnor and Bruce Hawkins! She wished both would sink to the bottom of the blue Caribbean!

Devora turned to look toward the plaza garden aware of a strange lull in the fighting. Her breath paused when there came the sound of footsteps, the clink of metal. The tunnel — she would go for the old Señora and they would escape together!

She turned around and started up the

stairs, but the soldier's warning proved all too real: The pirates were inside the hacienda. Several must have managed to fight their way up the upper chamber balconies and were surging down the corridor, opening chamber doors as they went to see what booty they might cart off. One already had some silk garments sewn with pearls thrown over his shoulder, and another carried a silver candelabra.

Too late! She would never get past them now. Bruce — where was he?

More footsteps followed, these from behind her, coming through the arched patio door. She whirled, confronted by three lean and savage men, hatred for anything resembling Spain coloring their faces. Her hair was the color of honey, her skin as fair as a lily, and while they were certain to notice, their lust would not treat her the better for being an Englishwoman.

Into the governor's salon they surged, stepping over the fallen bodies of dead Spanish soldiers as they progressed. A broad-shouldered man saw her and stopped. Devora stared into the face of a man as swarthy as any Spaniard, cruelly handsome, with the chest of a bull. He wore numerous chains of gold around his neck, one with a large emerald contrasting hideously with his blood-splattered, baked-brown jerkin. He gripped a broad-blade cutlass in one hand, a large pistol in the other. His almond-shaped eyes latched hold of her at once.

A leering, hawk-faced man beside him breathed, "Stab me innards, Capt'n Quinn, will ye look at that. That'un gotta be the wench Bruce mentioned all right."

"Aye, a wee, fair blossom just ready to be plucked. But not by Hawkins. Ah, this'un be your rare captain's share, Brethren."

Another man called, "Better think twice, Quinn! Ye knows how our capt'n don't see eye to eye wi'h ye when it comes to female booty! Hawkins was clear as water on a certain lass with the looks of 'er. Say 'e'd cut yer stinkin' liver out if ye touched 'er."

"Let Hawkins roast in Hades."

"You'll go there first!" Devora lifted the French pistol and took a step back, but men were also converging down the stairs, calling down to him, "Capt'n Quinn, d'ye see a sweeter palace as this? Why's we can be 'ere a week pickin' it as clean as a 'ound's tooth."

Others came rushing in from the patio, ripping tapestries from the walls, tossing treasures into bags like pack rats.

A Spanish soldier appeared above in the

hall and leveled both guns at the two pirates starting down with their loot. Devora saw a small, bright explosion smelling of sulfuric smoke. The shot knocked one man backward; a second blast sent the other pirate stumbling down the stairs. Devora gave a cry and cringed with loathing as his clawed fingers grabbed hold of her skirts as he tumbled past her. She looked down into his half-blown-away face and nearly gagged. He sprawled there, his remaining glazed eye staring blankly up at the angel painted on the ceiling.

The broad-shouldered pirate named Quinn growled his rage and, lifting both boarding pistols, blasted the Spaniard. He fell onto the rail and hung there, arms dangling. Devora let out a high-pitched scream, leaning back against the side banister.

In three strides Captain Quinn was beside her, snatching the French pistol and tossing it down the stairs with disdain. She jerked her head away from the stench of rum and sweat. He lifted her as if she were a rag doll and, turning, took two stairs up, but abruptly stopped.

"Going somewhere, Jago?" came Bruce's smooth voice. He stood above on the landing with rapier in hand, his buccaneer shirt torn and stained, his handsome face unsmiling, his eyes smoldering with temper.

Bruce! Oh thank You, Lord! prayed Devora.

"Ye think I'll be takin' orders from ye, Hawkins?"

"When you and your crew signed on with me, you swore you would refrain from your filthy manners. You've as much truthfulness abiding in you as Lucifer. You'll obey captain's orders all right, unless you want to make your grave tonight with the Spaniards."

"Why — I be thinkin' ye mean it."

"Put her down nice and easy, Jago. That's it," he said when Devora felt her feet back on the stairs. "Now," Bruce warned him, "go dunk your thick head in a barrel of water and sober up. My orders were clear: no rum, no women. These are all wives and daughters of gentlemen."

"Weren't this way with Morgan! A wench be a wench, says I!"

"That's half your problem; your brain is so thick you can't tell the difference between Kill Devil rum and French wine. Now move!"

There were chuckles from the crew of the *Revenge*, but dour looks from the men of Captain Quinn's *Top Gallant*.

From the corner of her eye, Devora saw a

dark, sullen scowl on Quinn's face. He stepped back, mocked a pretty bow up to Bruce, glanced at Devora, then turned to prowl his way out of the salon into the night.

She heard Bruce's bootsteps coming down the stairs, but refused to look at him. "Did I not order you to stay in your chamber?"

"I'm sure that would be more convenient for you, Captain Hawkins! That way your men could loot and kill and burn churches, and I wouldn't know about it!"

"Cap'n! Ye've unwanted company!" called one of his crewmen.

Devora's eyes widened. The Spanish castellan who had been in command of the fortress La Gloria was standing in the middle of the salon, his sword in hand. He was a strong man, and a look of disparagement was etched on his face. He flipped the point of his blade toward Bruce with scorn.

"The English dog comes, eh, Señor Hawkins? Here you will die."

Bruce turned, pushing Devora behind him, but when the two men looked at each other, the castellan sucked in his breath. "But it cannot be! *You?*"

Bruce retorted something in Castilian, but his voice was so low that she could not make out what he said. She doubted any of his crew understood or spoke the language.

The castellan Don Carlos took several steps back, a hot look of excitement turning his face ruddy. "I cannot remain silent! My honor demands I report this to Viceroy Maximus!"

Bruce drew the pistol from his leather baldric. "Then it is your death or mine. I ask you to yield, friend Carlos."

They know each other? The thought raised itself within Devora's dazed mind.

Don Carlos shook his great head and drew in a breath, throwing back his shoulders. He shouted, "Don Nicklas Valeee —" and as the name slipped unfinished from between his lips, a blast from a boarding pistol struck his chest. He stumbled forward and fell to his knees. His wide eyes looked up at Bruce, who turned his head sharply in the direction of the pistol shot. Lieutenant Hakewell stood with his smoking pistol still leveled at the castellan. Bruce stared gravely down at Don Carlos.

Devora felt her knees buckling as her stomach churned with nausea. She sank slowly against the banister, turning her head away.

Friar Tobias Valentin walked across the polished tile floor, his sandals clicking, the edge of his brown habit swirling, and stopped before the castellan. Then Tobias looked over at Bruce. Bruce walked slowly to where the man lay.

"It was his death or your own," said Tobias. "He would not keep silent."

Devora watched as a look passed between Tobias and Bruce, and then Bruce turned and walked to where she was. His eyes narrowed. "Do not look at me that way. I am a soldier. In battle, men die. Others live."

"You make excuses for yourself. I will not hear them."

"Did I not tell you to go up to your chamber and stay there? I did not want you to see this," he said, frustrated.

She turned, holding back her feelings, and looked up the stairs. "Your vile crew is crawling about, Captain Hawkins."

His eyes flickered green and hard. "I've given orders they are not to molest the bedroom chambers, madam."

"And of course they follow your orders! Like that foul Quinn?"

"He is not a member of my crew. He captains his own ship and men, as does Captain Jean le Testu. He will not bother you again. Nor will the others. You have my word."

"Your word?" she breathed, her voice stiff with meaning.

His lashes narrowed. "My word, Lady

Ashby, happens to be of more honor than yours! You will go to your chamber as ordered!"

"Who are *you* to dare tell me what to do, sir?"

A humorless smile touched his lips. "Your future husband, perhaps."

His temerity was outrageous. "Such preposterous arrogance. Nay! Never, Pirate Hawkins!"

A lank old pirate with a grin came scurrying through the open door. "They've all fled like a pack o' slippery eels," he said gleefully, slapping his thigh. "We has the place in surrender! What say, Captain? Can we take our pay of goods now?"

Devora turned a challenging look at Bruce, but his unrelenting gaze refused apology.

"No, Githens. Not yet. The booty comes later. No man is to take a piece of eight until the prisoners are loosed from the dungeon. You'll stay sober and on guard. Is that clear?" And he turned sharply to the group of buccaneers that loitered about uneasily as though they knew his mood was riled — as though they had experienced his disappointment in them before.

"That goes for all of you. And the first man I see disobeying an order will dangle, is that understood?"

"Aye, Capt'n," said Githens, scratching his chin as he looked from Bruce's angry countenance toward Devora. "We understand wots got ye riled."

Devora whipped about, looking up the stairs, wincing at the sight of the fallen men sprawled in her path. Bruce might think the upstairs chambers were safe, but she had her own conclusions on that. "I won't go up there!"

"Githens! Hucks! Take the bodies away. Then guard Lady Ashby until I release Bonnor."

"Aye, Capt'n," said Githens. "But Tobias already silenced the fancy governor. They's down in the dungeon now."

Devora watched Bruce until he had left the salon, then looked at the tall, older man named Githens. His bushy gray brows stuck out like shortened cat whiskers above laughing, deep-set eyes. His gray locks hung loose beneath a yellow head scarf, and he hitched up his faded calico knee pants. "A gallant captain, Hawkins. Don't come no better. A king's man, he is."

Devora walked away, ignoring his chuckle. Her father, Lord Robert, was still below in the dungeon. She didn't trust either him or Bruce in the same room together. She glanced over her shoulder and, seeing that the two men named Githens and Hucks were heaving the bodies over their shoulders to carry them outside, she glanced about the salon. The other men in his crew also waited out on the patio.

Devora waited until they were carrying the bodies outside, then she went quickly and retrieved her French pistol. She looked in the direction where Bruce had gone a few minutes earlier and followed.

She ran through several chambers. The dead lay strewn all along the route. At last she came to the back of the house, where a small door stood ajar. She heard muffled voices from below. Evidently, this must be an entrance to the prison house. She listened intently to hear the voice of her father, but did not hear it.

Gingerly, she started down the short stone steps.

14

Swept Away!

Torches were lit on the stone wall, and the flames weaved in the draft.

"Who is he, Capt'n?" came an inquiring voice.

"Earl Radburn, the new English ambassador. About as trustworthy as a shark smelling blood," came Bruce's voice.

So he did have her father! Just what did he expect to do with him? What if he intended to kill her father once he had Kitt Bonnor released?

Devora, her pistol hidden behind her skirt, proceeded down the steps, making certain her slippers made no sound on the slimy stone. The air stank horribly, and she heard groans and mutters that turned her blood cold. When she was halfway down the steps, she saw all manner of wicked instruments used to make prisoners talk. Bruce was releasing a man from the rack while Kitt Bonnor, now armed with scabbard and baldric, was helping some pathetic former prisoners.

"I won't forget this fair delivery, Bruce, nor will the others once they come out of their stupor and understand they are free men again to sail on the *Revenge*."

"You can save your thanks until we all get out of here."

"He's right," said Friar Tobias, using a key on the chains that bound one of the prisoner's feet. "By now the rider on horseback has reached the garrison inland. Hundreds of soldiers will soon be swarming."

"God bless ye, Friar," groaned one of the prisoners, and began to weep.

"Aye, my lad, you'll be all right now," said Tobias. "We'll soon have you out of here."

Devora stopped, stunned by the sight of the liberated English prisoners. Were they even alive? She stared at thin and indescribably dirty men with white, skeletal faces and dark circles beneath sunken eyes. They looked about them from behind matted, dirty hair. Mostly naked, or wearing what remained of tattered breeches, they blinked at their captain and Tobias, still half-stunned by their release from ponderous gyves and chains.

Devora turned her head away. No wonder Bruce was angry. These were his men, and

Kitt Bonnor would have suffered an even worse fate at the hands of the viceroy's interrogators.

"There's naught I can do for the men until we're aboard ship. My chest of medicines is still in the Señorita's chamber upstairs."

"Be quick about it, or you won't be the only one sailing as a prisoner to Cadiz," warned Bruce. "Hakewell, get these men out of here and on ship."

But the buccaneer named Hakewell, who looked to be his lieutenant, was pointing a dagger beneath the heavy gullet of the blindfolded Governor Toledo. "He's passed out. The coward. After what he did to Tommy, for a single piece o' eight I would pluck him open like a cobbler."

"Enough, Hakewell," said Bruce with a steady voice. "He's not the fiend who split Tom's tongue. And nothing you do to Toledo can restore Tom's ability to talk. Take the boy to the ship and leave him with Kitt. He'll snap out of his daze once he sees his brother again. There's a few questions I want to ask our gracious governor when he awakes from his faint."

Devora glanced about, reminding herself what she had come here for. She did not see her father, but Governor Toledo was bound and blindfolded across the prison room. Why had Bruce ordered him blindfolded?

Kitt came bounding toward the steps to go up and find his satchel. He stopped when he saw Devora.

"You've company, Bruce."

Bruce turned, sword in hand, and saw her. Whatever flashed across his mind was not revealed.

Kitt bowed to her, a smile on his face, and went past her up the steps to find his medical satchel. "You won't find it in Margarita's chamber. I took it to my own room, two doors down."

"Obliged, Miss Devora," and he rushed up and was gone.

Devora looked back at Bruce. She took another step down and lifted the pistol, aiming it at him. "What have you done with my father? If you've harmed him —"

Bruce walked toward her and looked up, resting one boot on the bottom step. He looked pointedly at the pistol. "First a dagger and now a pistol. You never cease to amaze me."

"Where is he?"

"You must mean the fair and loyal English ambassador," he asked innocently.

"You know who I mean. Yes, Earl Robert Radburn."

"Unfortunately, he is unharmed."

"Unfortunately!"

"Not a relative, I hope?" he inquired lightly.

"Yes, a relative, Captain Hawkins. My father."

He stopped, his gaze flicking over her, all jesting gone. His face grew sober and reflective as though something had crossed his mind he had not thought of until now.

"Your father, you say?"

She thought he might be afraid now, for Robert was a powerful man of influence in Madrid and England. She smiled victoriously. "Yes, and while I commend you for rescuing these pitiable men, I do not think Whitehall will share in the celebration. When this deed of yours tonight reaches King Charles, he'll have every member of the High Admiralty after you to see you hang."

"Now let me get this matter straight. Did you not tell me in Barbados that the ambassador was not your father when I inquired?"

She moved uneasily. "I confess I did not explain everything. You see, he's my stepfather — not that it should matter to you."

"It may matter a great deal more than you think."

She had noted that at the mention of Lord

Robert, Bruce had come alert. His gaze flitted over her again. "Ah, I now understand. So you are the 'English treasure' he bargains with the viceroy to marry his son. My memory faults me — what was this despicable don's name?" Affecting innocence, he turned to Friar Tobias and Lieutenant Hakewell for an answer.

Laughter sounded from Hakewell, and Tobias quipped, "Nicklas Valentin, I think. A definite rogue, and a bloodthirsty pirate."

"You sound as if you have strong feelings in the matter, Friar," said Bruce wryly. He turned back to Devora, who watched the exchange with uneasy curiosity. She took a careful step back, still aiming the pistol.

"So that is why you spoke disparagingly of Nicklas Valentin's arrival from Madrid when I met you earlier in the plaza garden," said Bruce.

She thought she would choke over the expression on his face. Why did he appear so interested in Nicklas Valentin?

"I do not see that it is of your concern, Captain Hawkins."

"Oh, but it does concern me, madam, more than you know."

Tobias chuckled. "Why don't you tell the Señorita?"

"Quiet, Tobias, we mustn't rush things,

you know. And I'm rather enjoying myself."

"Tell me what?" she asked warily, and saw the amusement in Bruce's eyes.

He spread a hand. "Any woman who has so bitter a grudge against this fellow baits my curiosity. I want to know why you are so set against him."

By now he had climbed the steps and was just below her. In a quick gesture, he plucked the pistol from her hand and stuffed it inside his shoulder holster. "You won't need it any longer." He bowed his dark head. "In my presence and Tobias's, you will be quite safe."

In his presence? Wasn't he going to leave? Hadn't she just heard him tell Kitt they must hurry before more soldiers arrived?

"No need to fret over Lord Robert. He's safe enough. Merely cooling his heels in the dungeon overnight. Maximus will have the tarnished honor of releasing him and the governor. From what I've heard of the ambassador, he likes to send others to the dungeon. He is merely tasting the bitter cup himself for a change. One night is less pain than he's inflicted on others."

"Your feelings concerning my father are unfair, Captain Hawkins. He only arrived a few weeks ago from Madrid and would have nothing whatsoever to do with what's befallen members of your crew. I admit it is a tragedy . . . I do hope they will recover. . . . But Lord Robert is not to blame for the Inquisition."

"You are right, but he is involved in more than you know. And when you find out how much, I am confident you will agree with me."

"You are a very confident man," she said with a faint smile on her lips. "But, Captain, what are you going to do with me? Place me in a dungeon as well until Viceroy Maximus arrives?" Of course she knew he would not.

He smiled. "Forbid. No, indeed, I am making up my mind at this very moment, madam. Perhaps I shall take you as a prisoner. Naturally, you will be well-treated."

A prisoner.

"About this soldier from Madrid named Don Nicklas Valentin," he continued in an easy voice. "Forbid that I should leave you to this dreaded fate of marriage. Being a gallant man, I have decided to make your woeful plight my own. No need to thank me now. You can do so when I land you safely on the shores of Barbados."

The faint smile disturbed her. She took another step back, holding to the railing. "I would not make so great a burden to you, Captain. You dare not show yourself in Barbados lest Governor Huxley hang you," she said with deliberate emphasis.

He smiled again. "No burden. No, not at all. A mere kindness on my part. I so detest seeing a lady languish on Spanish soil. And I have heard that Nicklas Valentin is not an easy man to get along with."

She looked at him, trying to read behind his words, but his motives completely bewildered her. There was a hint of amusement in his smile, but why was it so? He wouldn't take her aboard the *Revenge*. It was just a malicious jest on his part.

"Did I not hear you in the garden earlier speaking a wish into the trade wind?" he asked.

Wary, she tried to read past his own guarded manner.

"If my memory serves me well," he continued, "you wished for one to come, to sweep you away from this ruthless don, whom you bade to remain forever in Madrid. Alas, that heartfelt wish I cannot ignore." He bowed. "Here I am, at your service, ready to save you from this shameless fate."

She heard soft laughter from the others below. "I do not wish you to save me, Captain Hawkins. Worry not yourself. You have concerns enough, surely. You will be caught one day soon and face the gallows."

"Until so dark and bleak a fate, forbid that I should be selfish enough to ignore your quandary. I have arrived at a most interesting moment in time." He turned and looked at Tobias, who watched him with a smile. "Do you not agree, Friar? Should we not make it our duty to save her from a man with a reputation as one of the most ruthless and despicable of King Philip's soldiers?"

Devora's hands formed fists. She trusted Tobias, but he looked to be dedicated to Bruce. "Nay, your concern is too much a risk," she said. "I would not ask so much. Leave. Leave now! The soldiers from the garrison may soon be here."

"You wish to escape, and having met this man Valentin, I must agree. I may be able to grant your wish to escape this marriage. Would you turn down the opportunity?"

He has met Nicklas Valentin? When? she wondered. And how could he grant her wish to avoid him? Such arrogance. And she began to think his smooth talk was a way of taking her off guard. Could she trust him or not? At the moment, after the horrors of the night, she wasn't certain.

"Stay away from me," she warned bluntly.

"As I told you, how can I? Our future, so it

seems, is intertwined. Friar Tobias surely agrees."

"You waste time! Take your pirate friend Kitt Bonnor, any jewels you wish. Here!" She pulled off her ear bobs and a brooch and handed them to him. "Take them and depart while you have your head in place."

He laughed and waved his hand at the jewelry, apparently in no hurry. He now watched her thoughtfully. "What you may have heard from the ambassador and the countess about Nicklas Valentin is of great interest to me. I am by nature a curious man. But there is no time to talk comfortably here. So we will debate your future on the voyage back to Barbados, for I will bring you there."

He held her gaze even as he spoke to one of his men. "Hakewell! Tell the others to take their pickings, but make haste. Lady Ashby is right; more soldiers will arrive from the garrison. The longer I show my face in these parts, the easier for someone to remember me."

"Aye, Capt'n."

"Tobias — take Lady Ashby to my ship."

He couldn't mean it. He was trying to frighten her. But as their gaze held, she had the horrid notion he was not bluffing, nor would he relent, though she or Tobias requested him to do so.

"You can't — you wouldn't —" she began lamely, and heard the friendly old pirate named Githens chuckling gleefully from above her on the steps.

"We have so much to discuss, madam," Bruce told her. "You see, I have grown quite interested in why your father hopes to arrange a loveless marriage with Maximus's son."

Bruce smiled and bowed low. "I do this, madam, for your ultimate good, of course."

"My good! You vile rogue!" She slapped him, her hand making a ready connection that left her palm stinging.

His green eyes flashed hot, and she saw him grit his teeth, but retain his exaggerated suavity. "Lock the little leopard in my cabin, Githens. And make certain you borrow a goodly roast and a few fat geese from the governor's rich store. I should like a pleasant feast when I entertain the ambassador's daughter at the captain's table."

Laughter filled the dungeon. "Aye, Capt'n!"

Devora's heart fell in a splatter at her feet. She looked at Friar Tobias for support, but he spread both hands as though he were helpless.

"Lord Robert will hunt you down and see

you hang at Execution Dock!" she told Bruce. "Or Nicklas Valentin will come and find you. I have heard he has come from Spain to track you down and see you brought in chains to stand before King Philip."

His brow lifted at this astonishing news, then he stepped aside and extended an arm to allow Githens to pass.

"Careful with her, Hakewell. We wouldn't want to give the future bride of Don Nicklas Valentin the impression that Captain Bruce Hawkins is less of a gentleman than he."

Then he was gone, walking over to the bound and blindfolded governor, who was now stirring awake.

"Hawkins, you'll die for this."

"Ah now, my friend, you are in a very dour mood. I have come to tell you thanks for your hospitality. My men will long remember. You will be sure to give Maximus the finest wishes from Captain Hawkins. Tell him we will meet one day face-to-face. Until then, we shall take a few mementos with us to commemorate two years in your dungeon. A fair and just wage, seeing as how I leave you alive."

The governor struggled uselessly to free himself. Bruce gave a pat to his belly and walked away.

Hakewell pled for Devora's cooperation. "I'll not be wanting to hurt ye, miss, so keep your claws in. If'n there be a bruise on ye, the capt'n will send me tarping on the yardarm."

It would be nice to muster a faint, thought Devora, but her mind remained alert as her wrists were brought behind her to tie.

"None of that, Hakewell," said Bruce, walking by. "I am sure she will go peaceably. Do I have your word, madam, or must I pain myself to order you bound?"

Her violet-blue eyes narrowed. "I shall go peaceably, but only if Tobias escorts me aboard your foul ship."

He bowed. "Tobias?" he called. "Take her away."

Tobias walked up and took Bruce aside, and she heard him say in a low voice, "Are you sure you want to bring her? It will mean profound complications. What will you do when she finds out the truth?"

"I haven't decided. I shall find out by the time I bring her to Barbados. You must admit that having her aboard will answer many questions I will never discover if we part company now."

"Is that your only reason?" came the wry inquiry.

"My good Tobias, what else would motivate me to return her to Barbados?"

"And if we do not go immediately to Barbados?"

Bruce tapped his chin, and when he looked over at her, she pretended she hadn't heard and turned her head away.

"Then I will bring her to Tortuga."

Her breath caught, and her head jerked in his direction. Tortuga! And what had Tobias meant about her discovering the truth. What truth?

Bruce's gaze remained thoughtful as he looked at her, but a faint smile touched his mouth. Then, with rapier in hand, he charged up the steps, calling orders to his buccaneers.

Tortuga! she thought, dazed. *The island of buccaneers!*

15

Buccaneers at Odds

Devora mounted the dungeon steps in the company of Friar Tobias. "He can be a rogue, but you've nothing to fear aboard his vessel," he told her. "Bruce would put himself at risk before allowing anything to happen to you. He'll either see you safely home to Barbados, or —" He stopped, as though even he did not know how to finish his statement.

Devora looked at him, lifting her skirts as she walked. "You saw what they did here tonight, what happened to the Catholic churches and the priests and nuns!"

He rubbed his chin, troubled lines showing on his face. "What happened tonight, Señorita, was not Bruce's doing, but the work of Captain Jago Quinn, an outright pirate."

"So Bruce has said, but he sailed with him, knowing what manner of sea rover he is."

"You may not accept this as an answer,

but he had little choice. Bruce is short-handed of men, and when we arrived on Tortuga, we found out that many of the buccaneers — men of the decent sort — were gone on expedition with Henry Morgan. Captain Jean le Testu is not a bad sort as buccaneers go, but he would not sail without Quinn. To rescue Kitt and the others, Bruce needed both captains. Now, however, he is much displeased with Quinn."

"As well he should be," she said, but felt she understood Bruce a little better. "You, too, are a puzzling man. You are the brother of the viceroy, yet you befriend the English buccaneer whom he and your king deem to be a great enemy to the rule of Spain in the Caribbean."

Tobias frowned at his thoughts. "May it suffice to say that, like Bruce, I too find my conscience at war with the policies of Maximus."

His reply raised more questions, rather than providing satisfying answers. Which policies troubled Bruce? Did this mean there was more to his behavior as a buccaneer than simply attacking for vengeance or booty? That there was, served to make Bruce more intriguing. And she wondered why a man like Tobias would even know him. Where had they met, and when? Their friendship was based on more than the fact that both men disliked the Spanish viceroy.

She had no more time for questions. As they walked into the salon, Tobias held out an arm to stop her. She looked ahead.

Instead of an orderly retreat back to the longboats, she saw men spread about the large room as though uncertain of which side they were on. They looked to be the lieutenants of the three captains who had attacked the governor's headquarters. Bruce stood facing down two swarthy men, one of which she recognized as the odious Captain Jago Quinn. He had returned with the captain that Tobias called Jean le Testu. The French buccaneer had a relaxed and almost graceful air about him, but there was no mistaking the dangerous, cunning face and restless dark eyes. He held a rapier, as did Quinn. Bruce and Kitt faced them, swords also drawn, but with the points held in an unthreatening position. There appeared to be an argument, and from Bruce's determined face she guessed he would not relent.

With Tobias's hand on her arm, she stepped back, but she could still see and hear everything that was going on. Her heart began to race again, for as she glanced about, she saw a glittering hoard of plunder piled on the floor and guarded by several men. From the way they eyed one another, she guessed that each guard represented a different captain. Hakewell she recognized as Bruce's lieutenant.

"Why has my order to move out been ignored?" demanded Bruce.

Quinn still wore a dark scowl from earlier when Bruce had restrained the pirate's greed, and if anything, he looked in search of trouble. The French captain, however, faced Bruce in a friendly manner.

"You're in too much hurry, Hawkins," said Quinn. "My men have fought well, and they have a hankering for some satisfaction on the Spaniards before we up and leave the Isle of Pearls."

"Don't be a fool, Jago. By now some stalwart Spanish soldier is racing to the garrison inland. Soon this place will be crawling with fresh soldiers."

"There ain't no hurry, Hawkins. It's a sure 20 miles to Nombre, and we ain't wrung all the purchase from these fat, gilded dons — and their wenches," said Quinn.

"Ten miles," corrected Bruce, looking bored with Quinn's exaggerations.

"Har! And wot makes ye so sure, eh?"

"I know the Main better than either you

or Jean. It's foolish to remain and risk another attack."

Captain le Testu remained silent, but rubbed his chin, his eyes bright with musings.

"We do not need the last dernier extracted from the hapless victims of your greed."

"Victims, he says!" mocked Quinn, casting an eye toward le Testu.

"We have accomplished what we came for," said Bruce. "We have Kitt and the crew, and enough purchase to satisfy a reasonable man."

"Are ye suggestin' I's not reasonable?"

Devora watched Bruce gesture with disdain toward the large mound of treasure. "There is more here than you'll likely see again. Chevalier de Fontenay will not be disappointed. By the time the purchase is divvied up according to the articles, there will be enough to satisfy even the most rapacious among the Brotherhood."

Captain Quinn turned to his lieutenant and gestured. Devora watched in horror as a moment later a long succession of heads of wealthy families were herded in, frightened but refusing to cower as Quinn's two pirates goaded them forward with their cutlasses.

Quinn leered derisively. "They's going to

taste the governor's sweet torture chamber below before we goes. An' if they don't tell us where the secret route is where the fat wenches have run to with the family gold and jewels, they'll be screaming for mercy before the sun comes up."

The buccaneers moved restlessly, glancing from one captain to the other.

Devora's eyes swerved toward Bruce, but she could tell nothing by his countenance. She felt Tobias tense beside her, and she expected him to surge forward and object to Quinn's plan, but he too remained silent. Was his confidence in Bruce?

Bruce turned and looked at the Spanish dons herded together, their wrists tied behind them.

"They ought not to be standing," gritted Quinn. "Knock 'em to their knees."

The two pirates glanced toward Bruce, and Kitt who stood on the stairs.

"There isn't going to be any torture of the citizens," said Bruce. "Not as long as I'm captain of this expedition."

The dons shot him a surprised glance, but Quinn's eyes narrowed.

"And why not? You saw the instruments below," he snarled. "Tell him, Kitt, or didn't Hawkins see wot was down there?"

"I saw," said Bruce evenly.

"An' ye ain't goin' to do anything to these devils? An eye fer an eye, tooth fer a tooth, thumbscrew fer thumbscrew, rack fer rack, boot fer boot, says I! Who do you think built the torture chamber, eh? Then they'll taste it themselves — including that greased pig of a governor downstairs! He'll talk all right, and he'll call for his Señora to bring her jewels, or he'll die screaming."

Quinn stepped forward, gesturing for his crew to follow him down into the dungeon.

A faint sound of a boarding pistol being drawn from its baldric brought Devora's eyes to Bruce. Both of his pistols were aimed at Quinn.

"One more step, Quinn, and you'll be left here with the dead."

Quinn's eyes boiled with hatred. "You can't shoot us all, Hawkins. And the others agrees with me. We had a meeting. If you got no stomach for it, then you take your crew and sail for Tortuga. The *Top Gallant* and *Defenseur* is stayin'."

By now, many of the other buccaneers had heard of the quarrel, and she saw them gathering outside in the patio.

"Is this so?" Bruce asked Jean le Testu.

The Frenchman rubbed his chin and shrugged his shoulders. "I have no wish to hear screams, monsieur, but . . . Jago, he has learned from one of the dons here," and he gestured to the prisoners, "that the Spanish pearl fleet arrived only days ago to haul casks of pearls aboard. It is a pity, mon ami, that we should leave without our ships taking a casket apiece. The pearls on this island are some of the finest on the Main."

"Pearls are one thing, Jean. Rounding up Spanish citizens for Quinn's diabolical pleasure is quite another. I cannot allow him to bring them below. Need I remind you and the others that you signed articles with me, not Quinn?"

"That is so, Monsieur Captain, but you knew I had signed articles with Quinn first."

"I and my crew will fight if necessary," warned Bruce.

"One would think ye was one of them stinking dons the way ye acts," said Quinn.

Bruce looked at him long and hard, and Devora noticed the spark of green fire in his eyes.

"Alas! Surely we can come to some agreement, Monsieur Captain," said le Testu. "This need not end in blood."

Kitt straightened from where he had been leaning against the banister, his voice deadly calm, matching Bruce's.

"There can be only one lead captain. You both signed articles with Bruce. Are you now turning traitor?"

Bruce walked forward, facing both Quinn and le Testu, rapier in hand, careful to keep his distance. Kitt joined him, as did Hakewell and a few others. But an equal number of dangerous-looking men slipped from their various places to side with captains le Testu and Quinn.

Quinn leered, satisfied. "Yer outnumbered, Hawkins."

Whether Bruce was aware of her, Devora couldn't tell, for he didn't glance her way. But he gestured a hand toward Tobias, who took hold of her arm to lead her away. As Tobias did, Devora saw the men spread cautiously about the large room to position themselves. Her heart leaped in fear to her throat and was beating so fast she could hardly breathe.

"Quickly," whispered Tobias, "before the fiends take note of you, adding you to their booty. This way!"

He was hurrying down a corridor in large strides, and Devora ran to keep up, too afraid to even speak. How could Bruce and Kitt defend themselves against so many?

Tobias came to a side door, and after fumbling a moment with the lock, unbolted it and threw it open.

The hot tropical night wrapped about her,

smothering her as she followed him down a pathway through the backside of the garden. After a minute they came to horses, saddled and waiting — at least six. She guessed these were meant to bring them to the longboats.

"Can you ride, Señorita?"

"Yes, Tobias! But what about Bruce and Kitt —"

"Quick, up with you, my girl."

She mounted easily, grabbing her reins and turning the horse in a half circle to ride.

Tobias raised bushy brows of surprised pleasure over her skill. "Ah, I see you know horses. You are no coddled Señorita from the parlor. Bruce will be pleased." He swung his hefty frame into the saddle and turned the horse's head to ride into the dark, sweltering night.

"Do not concern yourself for Bruce or Kitt. If it comes to it, they can fight circles around Quinn and his pirates."

She wondered that he had not mentioned Jean le Testu.

Tobias flipped the reins and galloped down the road, gesturing for her to ride beside him. They raced ahead in the night past palm trees, but not toward the bay's glittering water, as she would have supposed, had they been riding toward the ship. She realized the *Revenge* would not be anchored in the open bay where it would be visible from the fortress La Gloria. The castellan would have spotted the three vessels long before they could have managed to land the buccaneers. The ships must be anchored farther down the Main, out of sight in some sheltered cay. Bruce must have come ashore by longboat and marched overland through the steamy jungle to surprise Governor Toledo and his garrison of soldiers.

Devora guessed she must be right when they rode out of town and came to a small, dark pathway that led into the thick tropical foliage.

"There is a river," Tobias called over his shoulder. "The San Luis River. The longboats wait there, hidden in the shrubs. We should be safe here until Bruce and Kitt come with the crew and booty."

Devora shifted uneasily in the saddle, glancing about at the thick, dark, over-hanging trees, hearing strange cackles and screeches. The moon was hidden now, and it was so dark she could just make out the large frame of Tobias ahead of her on the path.

She rode along in the deep, hot darkness, hearing her own breathing and glancing off into the vines. She slapped at a cloud of mosquitoes and soon felt their bites. Hot and dripping with perspiration, her hair clung to her skin.

Tobias quickened his horse's trot.

When a vicious snarl echoed farther back in the jungle, her horse grew skittish and she struggled to keep it on the path. A panther?

Tobias drew reins and slowed, glancing back to see if she were all right. "We must move with speed and avoid the panther," he warned.

Devora looked up into the black, twisted branches, half expecting to see glowing amber or emerald eyes. With a prayer in her heart for their safety, she urged the nervous horse forward onto the damp earth.

They had ridden perhaps an hour before she began to hear the sound of the San Luis River. Soon the path began to follow the tall shrubs and vines that grew wildly on the riverbank. The trees were not as tall here, and the full yellow moon appeared in the velvet-black sky. The smell of the river, of plants and night flowers, accosted her senses. They were finally out of the mosquitoes, and the air was a little fresher. She could hear hundreds of insects and frogs, and shivered as she also imagined tarantulas and poisonous vipers hanging from low tree branches that extended out over the river.

They rode on. As the path widened, Tobias fell back to ride beside her. "It's not far now," he told her.

"What of Captain Quinn and the Frenchman? I don't see that coming here will help us escape them. Aren't their longboats waiting at the river as well?"

"They are. There is only one route out to the Caribbean — the San Luis River. But if my guess is good, Señorita, only the French captain will return with Bruce."

She looked at him, her fingers tightening on the reins.

Devora was impressed that Bruce had refused to turn the Spanish prisoners over to the diabolical Captain Jago Quinn. There was much more character in Bruce Hawkins than she had first thought. That Tobias associated with him no longer seemed odd. Still, she wondered how the two men had met.

✳ ✳ ✳

In the salon of Governor Toledo's hacienda, Bruce spoke to Jean le Testu, for of the two captains he was the least unreasonable.

"Our fight is with Madrid, and not with the hapless citizens on the island. Come, Jean, you are known to be a gentleman. Will you insist on needless torture, and thereby the necessity of our crossing swords? For surely, if you do not seize the advantage from Quinn, he will lead you into a fight that will leave many of us dead among our enemies!"

"Ye always was a smooth talker, Hawkins," said Captain Quinn with a sneer. "Pay him no mind, Jean. He thinks to squelch us with threats. He won't fight. He's outnumbered."

Bruce looked at him sharply. "You are wrong, Jago. There are some who will fight a losing battle only because it is right. I have not fought against Madrid and her atrocities, only to have those sailing with me now commit the same," he warned. "If you insist, we will fight, and only a few in this room will survive. You will not be one of them."

Quinn glanced toward Kitt who held steady, his point lifting to show he was of one accord with Bruce.

Jean le Testu's dark eyes moved restlessly, looking from Bruce to Kitt, then back again. He gestured a hand, and stepped lithely away from Quinn, rapier in hand.

"He is right, Jago. It is foolish to fight among ourselves. If I were not friends with Hawkins and Kitt, I would not have joined this venture. Enough! A fight here and now will benefit no one except the Spaniards. As I say, Monsieur Hawkins, I wish no cruel sport with these hildagos — only pearls."

"Señors," breathed one of the dons, "You shall have all the pearls you desire if you let us go. I will see to it. I can bring you there tonight."

Bruce saw the flaring interest leap into Quinn's eyes. Kitt came up beside Bruce and said in a low voice, "I suggest you let them have their pearls. They're right about that Spanish fleet having landed a few days ago. I overheard the guards in the dungeon talking about it before you arrived on the *Revenge*. Indian divers are gathered not far from here on the shore."

"I intend to do just that, but striking a bargain first to release the prisoners."

Bruce turned and offered a light bow. "All right, my captains, you have heard the Spaniard offer his cooperation. We shall stay long enough to gather the pearls on the condition we take no prisoners." He gestured to two of his crew above on the stairs. "Githens! Bring the hildagos to a chamber and lock them in for their own safety." He turned to the Spaniard. "Come, Don Pedro, lead us to the pearl fisheries."

The don looked at him sharply, surprise in his dark eyes. "Señor Hawkins, how did you know my name?"

A moment of awkward silence followed.

He knew Don Pedro because he had heard of him in Madrid. . . .

Bruce affected indifference over his slip. He saw Quinn's crafty gaze shoot in his direction.

"Aye," said Quinn suspiciously, scanning him. "How is it ye know him, Hawkins? How come you know a Spaniard? Ye talk as if yer one of 'em!"

Bruce smiled disdainfully. "Ask these hildagos if Captain Hawkins is one of them. They would as soon put me on the rack as look at me."

"Yet ye'll spare their stinking hides!"

"That, Captain, is a matter of Christian conscience that does not concern you, nor could you ever understand."

"Bah! A conscience hassled by that Tobias. Ye can have it. We'll take the pearls, won't we, Testu?"

Bruce could feel the inquisitive gaze of Jean. "You have not answered, Monsieur Hawkins. How is it you knew Don Pedro?"

Bruce gave a careless wave of his hand. "I have known all along about the Spanish pearl fleet arriving, and that you, Capitan Don Pedro Sanchez —" and he bowed in his direction — "were in command of that fleet. You were invited here tonight as a guest of Governor Toledo."

Quinn stepped forward, glaring at Bruce. "Why, you traitorous piece o' shark bait! Ye knew all along, d'ye? An' ye waren't even going to tell us, so ye could keep it all to yer own ship!"

"I've had about as much of you as I can swallow, Jago."

"Good, says I. Then I'll be mincing ye for what ye deserve, not only for keepin' the pearls a secret but for yer traitorous killing of Tom on Tortuga. Ye think I forgot?"

"I've been waiting for you to make it clear, Jago. If you want a duel here and now, far be it from me to disappoint you. You shall have it."

The room grew silent as the buccaneers moved out of the way. Quinn cocked an eye, more cautious now, and hesitated. He glanced at Jean le Testu, who turned away as though he would have no part in a matter that Quinn had brought on himself.

Quinn glanced around at the buccaneers, all watching in grave silence. Finally, Quinn's two officers came up beside him and tried to restrain him, giving him an excuse to back down. "Let's get to the pearls," he snarled, and turning his back to Bruce, he strode out into the patio followed by members of his crew.

Bruce looked after him but did not sheath

his blade. Once the treasure was carried away under guard, Captain le Testu followed Quinn. Soon the salon was empty except for Bruce, Hakewell, his lieutenant, and Captain Kitt Bonnor.

" 'Twill surprise me if ye've seen the end of the matter," Hakewell murmured, looking toward the patio, where footsteps died away on the adobe bricks.

Bruce knew he hadn't — that he would one day need to deal with Quinn. "Where is Tupac?"

"With the crew from the dungeon. We got 'em into some wagons ready to start out for the river."

"Tell him to move out. News of what happened tonight will soon reach every Spanish garrison in the vicinity. By tomorrow we'll be fortunate if we can escape to the boats."

"Aye, Capt'n," and he strode out to find the Inca.

Kitt looked at him. "You nearly slipped mentioning Don Pedro like that. Both Jean and Quinn are suspicious. Pedro, too. Did you notice how he looked at you? As though searching his memory. What if he remembers you from some function in Madrid — that military academy you went to, for instance?"

There was always that possibility, but it was a risk he had to take.

Kitt frowned. "What if he suddenly remembers where he saw you?" When Bruce simply frowned, thinking, Kitt went on. "What about Maximus? Tobias is sure your father will arrive soon."

The room was sweltering. Bruce wiped his perspiring forehead on his sleeve and looked at Kitt dourly. "You raise too many problems. Did Tobias get away with the ambassador's daughter?"

Kitt smiled. "I thought you would be concerned about that. Yes. A good-looking woman, isn't she? I saw her around Bridgetown but never had the opportunity of meeting her. I was too busy attending to the governor's gout."

Bruce scanned him, but Kitt didn't appear to notice. He said thoughtfully, "If only I can discover what causes gout to come and go. An interesting disease, gout . . ."

Their eyes met; a faint smile showed on Bruce's mouth. Kitt cleared his throat, settled his new Spanish hat on his head, and walked out.

Bruce looked after him, then sheathed his sword. He stood for a moment, one hand on hip, thinking of Devora. Then he turned his mind willfully to the pearl fleet and walked from the hacienda toward the beach.

The moon shone above the Caribbean, and the bay was calm, the trade wind ruffling the water.

16

Pearls and Peril

The sun came up above the Caribbean, showering red and gold across the horizon. Bruce stood on the beach, his broad hat with its white ostrich feather curling about its brim, the breeze tugging at the billowing sleeves of his shirt. His hat was lowered to shade his eyes against the rising glare, and he lowered his brass spyglass, contemplating what he had just seen. He drummed the fingers of his free hand against his leather bandolier, which was worn crisscross over his shoulder and chest, the silver butts of two boarding pistols glimmering as did his eyes.

Githens — a tall, skinny older man who was spry and wiry, and a trusted second lieutenant — strolled up from where barrels and booty were stacked on the shore and being loaded onto some mules. His long arms swung in rhythm with his stride, and his high, crackly voice cheered the breaking morning.

"We's ready, like you said, Cap'n Bruce."

"Did Spragge return?" he asked of a crewman he had sent ahead as a scout.

"Say's there ain't no sign of no Spaniards comin' yet." He gave a chortle. "Maybe we sceered the daylights out of 'em enough to send 'em fleein' to the mountain. Say, what ye be lookin' at?"

"Don Pedro," replied Bruce, not moving from his vantage point. He lifted the spyglass again and focused it ahead on some palm trees farther down the beach. "And Captain Quinn."

"Quinn?" he repeated with wonder. "So that's where the mangy rodent took to. Kept an eye on him like you said, but he gave me the slip."

Bruce passed him the instrument. "What do you think, Gith?"

Githens raised a roughened brown hand to hold the spyglass and squinted ahead. He made a noise in his throat. " 'Tis Quinn all right. How come he's so friendly with that Don Pedro? Only last night he wer ready to use thumbscrews on the poor devil."

"Hmm . . . I would say his friendly demeanor is rather unusual, wouldn't you?"

Githens hitched up his knee-length cotton drawers. "Quinn's acting 'bout as friendly as a hungry shark. Tickles the curiosity to know what the bloke is after."

Bruce thought he knew. Quinn had been suspicious since last night about his familiarity with Don Pedro. Was he asking him how much he knew about Hawkins? Bruce was irritated with himself. If he expected to keep up his identity, he had better avoid any more slips of the tongue.

"Looks as if Don Pedro is a bit more friendly himself, doesn't it? The question is, Why?"

Githens grinned. "I be figurin' ye need no invitation to find out."

Bruce pocketed his spyglass. It had probably been Quinn's intention to finish his meeting with Don Pedro before sunrise. Had Bruce not been suspicious of Quinn, he would not have noticed the meeting. He felt the heat of the sun beginning to beat upon his back.

Don Pedro was leaving Captain Quinn and walking toward a thicker group of trees. Then Bruce watched Quinn cut across the beach toward the crewmen loading the mules. Quinn, he could confront later. He hadn't noticed Bruce, and when Quinn disappeared among the pirates, Bruce turned to Githens.

"Find Kitt," he told him. "See what Quinn is up to. I'm going to have a talk with Don Pedro."

Bruce walked up the beach, his boots

sinking into the dry sand. When he emerged from the cluster of trees, he saw a small church building left unmolested the night before. Built of red stone and shaded by palms, it sat in silence.

Bruce paused at the church door, letting his eyes adjust to the dimness. The candles had long since burned out and, while the structure was intact, the pirates had robbed every ornament of silver and gold. He did not see any priest, but Don Pedro was kneeling before an altar. Bruce walked silently down the short aisle to the front, where the Spaniard knelt at the rail, and stood in the flickering light coming in through a high window. Don Pedro raised his head, his dark eyes widening when he saw him looking down upon him, unsmiling.

They stared at each other, then Don Pedro stood nervously.

"I am in your debt, Captain Hawkins. They would have killed us last night if you had not intervened. I — I have not forgotten your kindness, Señor."

Was he trying to tell him something? Bruce tried to read his eyes. He studied the perspiring face. The man licked his lips and wiped them on the back of a trembling hand.

"I — I told him nothing, Señor Nicklas, I swear it!"

So he knew. He remembered him. Bruce weighed the look of anxiety in his eyes.

Don Pedro took a step back, halting. "I will say nothing, Señor, I vow!" And he fell back to his knees, clutching the altar rail.

Wary, Bruce continued watching him, knowing there was a chance he would betray him to Maximus when he arrived.

"You recognize me then?"

Don Pedro swallowed. "How could I forget, Don Nicklas? You and your brother Favian attended the academy at Madrid. We were never friends, but I saw you about. You rode with honor, fought with honor. You and Favian Valentin were always on the tongues of the other students. We tried, but always we could not measure up to you, and now —" He stopped, his head lowering as though it was too painful to go on.

"And now you know me as the English pirate Captain Hawkins of the *Revenge*," finished Bruce, his tone expressionless.

Don Pedro nodded in silence and kept his head bent.

"You cannot comprehend," said Bruce. "I will not try to make you understand my reasons."

Silence filled the church, except for the

wind outside rustling the palm fronds.

"Maximus will arrive, maybe today," said Bruce.

Don Pedro looked up at him, fear in his eyes. He crossed himself. "I swear! I will say nothing!"

Bruce sighed. "Understand, Pedro, I cannot take that chance. In fear for your life you vow, but once I am gone and the viceroy arrives, it will be your duty to inform him about Hawkins. I would be disappointed in your allegiance if you did not. And so —"

"And so you must kill me, Señor Valentin?"

"Ah, Pedro, you pain me sorely. Yet I cannot leave you here alive. I must take you with me."

Don Pedro sucked in a despairing gasp. "Señor, but no!"

"I've no choice. But first, what did you tell Captain Quinn?"

"Not a thing, Señor, I swear it."

"I believe you tell the truth. What questions did he ask about me?"

"Everything, Señor. Where we had met before, how long ago, what I knew of you. I denied it all. He must have believed me because he left satisfied. I feared he would thrust me through, but I think the French captain warned him earlier against it. Señor,

I beg! Leave me here!"

"Understand that I cannot risk leaving you here. You will come with me."

"I — I am a prisoner then?"

"You may say that. You will be kept below in the ship until such a time as my situation permits me to release you."

"And if that time never comes, Señor Valentin?"

"You must *never* call me that, Don Pedro! Lest you force me to keep you gagged for many weeks."

"Yes — Señor Hawkins, I will remember."

Bruce heard footsteps coming and turned toward the doorway, where the lank figure of Githens stood.

"Get up," Bruce told Don Pedro. "We must go." He turned. "Gith?"

"Aye, Capt'n?"

"Get Hakewell and Spragge. We've a prisoner. I want him bound and gagged."

"Aye, Capt'n. Hakewell's right here. We has news for ye about Kitt."

Bruce took the Spaniard's arm and led him out of the church, turning him over to Githens. If he and Hakewell were surprised that the don was to be taken prisoner, no one questioned his action.

"What about Kitt?" asked Bruce, still thinking of Don Pedro. If it hadn't been for

314

Quinn rounding up Spanish citizens last night, they would never have met.

Hakewell frowned. "There's likely to be trouble. I saw Kitt go off alone last night to meet with some of them Indians. Said he was seeking a cure for gout. He shoulda been back by now."

A flicker of impatience crossed Bruce's brow. "Gout! He's probably out collecting leaves and bugs and forgot the time. If he gets caught by the Spaniards again, this time he can stay in the dungeon," he said flatly.

"Aye, Captain," Hakewell hastened to say, evidently aware of Bruce's mood.

"You and Gith see to the prisoner. Keep him away from the others, especially Captain le Testu and Quinn. Start out for the river. Kitt and I will catch up. This entire venture is turning into a catastrophe."

"Aye, Captain, but we sure got us some fancy pearls," said Hakewell with a grin. Then, seeing Bruce's unsmiling face, he sobered. "A catastrophe, Captain, to be sure," he agreed soberly.

Bruce headed toward the pearl fisheries, where Governor Toledo's Indian slaves lived and worked as divers in the pearl beds. Kitt had a mind of his own when it came to bartering with the Indians. *If Kitt is anywhere nearby on the island, it will be there*, he

315

thought, since that was where the Indians gathered and lived in huts. Bruce took the trail that would bring him in perhaps a quarter mile to the pearl beds, all the while irritated with Kitt. Kitt had already told Bruce that he had made the acquaintance of a certain friendly Indian on his first voyage to the Isle of Pearls, and he was evidently determined to meet with him again, despite the dangers.

Bruce frowned as he strode along in the hot morning, a blue sea and palm trees on his left. Soon his strides slowed, for the sand was deep. When at last he neared the fisheries, he saw with relief that Kitt was there with some of the Indian slaves. They were out in the pearl beds in canoes. Bruce restrained his irritation and stood, hands on hips, looking evenly at Kitt.

"You should have returned hours ago. Are you waiting to welcome Don Maximus Valentin?"

Kitt urgently gestured him closer to the fisheries. "I've not found the cure for Governor Huxley's gout," he called, "but the juice of the bansanuco plant is an excellent antivenom. It's said to be effective against the bites of the tabobas and coralis snakes."

Bruce walked up and stood on the bank, watching the two Indians hold the canoe steady with their oars. Seconds later a young Indian boy splashed up to the surface over the oyster bed. He slipped his head out of a carrier that had two pouches containing oysters, and another diver emptied it into a reed basket that was underwater. Then one of the men in the canoe lifted the basket and dumped the oysters with a clatter onto the already-brimming heap of shells.

Kitt called to Bruce: "And, I've learned that the mechoacan fronds when boiled in white wine are useful in dissolving an excess of phlegm."

A few minutes later the canoe docked and the Indians came ashore, their copper-toned, naked bodies rippling with muscle as they unloaded their catch.

Kitt came up to Bruce, apparently unaware of his captain's restrained temper. "And Habillus roots, ground and dried, make an excellent purge."

"I'll remember that," gritted Bruce. "But if you don't want to meditate on your great finds back in Toledo's dungeon again, I suggest we make haste for the San Luis River."

"You're right. I suppose I'm a trifle late." He dug something out of his trouser pocket. To Bruce it looked like a piece of slime. "Perfect for sword wounds. Stops the bleeding."

A half-dozen more Indians arrived, carrying a long leather pouch that bulged with pearls.

Kitt knelt on one knee and arranged a bag of trinkets on the small blanket. At once the Indian's interest was caught as sunlight caused the brass-looking glasses and colored beads and bangles to glitter. Kitt exchanged his wares for the bulging bag of pearls from the oyster beds and stood, slinging the canvas bag over his shoulder. He met Bruce's gaze.

"You're certain you have enough?" asked Bruce.

"I'll need to buy property in Bridgetown to set up medical practice," Kitt explained with a wry smile.

"You're more likely to hang on Execution Dock. Let's go."

As he turned away, one of the young Indians gestured toward Bruce's hat. It was clear he wanted to barter. Bruce glanced, intrigued by the Indian's bow and arrows. They had once used a type of poison to kill their victims, before the Spaniards had turned them into slaves. He had heard that even now the Indians managed to kill a Spanish soldier now and then, but when they did, five Indians would be taken at random and killed.

Bruce gestured to the bow and arrows, offering him an ebony-handled dagger. The somber black eyes of the Indian measured him, and for a good minute he did not move. Neither did Bruce. Bruce had about decided he would not make headway, when the Indian gestured to his wide-brimmed black velvet hat, the plume long ago wilted from sea spray.

Bruce removed his hat. The Indian with deft fingers retrieved both the hat and dagger and handed him the bow. Bruce gestured toward the arrows, holding up two fingers. The Indian hesitated, then, with an expressionless face, relented.

Some 20 minutes later Bruce and Kitt left the sandy beach and palm trees and went to where horses waited to bring them inland to the river. As Bruce put his foot in the stirrup, he heard some leaves rustle. A sense of danger alerted him at once. He had only a moment to shout — "Kitt, watch out!" — before a pistol shot blasted the humid morning air. A parrot cawed and flew away into a banana tree and Bruce, unhurt, turned to face his challenger.

Captain Jago Quinn stepped from the leafy bushes, his boarding pistol still smoking, a look of surprised dismay on his face.

"You're a miserable coward, Jago," scorned Bruce. "You would try to kill me with my back toward you." He whipped out his blade. "I will give you more chance than you were willing to give me — you and I, here, and now!"

Quinn wasted no time. Trying to seize the advantage, he came at him, his sword smashing against Bruce's. Bruce parried the blow and moved in quickly, with a surging thrust that nicked his opponent's throat, drawing blood. Quinn, now on the defensive, was driven back toward the bushes, fighting for his life.

In the morning's hush the deadly clash of steel rang. Bruce lunged, feinted, and lunged again, his glimmering blade whipping past Quinn's and then beating it back with one fierce blow after another. Quinn continued to retreat toward the open sand. Bruce pressed him harder until Quinn's face was dripping with sweat. He shook his wet hair from his eyes and tried to thrust, going for Bruce's stomach, but Bruce deflected Quinn's effort, providing an opening as his sharp Toledo blade whispered past Quinn's, and he rammed it through the pirate's chest. Quinn lurched and twisted, and Bruce pulled back his sword, looking down grimly at the man sprawled on the white sand. The eyes stared empty toward the sky, a look of eternal horror upon his face.

Bruce wiped the sweat from his eyes and looked at Quinn with both pity and loathing.

17

On the Caribbean

Devora rose from a cane chair beneath a temporary sailcloth awning on the upper deck of the *Revenge*, and cast a longing eye toward the west, wishing for even a breath of wind. She dabbed the sweat from her throat and swished her lifeless pink feather fan, tucking a few wisps of her honey-colored hair back into the strict confines of her chignon. She looked glumly at the fan. Of all her belongings, it was the only thing she had been able to bring with her, she thought wearily. She glanced toward Captain Bruce Hawkins on the ratlines. She supposed he was looking for a ship, but why that would be, she had no idea.

Bruce stood above the deck, hugging the ratlines while looking through the spyglass. They were two days out at sea from the Isle of Pearls and, from what she had gleaned, they were in somewhat of a difficult circumstance. The wind had ceased, and they were as stationary upon the Caribbean as though they had dropped anchor. Devora came down the steps, ignoring members of the crew who cast glances her way, for everyone knew Bruce had given her orders to stay near her cabin. She walked along the rail and, stopping below the ratlines, looked up at Bruce.

"Captain Hawkins!"

He seemed not to hear, and kept the instrument leveled out to sea. He was dressed in exquisite Spanish garb. His somber black doublet was open to the waist, and a broad sash of gold cloth, contrasting with the somberness of his other garments, was tied about his waist, where pistols were shoved. His cavalier-length dark hair was held back with a cord. He was quite the most handsome man she had ever seen, but she didn't want to notice.

She folded her arms and tapped her toe on the wooden deck. "I wish to speak with you," she called again.

"About what?"

Her eyes narrowed. "Alone, Captain; not shouting back and forth for the entire crew to hear!"

He lowered the spyglass, and she saw a smile, a flash of white teeth against his handsome face — and she steeled herself against her emotions. *I don't care a thing about this pirate,* she told herself abruptly. He swayed on the ratline with one hand, looking down at her.

"Have you changed your mind about feasting with the captain, madam?"

"I shall take my supper in my cabin again alone, thank you."

"Your stubbornness is affecting your good health. You're not eating well," he called airily. "By the time we reach Barbados again, your frock will be drooping on you like a barley sack."

She whipped about and walked brusquely to the steps and climbed quickly, her mouth set in a tight line. As she brushed past two crewmen, they offered bows. Devora walked back to the awning and stood watching as Bruce climbed down from the ratlines and said something to the crew. Hearing their laughter, she fumed, and seeing that he was coming up the steps, she turned her back, arms folded, staring out at the glassy, blue-gray Caribbean.

She heard him come on deck and step under the awning. Devora turned, making certain her expression revealed nothing of her inner turmoil.

He leaned against the rail, and seeing the bowl of fruit he had sent to her earlier, he chose a bright orange and began to peel it.

Their eyes met, and she felt a slight flush warm her cheeks.

"I've come at your beck and call, madam. You wish to speak with me?"

The amusement reflected in his eyes, and Devora, to cover her feelings, folded her arms impatiently.

"How long do you intend to keep me a prisoner aboard your ship?"

Bruce tossed the orange peel over the side. She saw a shark come at once to see what it was, then go deeper below the water. She shivered.

"Without wind," he said tediously, "there is little I can do."

"Are we doomed to drift in this sweltering heat until the sails turn to rags?" she asked in a tone of voice that she knew unfairly delegated all blame to him.

"Do you suggest we risk the sharks and swim to the Main for a stroll among the palm trees, Lady Ashby?"

She gave a short laugh. "The Spaniards would catch you, Captain, and bring you back to Governor Toledo. I tremble to think what may happen to you at his just hand."

"Do you?" he asked, deliberately misreading her concern. "Then tremble no longer, Señorita, I will be sure to spare myself for you."

He handed her a juicy section of orange, which she refused.

"Scurvy is a very unpleasant disease," came his lightly taunting voice. "Citrus fruits are known to prevent it. But then, maybe you would prefer the care of the physician."

She pretended she didn't understand his insinuation. For the last few days she had spent some time in the company of Kitt. It seemed to irk Bruce; she could almost think he was jealous. But of course, that was absurd. She and Bruce hardly knew each other, and any attraction between them was mostly physical, she warned herself again. Physical attraction, so Uncle Barnabas had told her in Barbados, was not enough to base a lasting relationship upon. She watched him eating the orange, and finally turned away with a lift of her chin.

"I fear it would serve you right if some Spanish warship came upon you and sank the *Revenge*," she said.

"If any of King Philip's galleons happen to come upon us with a show of strength, dear, it will be the galleon that will become prey to the sharks, not my ship. I have guns enough to rip her apart."

"And you think that's something to brag about? Killing Spanish soldiers?"

"That depends."

She looked at him. "On what, may I ask?"

"On their intentions, of course. If the Spaniards intend to turn against hapless Protestant colonists, I will most happily sink them to the bottom. If that offends you, Lady Ashby, perhaps it's because you are ignorant of their ways."

"Captain Hawkins, I am certainly not ignorant of Spain's claim upon the West Indies, nor of the presence of the inquisitors."

"Then I suggest you favor the poor Spaniards, because Lord Robert prefers them so that he can plunder the Peruvian silver mines."

Her violet-blue eyes turned warm with temper. "Never mind Earl Radburn. By now he's out of the miserable dungeon you put him in and making plans with Viceroy Valentin to search for you and bring you to Madrid. If I were you, sir, I would be worried."

He smiled. "I am very worried, but mostly because the wind is not cooperating. As you say, it sometimes seems as though the sails will rot before they are ever filled again." And he looked up toward the brazen sky.

She scanned him. The goading tone in his voice had turned serious, and she let down her guard. "What were you looking for from the ratlines? Not a Spanish ship?"

"There may be a ship out there from Cartagena . . . I've a notion it could be the viceroy's flagship."

She looked at him, stunned, and gripped the rail. "You're not serious?"

"Quite. Fortunately, his ship, the *Santa Maria*, is as helpless as we are until the wind blows. We'll do everything I can to avoid her, but I may not be able to do so."

The seriousness of the thought silenced her. If the viceroy caught him, Bruce would surely hang.

He must have read her alarm for he calmly changed the subject back to the weather. "It's like this sometimes when we're waiting for the trades. But I'm sure there's a wind in the making."

Devora walked to the taffrail and, shading her eyes, stared out upon the glassy-smooth sea. She could almost think they were alone in the world, doomed there forever. They hadn't seen another ship since leaving the Isle of Pearls — not even the two ships belonging to captains le Testu and the odious Quinn. Kitt had told her that Bruce wanted to give them the slip and had passed them in the night. But that had all been before the winds ceased to blow and they had become all but stuck, so it appeared, in the still sea.

The heat in the cabin was oppressive, but on deck, with the sun beating down, it was also unbearable, and she stepped back into the patch of shade from the canvas awning. Silence surrounded them except for the normal shipboard noises, and now and then a plop coming from the water where she had seen sharks. She shuddered.

A rivulet of sweat ran down Devora's throat, and she automatically moved to blot it. She had prayed fervently over the last few days that somehow the Lord would intervene in her circumstances, but after they had taken to sea and she was locked in her cabin, she had resigned herself that by some strange providence she was a prisoner of Captain Bruce Hawkins. Not that she hadn't been treated well by him and his crew. Kitt, too, and Friar Tobias had all gone out of their way to make her feel safe and comfortable. Tobias had come to talk about the Lord and to pray with her, and afterward had assured her that the dreadful pirate Hawkins was in reality a distinguished and gallant gentleman. Devora might have laughed at that, except that each time she was in Bruce's commanding presence, she sensed that he was far from a crude and uneducated pirate.

On the fifth day in a still world, the ship

sat waiting for the moving of the wind. A wind that stubbornly refused to blow. As though from nowhere, Devora suddenly felt an ominous sensation steal over her in the sluggish heat of the morning, and she looked off into the haze, seeing nothing, yet almost expecting a great behemoth to rise up from the sea like the sea monster described in the Book of Job. Her imagination could see the water ripple and bubble as a great head rose from the sea and a mouth gaped open to swallow them whole, ship and all.

Devora shuddered and swished her fan again and almost laughed aloud at her foolishness. However, she had looked over the rail at other times and seen sharks. The creatures were real and dangerous enough.

"What did the countess and Lord Robert tell you about Nicklas Valentin?"

At the mention of the don's name, Devora came fast awake and looked at Bruce. He lounged there against the rail, watching her with an alertness in his eyes and a relaxed smile. "I should be curious to know. After all, I have taken great pains to deliver you from him."

"Perhaps I would prefer a Spanish don to an English pirate," she quipped.

"I've heard Nicklas has an English

mother," he said smoothly. "She was a granddaughter of Earl Anthony, a close ally of King Charles."

"You seem to know more about him than I do. Suppose you tell me what he is like," she suggested with a slight flippancy.

"I've heard so many things that I would only bore you."

"No, he does not bore me, he frightens me, but then —" She started to compare Bruce with Don Valentin, but he laughed.

"But the terrible pirate Hawkins frightens you more? I would think by now you would know you are safe in my presence. But from the way that your words scourge me, madam, perhaps I should have fear of you. After all, as I told you that night in the garden, your beauty is enough to capture the heart of any man — even the dread Hawkins, maybe even Don Nicklas Valentin."

"As I've told you, Captain, unfortunately I've little choice in the matter. The marriage is arranged by the Earl and Countess of Radburn, and with the viceroy's approval, I suppose I shall become his — his wife."

"A tragedy, no less," he said softly. "Naturally, you would loathe this cruel and heartless fate."

"It would not be my wish to despise him

unfairly, Captain. I do not want this marriage, but if God allows it, then I will make it my duty to honor him as best I can, for my Christian faith demands it of me. And I would try — try to learn to care for him."

"Would you?"

She looked at him surprised, almost certain she had detected a wistfulness in his voice. She found his alert gaze studying her. The look warmed her skin, and she looked away. "You need not concern yourself, Captain Hawkins. And even if you do keep your word and bring me to Barbados, I fear I shall only be brought back to Cartagena once Lord Robert comes seeking for me."

"You have not yet told me what Lord Robert said to you about Don Nicklas. If this man of military reputation should come seeking to arrest me, then I should like to know what to expect from him."

"You speak with amusement in your voice, but it will not be so when he has you in his clutches."

"Do you think so? Then Lord Robert assured you Nicklas would come to the Caribbean to search down Pirate Hawkins?"

"He seemed to believe so. That, and securing the safety of the treasure fleet. I suppose they think you bold and reckless enough to try to take the fleet."

"Perhaps I will not disappoint them. Would it disappoint you?"

She shrugged. "I already know you to be a pirate. Nothing you do surprises me, Captain. Anyway, once you set me ashore at Barbados, I will not see you again."

Strange how those words, once spoken, left a surprising void in her heart. Absurd!

"Would you ever think of me?"

"Such audacity, Captain!"

"But a fair and honest question, madam. I asked you if you would ever think of me."

She refused to look at him, but was aware that he had come up beside her and was standing too near.

"No, Captain. I should only be entirely relieved you — you were gone, and I was safely back home — at least until my father comes for me again."

"I see. So . . . you would not think of me at all — not even a little?"

The cad! "No."

"What if I suggested you do not tell the truth? That you find yourself as drawn to me as I am to you?"

She flushed. "Your ego is as bold as your sword, Captain. I shall go on my way, and except for this wretched adventure, forget I ever laid eyes on you —"

The strong touch of his hand closing

about her arm halted her tongue. "I think you are trying to deceive yourself." He turned her around to face him, and she was confronted by a warm green gaze that held her breathless. "Nor will I easily forget you, Devora."

Devora . . . The caress of his voice when speaking her name for the first time caused her heart to beat faster. Aware of his nearness, she tried to pull back, but he did not release her.

"What if I've decided that you are too precious to release to Barbados?"

Her throat went dry, and she said nothing. They stared at each other. She felt unable to pull away. Almost involuntarily, she found herself swaying toward him. His arm went around her waist, and he drew her toward him. She had lifted her lips toward his when the bos'n pipe shrilled.

Catching her breath, Devora jerked away guiltily. Bruce grimaced and turned sharply toward the taffrail. "Hucks! You insensitive clod!"

"Capt'n! We's spotted a sail!"

"I know! I saw it before you did!" He turned impatiently from the rail to look at Devora, but she had retreated into the cabin. She glanced back at him and found him standing there, hands on hips, looking as frustrated as she. She couldn't help but smile. His mouth tipped downward, then he turned abruptly and went down the steps.

It was afternoon when Devora ventured out again from beneath the sailcloth awning onto the uppermost deck. One of Bruce's lead crewmen approached her, hat in hand. "Afternoon, Lady Ashby. Name's Githens. Captain sends me to inform ye how a wind is on the way by nightfall."

Devora smiled hopefully. "I hope you're right, Githens, but you'll pardon me if I'm rather skeptical. How would Captain Hawkins know that?"

"Ye can smell it, lady," and he breathed in. He turned, pointing out to sea. "And out yonder, see that look in the sky?"

"Yes . . . I think so," and she squinted at what appeared to be a streak near the horizon.

"That's the beginning, says the captain, and he has hisself a keg o' experience to know what he's about. He's sailed more'n the Caribbean, and seen plenty."

She looked at him, curious. "Oh? More than the Caribbean? When and where, if you don't mind my asking?"

"Oh —" he waved his long arms and hitched up his trousers. "Around, miss. Can't say exactly."

She eyed him, her curiosity growing, for Githens appeared to be uneasy talking about it. Why should he be? Unless Bruce was a pirate in other parts of the world. "He appears rather a young man to have sailed and gathered so much experience," she said, fishing for answers. She leaned against the rail and, looking below, saw Bruce and Kitt in a meeting. Then Friar Tobias joined them and seemed to be arguing with them. Soon they were joined by Hakewell and another man whom she had heard was the chief gunner.

"I wonder how long he's been a sea captain," she said, and glanced sideways at Githens. He had noticed the meeting and looked suddenly excited. His crinkled eyes looked out to sea, but Devora doing the same could see nothing.

"Five years," said Githens. "That's how long he's been about."

She looked at him. "Five years is a mighty long time to be a pirate. I heard in Bridgetown that Captain Hawkins has only been terrorizing the Main for around three years. Did he sail the Atlantic?"

Givens scratched his chin and changed the subject, but he was not very good at misleading, and she saw through his ploy at once. So it was a secret where and what

Bruce had been doing when not based at the buccaneering stronghold of Tortuga.

"There's a blow comin' behind that stain in the sky. It's what the captain asked me to warn ye about. Don't venture out of yer cabin tonight."

"A storm in a stillness like this?" said Devora, surprised.

"It won't stay so, ye can be sure of it. It's likely to be a blowhard is the captain's guess."

Devora shaded her eyes again. "If it's a hurricane, shouldn't we return to the Main? Any stretch of coast will do us now."

"We don't know it's a hurricane, miss. An' he may yet try for land. Captain is knowing what he's about. He were captain of a whole fleet of galleons once and got caught in a storm in the Adriatic —"

He looked as though he had swallowed a cold, slimy fish.

Devora's eyes swerved to his. "Galleons? But only Spain has galleons. What do you mean, Githens?"

He flushed and stammered. "Said he could outsail any commander of a Spanish fleet, Lady Ashby. No need to worry now." He backed away from the rail. "If ye be excusing me, I had best get back down to the captain."

Devora walked to the steps and looked after him, her eyes narrowing. *Galleons?*

She stood silently for a long minute, thinking. Something was wrong; something was unusual. But what was it that tapped at the back of her mind?

She lifted her skirts and came down the steps. Bruce was still talking in low tones with Kitt and Tobias. She noted that Githens had slipped away to the other side of the deck as though he wanted to avoid his captain. She scanned Bruce, studying him carefully. She took in his features. Handsome, strong, tanned from the sun . . . very dark hair, brows, earthy — but he was very English — and those devastating green eyes —

His head turned and he looked at her. A brow lifted and his gaze swept her. She flushed and quickly turned away, embarrassed he had caught her relentless stare. After what had happened between them earlier, she feared he might think she was trying to lead him on. Quickly she walked away to the other side of the rail, ignoring the crew. She leaned her elbows on the rail and stared out at the darkening stain that seemed to drip across the horizon. How bad would the storm be?

Devora was more alarmed than she had

shown Githens. She knew what a hurricane could do, for she had lived through three of them since coming to the Caribbean. Although the *Revenge* appeared to be in fine, seaworthy shape, they could be battered to within an inch of their life if they didn't make it to shore. But how could they when they were in Spanish territory?

Bruce walked up and followed her gaze. "We may be able to avoid it."

She turned and looked at him. "You've not always been Captain Hawkins, have you?" she asked calmly.

He stared at her, his eyes taking in her face, as though measuring the depth to her question. He glanced over at Githens, and Devora saw his lieutenant scurry away. Bruce frowned.

"I told you in the governor's hacienda that I was Bruce Anthony. Hawkins is a name I picked up. It suited me."

"Yes, I can see it suits you for your present behavior, but were you Captain Anthony when you commanded a fleet of Spanish galleons in the Adriatic? Or should I say were you *Capitan* Anthony?"

She watched his every response. But if she had him in a corner, he wouldn't show it. He smiled and folded his arms. "Spanish galleons? Now, this is interesting! Pray tell, madam, where such an astounding notion as this came from?"

"Are you denying it?"

He folded his palms together, tapping his fingers against his chin as he watched her, his eyes flickering. "I never captained a fleet of Spanish galleons in the Adriatic."

As their eyes held, Bruce turned away casually and gestured toward the streak in the distant sky that colored the water.

"My guess is it's a hurricane. We'll need to head for the shore. I know of a cay near here where we might hold up, but the place could be crawling with the guarda costa.If you weren't with me, I would ride the storm out."

"You mustn't think of me."

He turned his head, an almost languid look warming his eyes. "I find myself thinking of you when I don't want to," he said quietly.

Her fingers tightened on the rail and she stared ahead, insisting to no avail that her heart cease its thumping. "If you wish to ride out the storm, Captain, do so."

"Why I should keep thinking of you is curious even to me," he continued, ignoring her effort to change the subject. "I've seen many others who are nearly as lovely. Maybe I would not have been drawn to you at all had we met in normal circumstances. The uniqueness of our relationship seems to be rather jolting, doesn't it?" he asked. "And memorable."

"You mean the dagger incident, then your band of pirates storming the hacienda?" she murmured dryly. "Yes, I quite agree. It's not something one quickly forgets."

He laughed.

She looked at him and against her will smiled, but it was a rueful smile just the same. She dare not let him know that she would always remember him, pirate or not. As they smiled, their eyes held, and the same quickening of her heart almost stole her breath away.

The first breeze of the Caribbean riffled toward them, stirring the once-glassy sea into ripples. As a gust of wind blew against her and the timbers creaked softly, her emotions touched his. His smile faded and his eyes embraced her, and it seemed their lips met.

The breeze picked up. She stirred to life, the spell broken when all at once he turned and as captain of the *Revenge* walked away, shouting his orders. The seamen rushed to unfurl the canvas. For the first time in days the ship began to move, and the helmsman shouted to Bruce, "Thar she blows!"

Devora felt the thrill along with them. She smiled and gripped the rail as the swells beneath the hull began to bear them along, thrusting the ship forward.

"Oh, that wind," she sighed to herself, turning her damp face toward the sky and closing her eyes with ecstasy. "May it bring me to where my heart longs."

Devora felt a sudden pain ripple through her, and she turned her head to glance in Bruce's direction. For despite her wishes to the contrary, she was falling in love with this daring and bold buccaneer. And now what? How could it ever be? She blinked back a tear and climbed the steps toward the awning and, as she did, she neared the captain's cabin. She was about to walk by when she thought again of what Githens had mentioned about Bruce commanding a fleet of galleons. Bruce seemed to deny it, but perhaps he had merely cleverly reworded her question? Had he served in the Mediterranean near Portugal and Spain? But that seemed absurd!

Who was Captain Bruce Anthony?

She looked back toward deck and saw that he was occupied with the crew. She hesitated, then tried the heavy oak door of the great cabin. It was unlocked. *No,* her conscience rebuked. But her desire to know more about him urged her forward, the temptation too strong. She told herself she had a right to know, since he had swept her away without her consent. The next thing she knew she was inside his cabin, glancing about at the dark overhead beams. The stern windows offered light, and there was an oil lantern swinging above the large desk, and she went to turn up the wick. The cabin was nicely equipped and furnished, and smelled pleasantly of cedar wood and spices. With heart pounding, she rushed to his desk and threw open the large drawer. Astounded, she stared at a black leather King James Bible. Her heart lurched with joy, and she reached her shaking fingers to caress the old leather. The pages were worn, showing he not only possessed a Bible but actually read and studied it. She winked back tears. He wasn't simply a pirate! Bruce was much more complex.

She glanced toward the door, then removed the Bible and opened it, looking for a family register. Her breath paused as a list of names stared up at her in delicate black ink — certainly not his handwriting, she thought. Her finger traced down the list:

Duke Roger Anthony
Lord Arlen Anthony
Lady Lillian Bruce

Lady Marian Bruce —

Her eyes shot up, wide and amazed before she could read on, for she heard someone coming up the steps and striding down the walkway. Swiftly she placed the Bible back into the drawer, shut it, and rushed out from behind the desk as the door opened. She had just a moment to back up against the side of the paneled wall before Bruce walked in.

She leaned there, palms against the wall, holding her breath. She watched him go to the desk and open the drawer, taking out a leather map and spreading it on the desk. Her breath held as he reached to turn up the wick on the overhead lantern but saw that it was already up. Devora bit her lip and closed her eyes. A moment later she felt his gaze and slowly looked up.

He stared at her, his expression telling nothing. Cautiously, she moved against the wall toward the door.

His eyes narrowed. He started out from behind the desk. She knew escape was impossible and stopped, glancing away. Then folding her arms, she sighed.

"I'm sorry."

"No you're not."

She lifted her chin, telling herself she would not be trapped.

"I had a right to know about you. You've abducted me."

He smirked, scanning her. "What sweet stories our consciences can come up with to defend our actions."

"You're hardly the one to lecture me on good and evil. You and your pirates just carried off stolen treasure from the citizens of the Isle of Pearls!"

He laughed unpleasantly, then unexpectedly went to an oak cupboard, took out a key, unlocked it, and hauled out a foot-wide silver chest. Another key opened its lid, and he ran his strong fingers through the jewels, scooping up a glitter of gold, silver, and flashes of every delectable color in the rainbow. He looked at her and smiled maliciously.

"Is this what you were looking for?"

"Of course not!" she breathed, shocked and indignant, but he lifted a brow, his eyes glinting green. She sucked in her breath. Did he think this, or was he deliberately goading her?

He sat on the edge of his desk. "Have a look."

"No thank you," she said icily.

He took her in, studying her face and throat. "There aren't many women with violet-blue eyes . . ." He pulled out several jewels and a necklace and straightening from the desk, came toward her. Devora watched his hand, seeing sparkling blue, as deep and wild and passionate as a sapphire night beneath the tropical moon.

"Here — a gift for abducting you. A good-bye, and a promise as well."

She swallowed. *Good-bye?* Her eyes came to his, wondering. There was no longer anything in his look that hinted of malicious teasing.

"Good-bye?" she said.

"Yes, you'll be pleased to know I've made up my mind. I'm not bringing you to Tortuga. You're too noble to go there. I've decided to be a gentleman and allow you to take leave of the *Revenge*. Don't ask me why — maybe because you're more of a distraction to me than an asset at the moment."

She tried to take all of this in, but his words bounced about her heart and nothing took root.

"I think I can get you to safety before the storm hits. I know this area of the Main fairly well. . . . I came to read the map to make certain my plans are possible before I told you. There's a village not far from here. Friar Tobias has agreed to bring you there and arrange transportation."

Her mind swirled. "To Barbados?" she

whispered. "But are we not far from there? Is it not wiser to wait until the storm passes, then sail on to Carlisle Bay?"

A hint of a smile was on his lips. "Yes, it would be — if I were bringing you to Carlisle Bay."

She searched his face. Was he saying he would not, but that Tobias would?

He handed her the sapphires. She looked into his palm and saw ear bobs and a necklace with several stones arranged into a cross on a gold mounting and chain. "I want you to have these," he said.

She shook her head. "Bruce, I couldn't —"

"I couldn't," she repeated.

His eyes sparked. "Do you think I would give you pirated jewels from the Isle of Pearls? What I offer you I have earned through many hard and torturous years of service." His voice softened. "They were meant for someone else, but I want you to have them, Devora. A gift. I want you to remember me."

She swallowed again and tears wet her eyes.

"You will remember me?" he said softly.

Her eyes rushed to his, and her lips quavered with the emotion that stuck painfully in her throat. "You know I will."

"As I will remember you." He enfolded

the jewels in her hand, then his hands closed about her waist, drawing her to him, and she went willingly, the world exploding as his lips took hers.

The moments slipped away, and when he let her go, he stared at her, then said with unspeakable calmness, "I'll bring you and Tobias to shore tonight. You better go back now."

She managed to get back to her cabin, and once there found that her hand was still gripping the jewels so tightly that the stones had left marks on her palms. She stared at the glittering blue, wondering how she could have taken them, how she could have permitted him to kiss her good-bye, and why it seemed that her heart had changed so drastically in the time since she had met him at the residence of Governor Huxley.

"I don't care," she murmured, full of emotion. "I can't forget him. I think I'm falling in love with him."

He would see her again, she told herself confidently. He would give up buccaneering and come to Barbados, settle down at Ashby Hall with Uncle Barnabas, and they would find love and contentment.

But she knew she only told herself this. She walked to the cane daybed and sank onto it, her heart defeated, and covered her face with one palm, the other holding the glittering blue gems that danced and winked in the light coming from the walkway.

18

Until Then . . .

By evening the wind had strengthened, and she feared that Bruce was right about a storm. The noise and shudder of the ship filled her ears and drowned out the steady beating of her heart. Tobias had come for her, and in the dark, starless night she stood below on deck, prepared to be rowed to the Main under the protection of Tobias, who was now garbed as a friar again. Bruce came forward carrying his weapons and, lifting her up into his arms, carried her over the side of the ship and down the rope ladder to the waiting longboat. He let her feet touch the bottom of the rocking boat, and held her still with one strong hand. She found a seat in the stern, and Bruce went to the tiller behind her, calling a low order to Githens and Spragge.

She looked at him, now a dark silhouette of strength and enigma, and she wondered. "What of the ship?" she said in a low voice.

"Is there no place to come ashore until the storm passes?"

"We will be safe enough. There is a sheltered cay ahead, and we will anchor there until it blows itself out."

He had not yet explained the details of where Tobias was bringing her, or why he chose to have them part this way instead of going to Barbados.

The boat's keel grated on the lonely stretch of beach with frothy waves and swaying palm trees. The rowers got out and sprang ashore, closely followed by Tobias. Bruce took her arm and edged her toward the bow of the boat. A moment later she stepped into the warm, wet sand, feeling the water pull and suck at her feet as it splashed around her legs and soaked the edge of her skirts. Bruce ran with her through the sand, to where some swaying palms were clustered. He turned her to look at him, and they were alone.

"There are friends here who will give you and Tobias lodging for the night. Tomorrow, a trusty man will ride into the village to find a coach to bring you both to Cartagena."

Momentarily dazed, she looked up at him, certain she had heard the name of her destination wrong.

"You mean Barbados," she whispered, her eyes searching his, but now not certain of anything, not even Bruce Hawkins. Her chest tightened and her breath came rapidly. "You *do* mean Bridgetown?"

Bruce was unsmiling, and his hands reached to enclose her upper arms. "No, Cartagena. Tobias will bring you to his brother Don Maximus Valentin, the viceroy."

She shook her head as if he were mad. "How could you betray me?"

"I do not betray you, Devora."

He did betray her! "You will give me back to the viceroy, to the Valentin family — to Nicklas Valentin!"

"Trust me. I will come to you there."

"Come to me? In Cartagena?" she cried. "You cannot. They will kill you. Oh, Bruce — how can you do this? Was I mistaken? I thought —" She dare not say what she thought, but he seemed to understand, for he brought her close and her hands gripped the damp shirt, afraid to let go, afraid he would forever slip away onto the Caribbean and she would never see him again.

"You were not mistaken. Can you not feel by the way I hold you that I will never let you go? I will come to Cartagena and take you away from Don Nicklas."

"Foolhardy! I will go with you now. You cannot enter the lion's den!"

"It must be. I must go to the port of Cartagena, and then to Lima. And for us to be together, you must go there. Fear not. Tobias will be there with you. And the viceroy will treat you well; he is now very proud of Don Nicklas. He will want you for his son so that he can make an alliance with Lord Robert."

Bruce drew her closer still, and she quavered with emotion and fear. "You are mad," she whispered.

He bent his dark head and kissed her passionately. "I will come again. Perhaps in less than two months. Wait for me with confidence. I promise, this is not good-bye."

Devora blinked back the tears, aware of only one thing: Bruce was leaving her. He was doing the unthinkable, turning her over to the Valentin family after all his words to the contrary at the hacienda on the Isle of Pearls. Why had he changed his mind? Why would he do such a thing?

"You will not come," she whispered.

"Little doubter, wait and see. Until then!" And he backed away gravely now, still holding her hand. "Our Lord keep us both in His hand until then!"

Devora stood, heart swelling as she

watched him run back to the boat. She watched him slip back out onto the water and slowly disappear into the stormy darkness.

"Bruce," she whispered, "I love you. . . ."

The Spanish trade winds rustled the palm fronds, stirring her damp dress and tugging at the tears on her cheeks. His words came once again to her heart, bringing the birth of expectation: "I promise, this is not good-bye."

The employees of Thorndike Press hope you have enjoyed this Large Print book. All our Large Print titles are designed for easy reading, and all our books are made to last. Other Thorndike Press Large Print books are available at your library, through selected bookstores, or directly from us.

For information about titles, please call:

(800) 223-1244
(800) 223-6121

To share your comments, please write:

Publisher
Thorndike Press
P.O. Box 159
Thorndike, Maine 04986